PRAISE FOR
PAUL IS UNDEAD

"A wonderfully inventive blend of comedy, alternative history—and flesh-eating. A post-modern gothic classic."

> —Mick Wall, author of *When Giants Walked the Earth: A Biography of Led Zeppelin*

"If you've ever wondered (as I have) how the story of the Beatles would have turned out if, instead of a quartet of working-class Liverpool lads, they had been a bunch of zombies, this hilarious book finally answers the question."

> —Michael Ian Black, comedian and author of *Clappy as a Ham*

"*Paul Is Undead* brings the Beatles back to life . . . and now they want braaains. Brilliant and hilarious. Two decaying thumbs up."

> —Jonathan Maberry, multiple Bram Stoker Award–winning author of *Patient Zero* and *Rot & Ruin*

"*Paul Is Undead* is the *Abbey Road* of Beatles zombie mashup novels."

> —A. J. Jacobs, author of *The Guinea Pig Diaries* and *The Year of Living Biblically*

"Investigative music journalist Alan Goldsher has ripped the mop-tops off the Fab Four, revealing the wormy undead belly of godless, noggin-gobbling rock 'n' roll. Read it, or die."

> —Larry Doyle, author of *I Love You, Beth Cooper* and *Go, Mutants!*

Paul Is Undead is also available as an eBook

PAUL IS UNDEAD

THE BRITISH ZOMBIE INVASION

ALAN GOLDSHER

GALLERY BOOKS

NEW YORK LONDON TORONTO SYDNEY

Gallery Books
A Division of Simon & Schuster, Inc.
1230 Avenue of the Americas
New York, NY 10020

First Gallery Books trade paperback edition June 2010

GALLERY BOOKS and colophon are registered trademarks of Simon & Schuster, Inc.

For information about special discounts for bulk purchases, please contact Simon & Schuster Special Sales at 1-866-506-1949 or business@simonandschuster.com.

The Simon & Schuster Speakers Bureau can bring authors to your live event. For more information or to book an event contact the Simon & Schuster Speakers Bureau at 1-866-248-3049 or visit our website at www.simonspeakers.com.

Designed by Jaime Putorti
Interior Art by Jeffrey Brown

Manufactured in the United States of America

10 9 8 7 6 5 4 3 2 1

Library of Congress Cataloging-in-Publication Data

Goldsher, Alan
    Paul is undead : the British zombie invasion / Alan Goldsher. —1st Gallery Books trade paperback ed.
        p. cm.
    1. Beatles—Fiction. 2. Zombies—Fiction. I. Title.
    PS3607.O48P38 2010
    813'.6—dc22   2010002218

ISBN 978-1-4391-7792-1
ISBN 978-1-4391-7795-2 (ebook)

PAUL IS UNDEAD

PREFACE

For some, the most indelible memory of their television-viewing lives was the moment Jack Ruby assassinated Lee Harvey Oswald in 1963. For others, it was Neil Armstrong's 1969 moon landing. For today's generation, it might be the fall of the Berlin Wall in 1989, or the World Trade Center attacks on September 11, 2001.

I realized television was more than sitcoms and sporting events on December 8, 1980, the night Mark David Chapman tried to lop off John Lennon's head with a silver scythe.

•

I was fourteen, parked by the tube in the basement of my suburban Chicago home, watching what I watched every Monday night during the winter months: *Monday Night Football*. The New England Patriots were down in Miami taking on the Dolphins, and I can't recall a damn thing about the game; all I remember is Howard Cosell's announcement right before halftime—and, like most music fanatics, I know it word for word:

"An unspeakable tragedy confirmed to us by ABC News in New

York City: John Lennon, outside of his apartment building on the West Side of New York City, the most famous, perhaps, of all of the Beatles, was chopped twice on the top of his spine, then rushed to an undisclosed location, where his skull was reattached and he was reanimated for the 263rd time. The damage was such that his head will now permanently tilt at a ten-degree angle. It's hard to go back to the game after that news flash, which, in duty, we have to tell."

I turned off the television. I went to bed. And I wept myself to sleep.

*

Ironically enough, I fell in love with Paul McCartney's solo stuff first—hey, I was five years old, and "Uncle Albert/Admiral Halsey" played on the radio all day, every day, so what can I tell you?—then I worked my way through the Beatles' catalog in reverse chronological order, starting with their swan song, *Abbey Road*, all the way back to their debut, *Please Please Me*. Since I loved almost every note of the catalog, I didn't factor their state of being into my feelings about them as a music-making unit. I mean, who cared if they were undead? My eighth-grade orchestra teacher was a zombie, and he was cool. Yeah, a couple of the shufflers at school—we called them shufflers, and for that, I still feel guilty—were a bit *off*, but I had no personal issues with the undead. The Beatles were just a rock group whose music I loved, and if they didn't have blood pumping through their veins, so be it.

When Chapman tried to take down Lennon, it dawned on me that I actually knew very little about the Liverpudlians, so I went to the Wilmette Public Library and borrowed the only four Beatles books on their shelves: Ian McGinty's *Scream! The Beatles Eat Their Generation*; Maureen Miller's *A Hard Night's Death: McCartney,*

Movies, and Mayhem; Eliot Barton's *Hypnosis, Liverpool Style*; and the uneven, clumsily ghostwritten Ringo Starr memoir, *Starr's Stars: A Ninja's Life*. Dozens more titles were in print, but the library refused to bring them in, assuming that nobody on the lily-white North Shore of Chicago cared about John Lennon, Paul McCartney, George Harrison, and Ringo Starr. I suppose I can understand their reasoning: My orchestra teacher notwithstanding, the adult zombie population of Wilmette, Illinois, circa 1980 was all but nonexistent, and none of them worked at the library. I'm not calling my hometown racist. I'm just reporting the facts.

Over the next few years, I scooped up any Beatles-oriented tome I could find, but aside from the purely journalistic bestseller *The Shea Stadium Riot: How the Beatles Almost Destroyed New York City* by *New York Times* crime reporter Jessica Brandice, all of these so-called biographies focused mostly on the music, rather than the men. That's understandable, as writers were hesitant to sit down with the band after Lennon and McCartney famously dismembered, castrated, and ultimately murdered *New Musical Express* staffer William "Guitar" Tyler back in 1967—and this after previously announcing that, in terms of proactive attacking, the media was off-limits. In the post-Tyler world, publishers and media executives decreed that their staff were required to conduct any and all interviews behind a six-inch-thick partition. (Half a foot of glass wouldn't stop a hungry Liverpudlian zombie, but it would slow them down long enough for the interviewer to make a getaway.) That sort of impersonal setup didn't lend itself to an intimate, revealing talk.

Come 1995, the year I became a "real" writer (as opposed to the previous decade, when I was a "fake" scribe who, when he wasn't trying to get work as a bassist, churned out a bunch of pretentious and clumsy crapola), the Beatles as individuals were all but forgot-

ten. John and his wife, Yoko Ono, as had been the case since that horrible Monday night fifteen years before, were holed up in their uptown New York fortress. Lennon rarely left the apartment, and when he did, he was accompanied by half a dozen highly trained USZGs (United States Zombie Guards), all six of whom were festooned with tommy guns and force fields. Paul was living on a farm in Scotland, surfacing every few years with a solo album that inevitably didn't do the kind of numbers he'd hoped for. (Paul was, is, and always will be a bottom-line guy, be it about record sales or body count.) George was the most visible Beatle, giving lectures to religious types and horror aficionados at various conventions throughout the world and having fun with his telekinetic powers—most notably when he created a music video featuring dancing tchotchkes that was a real hit with the first wave of MTV fans. As for Ringo, nobody had a clue; there were sightings from the North Pole to the South Pole and everywhere in between. Pop-culture junkies had stopped caring about Lennon's, McCartney's, Harrison's, and Starr's whereabouts or activities, and the number of fans who showed up at their local neighborhood Beatlefests dwindled each year. The music was still relevant, but the men, not so much.

But I *cared*. And I wanted the story. And I was a writer. And a tenacious one at that. So after a bunch of soul-searching, I amped up my health insurance plan and dived in.

I didn't have a book deal in place when I began work on this oral history in February 1996—an oral history in which I intended to focus solely on the men, rather than their songs—thus I had to finance it myself. In order to keep my bank account liquid while researching the Beatles all these years, I've ghostwritten thirty-one memoirs and twelve novels, none of which I can legally discuss. (Suffice it to say you've probably read at least three of them.)

In between these writing projects, I was doing loads of research;

I traveled to New York City, Liverpool, London, Edinburgh, Tibet, Los Angeles, Port-au-Prince, Nippon, Antarctica, Ibiza, and two locations I'm not at liberty to divulge. I spent a cold, wet night under a bamboo umbrella in the middle of a field deep in the bowels of Paraguay with Alexis "Magic Alex" Mardas, and a memorable, harrowing afternoon sitting next to Dr. Timothy Leary while he was on his deathbed. There were clandestine meetings in frightening locations, blindfolds, death threats, hallucinogenics, and in one memorable instance, I had to scale the side of a mountain in Osaka to speak with a Sixty-sixth Level Ninja Lord, with nary a copy of Lonely Planet's *Japan Travel Guide* to be seen.

Fifteen years later, I have the story . . . or, at least, I *hope* I do. I guess that's for all of you—the Beatlemaniacs, the musicologists, the reviewers, the undead, and the hundreds of thousands of attack survivors—to decide.

INTRODUCTION

Lyman Cosgrove and Ellington Worthson are considered among the world's foremost experts on Liverpudlian zombies. Their 1979 self-published book, Under the Canal: The Undead of Abyssinia Close and the Birth of the Liverpool Process, is the Bible of Liverpudlian zombie history, and if you can track down a copy, buy it, read it, and hold on to it for dear life, because there are only approximately two thousand of them in existence. Worthson died in 1990 at the age of ninety-three—the cause of death remains either a mystery or a well-shrouded secret—but Cosgrove is still undead and kicking, still living in a modest Liverpool flat, and, when I spoke with him in January 1999, still cheerfully waxing poetic about English monsters.

LYMAN COSGROVE: Over the years, dozens of historians have floated dozens of theories about how the Liverpool infestation started, and I can understand why there is so much conflict. We suspect that it began in 1840, but back then, nobody was keeping proper records, you see, so most of our theories about the specifics are conjecture. But isn't that the way it always was with the undead, pre–World War II? Hundreds of questions, and only dozens of answers.

We know for certain that the boat the First—the original Liverpool *nzambi*—arrived in was called the SS *Heartbeat*. (My personal opinion is that the vessel's owners used the whimsical name to mask the fact that it was a brutal, sadistic hell ship.) The slave trade was in full swing, and the captain, Arthur Smyth, was a greedy bastard of the highest order. He pulled slaves from the United States, from Haiti, and from Africa's northernmost coast, and, believing that a broken slave is a valuable slave, he and his merciless crew beat the tar out of them.

The ship could hold as many as two hundred, shall we say, passengers, but according to Smyth's journals, on his first trip to the UK, he sold only 142 men into slavery. It's fair to theorize that approximately fifty men were killed on the boat; their bodies were most likely thrown overboard. I'd venture to say that some of these men were still alive when they were launched from the *Heartbeat*. I have no clue as to whether any of them were undead.

We don't know, nor will we ever know, where exactly the First joined Captain Smyth's floating party. I've always felt that Tunisia was the most likely locale, but it's possible he was found in Haiti. My late partner, Ellington Worthson, floated the theory that the First came from the Louisiana bayou, but I feel the evidence he compiled didn't completely back it up.

The irony is that the First—and make certain you tell your readers that in this case, and in this case *only*, we spell it N-Z-A-M-B-I— was the least of the slaves' worries. According to the single published report, the First appeared to be relatively docile—and back then the Tunisian undead were quite docile; thus my working theory of his origination—and there wasn't a single *nzambi* sold into slavery. If the First launched an attack, and that's a big *if*, it would have been a light one.

Smyth was careless and sloppy, and more than once, he lost slaves, just literally lost them. It was documented that during an 1837 delivery, ten teenage slaves-to-be escaped soon after the *Heartbeat* docked. The following year, another eight, *gone*. My guess is that one of two things happened: either these eighteen slaves hid on the boat until everybody had disembarked, then sneaked out onto the dock and disappeared into the UK population; or they broke free from the chains that bound them together, chains that that fool Smyth acknowledged in his journals were less than satisfactory, and they ran. As for the First, I believe he hid, then escaped, the reasoning being that even if he managed to shed the chains, he couldn't have moved fast enough to elude his captors, as this *nzambi* hadn't yet developed the speed and strength that Liverpool zombies eventually became known for.

Liverpool entered the modern age in 1825, when the first locomotives rolled into town from Manchester. Come 1840, there were three train yards, where the *nzambi* could not only hide undetected but also find unsuspecting living humans to feed on. (Another characteristic of the Tunisian zombie is its lack of hunger; therefore, the First could get by on just a handful of brains a year should it so choose, a factor that helped keep him out of the public eye. If he had been, for instance, a run-of-the-mill Norwegian zombie who couldn't survive on less than one brain a day, the bobbies would have used all of their limited resources to track the First down. Not that they would have had the wherewithal to do anything to him once they found him, but still.) But the railroads boomed at the turn of the century, and it soon became more difficult for our *nzambi* to stay hidden, so when the Liverpool sewer system was completed in 1929, the First went underground, both literally and figuratively.

Fearing detection if he left the sewers, the *nzambi* had to be extremely stealthy in order to acquire his nutritional fix: He would climb up through the sewage line, procure and eat the first brain in sight, zombify the victim, then maybe drag the undead body back into the sewers—or maybe not, depending on his mood. With few exceptions, his bounty, once turned, were nonviolent, content to stay put, bask in fecal matter that defined the Liverpudlian sewers, and rely on the First's brain-hunting-and-gathering skills until they developed the ability to fend for themselves.

On October 9, 1940, just before midnight, the First surfaced for his evening meal, slithering out of a loo on the ground floor of the Liverpool Maternity Hospital. The hallway was quiet and empty. He wandered the floor until he came to a room housing one Julia Lennon, who had just endured a thirty-hour labor. She must have looked wasted and unappetizing, because the First walked right past her and snatched up her newborn boy.

●

Julia Lennon died on July 15, 1958, and was reanimated by her son the following week. She still lives at 8 Head Street in Liverpool, the same place she's lived since John came home from the hospital. When I met with her in May 2003, one thing was clear: if you look past the shiny scars and permanent stitches, it's easy to glean that, once upon a time, this gal was a knockout.

JULIA LENNON: Johnny's delivery was rough. Now, this was seventy years ago, and me memory ain't so good, but I still remember a *lot* about the birth . . . but I don't think there's nothin' to tell, really. There was a lotta yellin', I was downright manky, and there was a lotta blood. And that's all I'm gonna say. It's not something I care to go on about.

Johnny was a beautiful boy, but he came out of me kickin' and screamin', and he kept it up for a good three hours. I tried to calm him—it was breakin' me heart to hear me baby raisin' such a fuss—but he wouldn't settle down, no matter what I tried. Singin' didn't do shite, and rockin' him didn't help, but finally he wore out, and come midnight, he fell into a deep sleep. For a while, he was dead to the world.

LYMAN COSGROVE: There's no question that spending years huddled in heaps of fecal matter affected the First's body chemistry, and living in gallons of human waste explains why the undead who were raised in the sewers of Liverpool have radically different qualities and powers than their brethren around the world. It goes without saying that these powers led to the development and evolution of the Liverpool Process.

Now, most who are acquainted with the history of either zombies or the Beatles are at least casually aware of the ins and outs of the Liverpool Process, but I've always felt it important that when I discuss the Process in any venue—be it a one-on-one chat such as this, or a lecture in front of a few hundred Beatles fans—I offer as many details as possible, because the more you know, the better you understand.

So. Step one: The Liverpool zombie subdues its victim, either by physical force or simple hypnosis. Being that Lennon was all of five hours old when he was attacked by the First, I feel comfortable in saying that the First used a spell on the baby rather than an assault. Violence certainly wouldn't have been necessary.

Step two: Either close or cover the victim's eyes. I don't know whether that's absolutely necessary to complete the Process or

simply a local tradition. I, myself, have successfully performed the Process over nine hundred times, and in each instance, just to play it safe, the victim's eyes were shielded. It's worked for me thus far, and I wouldn't try it any other way.

Step three: Bite the right side of the victim's neck, just below the left earlobe. (As that's a vampirelike transformative maneuver, many have suggested that the Liverpool *nzambi* originated in the Balkans, but I chalk it up to an evolutionary kinship with the sewer bats.) There's no rule as to how much of the neck needs to be bitten. Just as long as your tongue can fit into the hole, you'll be fine. It's not necessary to swallow the blood. For the most part, I don't.

Step four: Slide your expandable zombie tongue past the victim's ear canal, around the orbital socket, and into the area housing the cerebrospinal fluid. It's up for debate as to whether you should or shouldn't swallow the fluid. I don't know if drinking the fluid helps the Process, but it certainly doesn't hurt.

Step five: Collect the brain matter. You have only one chance— that neck hole closes up almost straightaway, and it's common knowledge that once a brain has been penetrated, it's edible for only three or so minutes, so it's essential to procure as much gray matter as you can, as quickly as you can. Upon initial penetration, you'll be closest to the cerebellum, and if you can get only one section, make it that one. If you can snake your tongue past the temporal lobe and get a piece of the parietal, bully for you.

Step six: Extract your tongue as quickly as possible. I can't stress this enough. The bite wound heals quickly, and you don't want to get your tongue stuck in there. Look what happened to poor Lu Walters.

Step seven is necessary only if you choose to reanimate your victim. Force your tongue through the roof of your own mouth—

which sounds difficult, but the more experience you have, the less of an issue it becomes—then maneuver it into the brain, then remove as much of your cerebrospinal fluid as you can, and since you're undead there isn't much to be had, then spit it into the victim's right ear. Including reanimation, the entire Process should take no more than two minutes. Anything beyond that, and there's a slight chance the victim will become a Midpointer. And Midpointing somebody simply isn't polite.

I'm 99 percent certain that John Lennon was the first infant the Liverpool *nzambi* killed and reanimated. I believe this explains Lennon's wild artistic talent and his heightened zombie powers. But maybe not. Maybe Lennon was just touched by God. Or the Devil.

JULIA LENNON: John was me first baby, so I didn't think anything of it when he refused me tit that first night. If he was hungry, he'd have eaten. I wasn't worried about the mark on his neck, neither. I figured it was a birthmark. I *did* get concerned when, right after I brought him home, his skin got grayer and grayer, until it was the color of the concrete road in front of our house.

LYMAN COSGROVE: Not everybody realizes that the region where a zombie is reanimated dictates everything from its powers to its appearance. For example, Brazilian and Argentinean zombies share identical undead characteristics save for their skin color: Brazil produces pale blue zombies, while in Argentina the epidermis is generally a sickly green. Another example: the zombies in the North African countries—Tunisia, for instance—remain docile, but by the time you work your way down to Botswana, you have tribes of death machines who kill up to seven people a day, without fail. I won't torture you or your readers with what goes on in Mexico.

I may be biased, but I feel that Liverpool zombies, save for the dreary gray skin tone, have the most interesting collection of powers in the world. Our physical strength rivals that of the undead who inhabit the Earth's poles, and our collection of psychic skills—hypnosis and telekinesis are my two personal favorites—is unmatched. Like the Australian undead, we Liverpudlians can immediately attach and reattach our extremities, except for the head, of course, which, as we know from John's very own case, is an issue easily solved via some quick and simple stitching.

The Liverpool undead are virtually impossible to kill, you know. The only way to end our lives is to shoot the bite scar in our necks with a bullet fashioned from a diamond. It takes an expert zombie hunter to make that happen. Only sixty-one Liverpudlian zombies have been put to eternal death.

Here's one of the odder things specific to the Liverpool Process: intense physical trauma caused by a living human or an earthly entity such as a car, a bomb, or a gun *can* kill us . . . but we won't die, per se. What happens is, we become stuck in a state between dead and undead, which, by all indications, is a miserable place to be. Those who suffer this horrible fate are called Midpointers. According to an informal 2009 study, there are just over one thousand Midpointers in the world. They're easy to spot, because they walk two inches off the ground and always have dark blue tears spurting from their eyes. As I said, a miserable place to be.

To me, the three best things about having been transformed by the Liverpool Process are that we can eat and digest human food without gaining weight or ever having to void our bowels or bladders—although we have been known to expel gas upon occasion—our physical evolution ceases at around the age of fifty (I've looked the way I look now since about 1958), and finally, I most enjoy the fact that despite not having any blood in our bodies, we can still get erections and have orgasms, although our ejaculate consists of a powdery substance that some joker back in the nineteenth century started referring to as *dustmen*—that, of course, being a combination of the words *dust* and *semen*.

Before you dive into your story, I can't stress enough that mentally, physically, and artistically, Liverpool zombies are strong. But from the moment he was reanimated, John Lennon was *stronger*.

CHAPTER ONE

1940–1961

John Lennon is an easy man to track down, but he's a hard man to pin down. He hasn't released a record of new music since 1980, thus he's not affiliated with a label, so there isn't a publicity manager you can call to set up an interview. He doesn't give a damn what people say about him in the press, so he has no need or desire for a PR person. He's a hermit who doesn't answer his phone, return emails, or leave the house. The only difference between him and fellow zombie recluse J. D. Salinger is that everybody knows where Lennon lives: The Dakota on 72nd and Central Park West, Apartment 72, New York City, America.

But if you make nice with the Dakota's concierge, and slip him a few sawbucks, he might deliver John a package. If you load the package with several boxes of Corn Flakes and ten pounds of Kopi Luwak—a painfully bitter coffee from Indonesia that costs almost six hundred bucks a pound—John might ring you on your cell. If you can persuade John that you don't have an agenda other than finding out the story behind the Beatles, and you don't have an axe to grind, and

you've never touched a diamond bullet in your life, John might invite you over to share a bit of that Kopi. And then maybe, just maybe, after a while, he'll talk to you on the record about his life and career.

It took me two years of rambling cell chats, bottomless bowls of Corn Flakes, and horrible java to get John to submit to a formal taped interview, but once I fired up the recorder, the guy was an open book. For the first two weeks in November 2005—while his wife, Yoko Ono, was out of town, natch—John talked. And talked. And talked some more. He was sometimes mesmerizing, sometimes hilarious, sometimes heartbreaking, sometimes sarcastic, sometimes infuriating, and sometimes violent (my doctor told me that with regular physical therapy, I will someday regain full motion in my left shoulder), but for those fourteen days, John Lennon was There. And thank God for it.

JOHN LENNON: At this point, nobody wants to hear about my childhood. *I* don't even want to hear about my childhood. My mum died, I brought her back to life, I went to Quarry Bank High, I drew cartoons, I mucked about with rock 'n' roll, I killed a bunch of people, and zombified eight of 'em. Big fookin' deal.

People probably don't want to hear about the skiffle days either, but sod 'em. If there's no skiffle, there's no Beatles.

Me and my mate Eric Griffiths took guitar lessons out in Hunts Cross, but the teacher wasn't teaching us anything we couldn't have taught ourselves. And the teacher—I forget his name—treated me like a leper. In retrospect, I can understand his reaction, because during my first lesson, my left pinkie fell off while I was trying to shift from an F chord to a D sus 4, but that doesn't give him the right to look at me sideways, for fook's sake. That's racism, pure and simple. I bet if Big Bill Broonzy or some other black man walked into his studio, he wouldn't have said a damn thing, but show him a zombie, and *ooooooh,* we've got an international panic. He was a right bastard, that one.

Anyhow, I got fed up with his attitude by the seventh lesson, so that night, after I packed up my guitar, I ate the teacher's brain, then threw his body into the River Mersey. The man weighed twelve stone, and getting him from his studio to Wirral Line and all the way down to the river was rough. If Eric hadn't helped, I would've had to leave the corpse on the train.

I started my first band in 1957, and I suppose my initial concern was our name. The biggest skiffle unit around was called Lonnie Donegan's Skiffle Group, and musically, we weren't nearly as good as they were, so we had to do something to make ourselves stand out until we learned how to play our instruments . . . like come up with a better name than Lonnie Donegan's Skiffle Group, which I figured wouldn't be that difficult, because Lonnie Donegan's Skiffle Group is a fookin' boring name.

First, we were the Blackjacks, but Pete Shotton, who was our washboard player for a while, didn't like it, and wanted us to change to the Quarrymen, which, of course, referred to our school, Quarry Bank. I pushed for the Maggots, but Eric nixed that because he thought it would draw too much attention to what he called my "situation." Then good old Lenny Garry piped up and said he thought calling ourselves the Maggots would frighten people—but Len was scared of his own shadow, so he wasn't the best gauge. I did see Eric and Len's point, however, so the Quarrymen it was. But I wasn't happy about it. I thought the Maggots was a brilliant name. Still do, actually.

The two Quarrymen gigs everybody talks about were in '57, at the end of June and the beginning of July, but the one that I personally remember the best—and the most important one, as far as I'm concerned—was that May, I think the fifteenth. It wasn't a gig,

really, just me and the guys muckin' about on the street in front of
Mendips, which is what we used to call my aunt Mimi's house over
on Menlove Avenue. But that's when the brilliant stuff happens,
when you're muckin' about.

I knew none of the local mortals would want to spend a beautiful spring day listening to a batch of local rugrats stumble through
"Rock Island Line," so I telepathically summoned all the undead
within brain-shot to come to Mendips and watch us do our thing.
Even though they were only a few dozen meters away, those
bloody shufflers took a good half hour to arrive. I know for
certain they could've moved faster, because they were zombies of
the higher-functioning variety (I guess they weren't motivated
enough) but that was fine, 'cause it took me a while to figure out
how to keep my left pinkie attached. Shotten suggested I tie the
finger to my hand with some twine. It worked, and off we went.
Cheers, Pete.

Our first tune was "Worried Man Blues," not exactly a number
you can dance to, but that didn't stop our audience from trying. It
was the first time I'd seen a gathering of undead try to dance, and it
wasn't an impressive display—only about half of them could bend
their knees, which made it tough for them to do the Mashed Potato.
I *will* say they were an appreciative crowd, though; so much so that
they begged to turn our bass player Bill Smith into one of their own.
I told them no way, he was my friend, and if anybody was gonna
transform him, it would be me.

But it wasn't.

I don't know who turned Bill, but if I ever find out, that arsehole'll
get a diamond bullet right up his bum. See, I hated it when my
mates got turned by somebody other than me—still do, matter of
fact. Think about it: it was *me* who started the modern Liverpool
zombie movement, and if a friend of mine needs to be finished,

then restarted, I deserve to do the finishing *and* the restarting, d'you know what I mean?

Bill left the band soon after his transformation, and I never saw him again. I remember in '61, Paulie told me he'd heard some bollocks that Bill was living underground. Even though I despised being anywhere near the sewers, I went looking for him. No luck; all I got out of the trip was a load of cack under my fingernails. I hated the fookin' sewers, and I wouldn't go underground for just anybody, but Bill was a good man, the kind of guy you'd walk through filth for.

Bill's gone now, mate. You'll never find him. I tried hard, man. Really, really hard.

•

Considering Lennon's swift and horrifyingly violent attack upon my person—a shockingly fast attack that I'll always consider myself lucky to have survived more or less intact—after I contended that George Martin was just as important to the musical success of the Beatles' final three albums as George Harrison was, I hesitate to question to his face the veracity of any of his claims, for fear of my life. That said, thanks to a tip from one James Paul McCartney, it took me a grand total of three minutes to track down Bill Smith, so one has to wonder how hard Lennon really looked. According to Paul, Smitty's always been an accessible zombie, always armed with smiles and jokes, always eager to gossip about his days as a Quarryman.

A cheerful sewer dweller who doesn't like to come aboveground for any reason other than to dine, Smitty would speak to me only on his home turf, so on August 3, 2007, I donned a biohazard suit and made the first of my three forays into the Liverpool sewers.

The local undead populous has done wonders with the place—there's a lovely Internet cafe, a well-stocked trading post/general store, and velveteen sofas and soft recliners wherever you turn—and if the ground wasn't covered with a two-inch layer of liquidized shit, decades-old piss, clotted blood, and chunky brain matter, it would be quite an enjoyable place to visit.

Like the majority of those who've undergone the Liverpool Process, Smitty is a gracious, gregarious sort and was more than happy to spend several hours regaling me with tales about what he called, "Me first band, me first life, and me first death."

BILL SMITH: Me mate Pete Shotten brought me into the Quarrymen, and Johnny and I got on right away. Even though Johnny was smarter and more popular than I was, we clicked. He was funny, and I was funny, and he liked the blues, and I liked the blues, and when you're a kid, sometimes a mutual love for music and similar senses of humor are enough to form a solid friendship, regardless of social status. Over the years, I've learned that it doesn't always happen that way. The cool kids gravitate toward the cool kids, the uncool kids be damned; that's certainly the way it is down in the sewers. The irony is that now, because of my association with the Quarrymen, I'm just about the coolest kid in the sewers . . . or, at this point, the coolest old wanker, I suppose. But none of your readers give an arse about my philosophy of life; they want to know the good stuff about me and John Lennon.

Okay, I remember in the summer of 1957—right after that first Mendips concert—Johnny and I were messin' about in Calderstones Park, eating sandwiches, watching the girls, and working out vocal harmonies on some Buddy Holly songs. Then out of nowhere, right while I'm singin', "Pretty, pretty, pretty, pretty Peggy Sue," he turns to me, smiling, and says, "Smitty, you're me best mate."

Back then, not too many sixteen-year-old males would show such affection for a mate, so I was a bit of surprised. But this was, oh, four years before he became prone to random bouts of violence, and the Johnny Lennon of 1957 was a sweet sort, the kind of guy who was so talented and funny that, well, let me just say, when a guy like that tells you you're special, you have to be flattered. So I told him he was my best mate, too.

Then he says, "I want to be best mates forever, Smitty."

Again, I was surprised, but remember, this was Johnny Lennon, man, *Johnny fookin' Lennon,* and when he gave you a certain look, you couldn't help agreeing with everything he said. *Everything.* If he gave me that look, then told me to climb to the top of St. Saviour's Church over on Breckfield Road and jump off, I'd have said, "You bet, mate. Shall I go headfirst?" (I now realize that's less of a cha-risma thing and more of a hypnosis thing.) So naturally, I told him I wanted to be his best friend forever, too.

I remember exactly what he said then: "I'm gonna do it. Right here. Right now. In Calderstones."

Those thin eyes of his were making me feel squiffy. I said, "Do what, Johnny?" My tongue had become thick, and I could barely get the words out.

He looked down, and when he broke eye contact, I snapped back to myself. I still think it was very gentlemanly for him to have stopped hypnotizing me and let me make my own decision. "Your brain, man," he said. "I'm gonna eat a bit of your brain. Just a bit. What d'you think about that?"

I didn't think much of it. See, I'd always wanted to find a wife and raise me a houseful of kids, and reproducin' would've been a diffi-cult proposition if me Jolly Roger could produce only dustmen, so I told him, "I don't think that'll work for me, mate." He looked like he was gonna burst out crying then, so I said, "It has nothing to do

with you. If I wanted to be undead, there's nobody I'd want to kill me more than you. You know that."

He said, "Yeah, I do know that," then started picking individual blades of grass from the ground and throwing them over his shoulder, one by one. We were both silent for a while, then, after a few minutes, he finally said something like, "Who's gonna help me get to the Toppermost of the Poppermost?" I asked him what the hell he was talking about, and he said, "Nothin', nothin', don't worry about it. Listen, Smitty, if I'm gonna be on this fookin' planet forever, I need to have people whose company I like, and that means transforming blokes, and how'm I gonna make that happen without gettin' all of England in an uproar? And if folks start thinking of me as, I dunno, the Killer from Menlove Avenue, or John the Ripper, nobody'll come to our shows. And how'm I gonna take over the world?"

Johnny was prone to exaggeration, so I let the comment about taking over the world pass. I told him, "I guess when you transform somebody, you're gonna have to pick your spots carefully. And it'd probably make more sense, instead of asking people, to *just do it*." The second that left my mouth, I realized I might've pulled a cock-up. John's eyes flashed red, and there was a small part of me that thought he'd consider *just doing it* to yours truly. He *was* a zombie, after all, and even if an undead individual has good intentions, they sometimes can't help being irrational. They get hungry, after all.

But he was a top geezer, Johnny was. He nodded and said, "You're right, Smitty." That's all. Just, "You're right, Smitty." Johnny Lennon, if you're reading this, you were the best. I suppose you think I'm a liar and an arsehole, but I think you're aces. Always have, always will.

Listen, don't get me wrong: I know and understand why Johnny wants bugger-all to do with me. See, I got turned in the fall of '57, a mere three months after those Quarrymen gigs, and he didn't do it. Her name was Lydia. If you'd have gotten one look at her back then, you'd have let her turn you, too. I'd introduce you, but she's hideous now, simply hideous. She oozes some kind of green shite from her ears, mate, and it ain't pretty.

Anyhow, long story short, I feel like I planted the seed. I was the guy who suggested Johnny take who he wanted, when he wanted. It probably would've happened sooner or later anyhow; there's no way a guy like Johnny Lennon would've gone through his life politely asking if he could turn you instead of *just doing it* . . . especially after he got famous. So yeah, wasn't *all* my fault, but I still feel bad.

A dapper gent who perfectly illustrates the Liverpool Process's "stop physically aging at fifty" axiom, Paul McCartney was sixty-four during our interview sessions in May 2003, but he could've easily passed for thirty. The guy was the Cute Beatle, is the Cute Beatle, and always will be the Cute Beatle . . . this despite the shiny green kiss-size scar beneath his left earlobe. What with those dewy eyes and apple cheeks, it's easy to see how, at the height of his musical and other-wordly powers, had he so desired, he could've hypnotized and sexually enslaved legions of teenage and twenty-something girls throughout the world. The key phrase there being "had he so desired."

As an interview subject, Paul was a toughie. Lennon was a compulsive truth teller, unconcerned with whose feelings he might hurt, what murders he might uncover, or which interviewer he might injure. Honesty wasn't the best policy for John; it was the only policy. McCartney, on the other hand, oftentimes seemed evasive—especially when it came to the subject of mass murder—and was hesitant to look

me directly in the eyes. (Two friends of mine floated the theory that McCartney was avoiding eye contact in order to keep from accidentally hypnotizing me. A good theory, but Paul McCartney doesn't do anything by accident.)

But here's the weird part: about half of what Paul told me sounded as if it was pulled almost verbatim from Harold Misor's controversial—and very poorly written—unauthorized biography from 1988, Macca Attack: James Paul McCartney Uncovered. *Beatleologists feel much of the book's biographical content was invented, and experts on the undead dismissed the zombie portions of the book as conjecture. Despite McCartney's numerous protestations, the public ate the book up, and it became a bestseller, and many of Misor's suppositions have been embraced as fact—possibly even by McCartney himself.*

Taking all that into consideration, my interviews with Paul raised numerous questions: Was McCartney's brain permanently altered by his LSD and marijuana consumption, and thus did Misor's tall tales became McCartney's memories? Was Misor's reportage actually on target? Did Paul calculatedly want to use my book as a platform to shape the Beatles myth the way he saw fit? Or was Macca simply messing with me for his own enjoyment?

In the end, it doesn't really matter. Paul's word is Paul's word, and we have no choice but to take it as gospel.

PAUL McCARTNEY: I died on July 7, 1957, and it was John Winston Lennon who killed me. When you say it black-and-white like that— or in ebony and ivory, if you will—it sounds ugly, y'know. Imagine that as a *London Times* headline, in bold, capital letters: LENNON MURDERS McCARTNEY. But that's what happened. And I suppose when you think about it, it *was* ugly.

We met the day before, John and I did, on July 6. The Quarrymen were doing a show at St. Peter's Church, and our mutual friend

Ivan Vaughan told me they were a nice little band, and there weren't too many nice little musicians, let alone nice little bands, in Liverpool, so I hopped the Woolton bus and made my way over.

Now, I'd seen a few undead individuals before—one of our neighbors over on Forthlin Road was a Midpointer, as a matter of fact—but never one as young or healthy-looking as John. The zombies I'd met had horrible complexions, just horrible, y'know; some reddish, some greenish, some with permanent blue tears dried on their cheeks. But not John. He glowed. Granted, it was a grayish glow, but it was impressive nonetheless.

After the Quarrymen show—which, erm, wasn't too bad, really— I borrowed a guitar (I believe it was John's) and played him a tune by Eddie Cochran called "Twenty Flight Rock." He stared at me and said, "Wow." That's all. Just "Wow." It was about the only time I've ever seen him at a loss for words. And I still believe that if we hadn't been in public, he probably would've murdered me on the spot.

I don't know if he was thinking of giving me a straight-up transformative bite, or tearing me limb from limb, but that look in his eyes told me, *I want you dead fast, mate.* What makes me say that? Well, erm, I *was* dead fast. *Very* fast. Eighteen hours later, to be exact.

JOHN LENNON: Of course I wanted Paulie dead. Anybody who played guitar that well should either be in my band, or sucking on maggots six feet under. Or both.

PAUL McCARTNEY: When I finished up the Cochran song, John invited me to bring my guitar over to Mendips the next day, and I said yes. I mean, he seemed like a good chap, y'know, and Ivan'd vouched for him, so why not? I figured we'd play some tunes, have a few

laughs, and I'd be on my way. I never even considered an attack. A whole lot of people heard John give me the invite, and if I disappeared, everybody'd know who did it.

I went over after breakfast. John answered the door wearing a blue-and-white-plaid shirt and those thick, clunky government-issue glasses of his. He pulled me in by my elbow—almost dislocating my shoulder in the process, y'know—and dragged me and my guitar to his bedroom.

After that, things happened fast.

JOHN LENNON: Rod Davis didn't want me to Process him. Neither did Lenny Garry or Colin Hanton or John Duff Love or Eric Griffiths or any of those other blokes who drifted in and out of the Quarrymen. Pete Shotten got so offended when I asked him if I could Process him that I thought he was gonna quit the band and get a job, just so he could afford to buy himself a gun and a handful of diamond bullets. None of the Quarrymen wanted it, none of my friends at school wanted it, and I was gonna be alone. It was disheartening, because I knew that, come the year 2040, when I'd be one hundred years old and not even in the prime of my undeath, there wouldn't be a single one of my Liverpool mates around to jam with. Paul wasn't a mate yet, but seemed like a good chap, and he was a helluva guitar player, better than anybody around, and Ivan'd vouched for him, so why not?

PAUL McCARTNEY: John didn't tell me the full details of my transformation until, erm, I believe 1962, but I'm not sure how good his reportage was, because when you're in the throes of brain-sucking, things can get hazy. To this day, I don't know how much of what I know about that afternoon is true.

JOHN LENNON: I wasn't going to muck about. I wasn't going to take any chances. No casual bites. No half-arsed fluid transfer. I decided Paul was the guy who could help me take over the world, and if I was gonna do him, I was gonna do him *right*. I suppose I went a bit overboard, but I knew I'd get only one chance, and like they say, better safe than sorry. In the end, it turned out brilliant anyhow.

With the Liverpool Process, when you're transforming someone, you don't need to take that large of a bite; the entryway only has to be big enough to fit your tongue, and since we Liverpudlian undead can make our tongues as skinny and as long as spaghetti, that's not a problem. You don't even need to take any of the victim's skin with you, but with Paul, like I said, I didn't want to take any chances, so my thinking going in was to take skin and veins and muscle, and lots of it.

PAUL McCARTNEY: The last thing I remember for certain was John jumping onto his bed, and then leaping off like he was diving into a swimming pool. And in this instance, yours truly was the swimming pool, an' that.

JOHN LENNON: I leapt off the bed, parallel to the floor, and landed right on Paulie. Of course, I went for his neck first, because from everything I'd heard, the neck-first approach had worked for over a century, so why mess with success?

I opened my mouth as wide as it would go, then bit off a chunk of his neck about the size of a scone. I wanted to keep the scone intact so I could slap it back over the wound; that way, none of the zombie cocktail could escape. I spit out the sconey thing into my hand and placed it gently on the floor—moving very quickly, of course, so Paul wouldn't bleed out—then did the usual tongue up past the ear and to the brain, and get the brain juice, blah, blah,

blah. I kept all the liquid in my right cheek, which wasn't altogether pleasant, but it wasn't *un*pleasant, either. Then, after I spit a bit of my goo into Paulie, I picked up Mr. Scone, jammed it back into the gouge, and sealed it shut with my tongue, as if I were licking an envelope. I'd never done the licking thing before—I never knew of anybody who did it, for that matter—but somehow, deep down at a gut level, I knew it'd work.

But I still had some goo left. Thus, the business with the arm.

PAUL McCARTNEY: Not too many people know this, but I was a right-hander before that day in John's bedroom.

JOHN LENNON: My thinking was, *better safe than sorry,* so why not take the leftover goo and spit it up into his arm socket?

It's fair to say that by '61, I'd become an expert at removing and reattaching limbs. But this was '57, and it was my first time taking off anybody's arm other than my own, and looking back on it, aesthetically speaking, I did a crap job, just dreadful. Part of it was indecision: I couldn't figure out whether to yank off his arm at the elbow, by a joint, or in the middle of a muscle. After a minute or two of deliberation, I tore off Paul's black jacket and went for an elbow tear. No idea why, really. Instinct, I suppose. Zombie nature, I guess. Who fookin' knows? Anyhow, it turned out to be the ideal choice for my purposes, but really, it was dumb luck; I could've just as easily gone for the shoulder.

Paul started gushing like a bloody geyser—there was spatter on the ceiling that Aunt Mimi wasn't too thrilled about—and I got kind of frazzled, so I didn't do any tidying up at the tear point, and it ended up all zigzagged. If it'd been four years later, we'd have been looking at a straight rip and a barely noticeable reattachment line, but I was new at that sort of thing. (I should mention that just because I figured out how to tear neatly doesn't mean I always *did* tear neatly. Sometimes neatness doesn't count. Sometimes sloppiness is called for.)

I laid Paul's forearm and hand where I'd put the scone earlier, then wrapped my mouth around his elbow and blew the rest of the juices up into his arm. For good measure, I snaked my tongue around his humerus bone and past his biceps, all the way on up to his clavicle. After all, I had to make sure that none of those precious fluids dribbled out, because I didn't want a brilliant musician like Paul to be a good zombie—I wanted him to be a fookin' *great* zombie.

I reattached his arm and licked it closed. Then I went over to the kitchen, tracked down a bottle of cooking sherry, threw down a big drink, which went straight into the hole in the roof of my mouth and into my brain, making me instantly rat-arsed, and I sat down at the table. I crossed my fingers and hoped for the best.

Ten or fifteen minutes later, I went back to my room, and there's Paul, curled up in a little ball, snoring away, sucking his thumb, looking rested, content, and slightly grayish.

I felt his forehead. It was ice cold. Success. Paul McCartney was as undead as a fookin' doornail.

PAUL McCARTNEY: John's often claimed that he set up my guitar for left-handed purposes while I was down for the count, but I don't believe that for a second, because I'm not entirely convinced he re-membered I was right-handed in the first place.

JOHN LENNON: How the fook was I supposed to remember if he was right- or left-handed? I'd only seen him play one fookin' song, and it was right after a Quarrymen show, and after most gigs, my head was in the clouds. Man, if Paul had an elephant trunk for a nose, I wouldn't have noticed.

The fact is, I didn't redo the guitar. Paulie did. And he did it the second after he opened his eyes. I could tell he didn't have any clue what he was doin' while he was doin' it. His hands were working of their own accord, and they were workin' blurry fast. It was a sight to behold. How he knew he'd become left-handed, I have no idea. The amazing thing was that he played even better as a lefty, so it turned out I'd made a solid decision.

PAUL McCARTNEY: John says that after I regained consciousness, we jammed on blues tunes for six or seven hours. That I can believe, because I remember when I woke up the next morning, both of my index fingers were lying under my pillow.

That's the moment I realized I wasn't alive anymore. And I wasn't a damn bit happy about it.

❖

Lennon claims he doesn't remember killing any of his Mendips neighbors, but he doesn't remember not killing them, either. I don't disbelieve him: being that he's eaten, transformed, or mortally wounded several thousand people, it's understandable he'd forget (or block out) a handful of capricious childhood murders.

But the stats don't lie: of the eighty-eight people who lived within a one-block radius of Mendips, circa 1957, eighty-two of them are dead. And of the seventy-nine death certificates I managed to track down, sixty-three of them list the cause of death as "unknown," and in four of those cases, the only identifiable part of the bodies uncovered were the victims' teeth. That's undoubtedly the work of a very, very potent

zombie. John Lennon wasn't the only zombie in the area, but he was certainly the strongest. You do the math.

Three years younger than his former neighbor John Lennon, Lawrence Carroll is one of the Menlove Avenue men who survived to tell some tales. A loyal Beatles fan and self-professed "nosy parker," Lawrence grew up on the corner of Menlove and Vale Road, a mere stone's throw from Mendips. His family moved to Brownlow Hill early that fateful fall, which likely explains why he was still amongst the living when I spoke with him at Bramley's Cafe in Liverpool during May 2002.

LAWRENCE CARROLL: I was kind of chunky and unathletic as a child, and I didn't have too many friends, so I spent a lot of my time wandering around the neighborhood and *watching*. I was a lurker, I suppose you could say. I hid behind trees and bushes and cars, and liked to pretend I was a newspaper reporter, or a spy. I always took notes on a little pad of paper, but very rarely saw anything of interest. Aside from John Lennon's periodic antics, the only thing that made an impression was the couple that I caught *in flagrante delicto* in the back of their silver AC Ace Bristol Roadster.

On July 8, 1957, a boy who I now know was Paul McCartney made his way down Menlove, to the Lennons' house. He was trying to run, but he kept stumbling; it was like his legs couldn't keep up with his upper body. It looked to me like the guitar case he was carrying was slowing him down, and I couldn't figure out why he didn't just drop it if he was in such a rush. It wasn't like anybody on our block would've bothered stealing it. Anybody except John Lennon, of course.

Paul was moaning so loudly that Mrs. Leary, who lived three houses down from the Lennons, stuck her head out her window and told him to stop that infernal racket. Once she saw he was undead, she slammed her window shut. I can't blame her, as I was frightened myself. But a good newspaperman or an honest-to-goodness spy wouldn't run away from a teenage zombie, so I held my ground. Granted, I was crouched down out of sight behind a thick bush, but at least I stayed.

Paul bashed his guitar case against the Lennons' front door over and over again, and yelled, "You get out here, John Lennon! You get out here right now, y'know! You get out here and take your medicine!" And he yelled *loud*.

JOHN LENNON: Paulie hadn't even been undead for twenty-four hours, so there's no way he could've known his vocal cords were considerably stronger than they were the previous day. I leaned out my bedroom window and chucked one of my school textbooks at his head, then told him to shut his gob and that I'd be there after I put on a shirt.

I never went outside without a shirt back then. Some zombies grow a lot of chest hair, and I was one of them, and it was embarrassing. It never dawned on me to lop it off until my first girlfriend, Thelma Pickles, gave me a straight razor for my birthday. It grew back faster than the hair on my head, so I had to shave it once or twice a week . . . yet another reason being undead isn't all it's cracked up to be.

PAUL McCARTNEY: When that textbook nailed me in the noggin, I felt rage, y'know. I'd never felt true rage before—maybe some very mild anger, or a bit of frustration—but I started seeing red, and then blue, and then purple, an' that. Literally. If somebody came across my path right at that moment, it's a guarantee I would've hurt them. Badly.

LAWRENCE CARROLL: It felt like Paul's piercing screams were ema-
nating from a pinprick in the center of my brain. If automobile
alarms existed back then, every car within five kilometers would've
been buzzing or beeping like nobody's business.

John finally came out the front door, and thank God, because
what with all the commotion, the next-door neighbor's schnauzer
sounded like it was gonna have a heart attack. Paul let out a
wordless roar, then smashed his guitar case against the side of
John's head. Then—and if I hadn't seen it with my own two eyes, I'd
never have believed it—John's head flew about ten meters in the air
and bounced off a lamppost. He was screaming *"Ahhhhhhhhhh"*
the entire time, and when his scream mixed with Paul's roar, it
was deafening, but also, in a weird way, lovely. Imagine the vocal
outro of "Twist and Shout" being played through ten thousand
stereos, all turned up to ten, and you'll have an idea of what sweet
yet terrible sounds I experienced on that hot summer day. My left
ear started to bleed, and I yelled, "Shut up, shut up, shut up!" but
naturally, they couldn't hear me over the sound of their own harmonized crowing.

John started running around like a chicken with his head cut
off—or a zombie with his head cut off, I suppose. His mouth continued to shriek, so I suppose his vocal cords didn't get severed,
but I don't know anything about undead science, so maybe zombies can't have severed vocal cords. In any event, it looked to me
like Paul was about to smash John with his guitar case again, but
before he could even lift it up, the right arm of John's headless
body ripped off its own left arm and swung it wildly at Paul.
Somehow, some way, headless John connected on the second
swing, and Paul went down, and went down *hard.* John's body felt
around blindly on the ground until it found its head, then he ran
inside, holding the head like it was a damned rugby ball. Paul was

facedown on the sidewalk, clutching what looked like a pair of sausages.

PAUL McCARTNEY: I was carrying my guitar in my left hand, and my two index fingers in my right, and I was holding on to those fingers for dear life. I can look back at it now and laugh, y'know, because reattaching fingers—especially index fingers—is about the easiest thing you can imagine.

JOHN LENNON: I wanted to glue my head back on the same way I'd closed Paul's wounds the previous day, but, as I immediately learned, when a Liverpool zombie's head is detached from its body, it loses the ability to alter the size and shape of its tongue, until the extrinsic muscles fuse back into place. So after I went inside, I tracked down my aunt Mimi's sewing kit and did some amateurish stitching, and voila, a working head for good ol' Johnny, almost as good as new.

LAWRENCE CARROLL: When John came back out about ten minutes later, Paul was sitting on the ground with his legs folded like he was meditating or something, staring at his guitar case. I knew for sure he was undead at that point, because had he been an average mortal, there's no chance he would've survived getting smacked upside his head by a zombie arm that'd been swung at one hundred kilometers per hour.

John hunkered down beside him and draped his arm around Paul's shoulders. I crawled out from behind the bush a bit so I could hear what they were saying. John was doing most of the talking, because Paul was sobbing so hard. John said, "Listen, mate, I barely know you, and you barely know me, and who knows if we'll even like each other next week, let alone next year? But you're a fookin'

great guitar player and singer, and I can sing and play a little bit too, and the worst thing that can happen now is we'll be able to jam together for all of eternity. When we take over the world, you'll thank me."

I assumed at the time that when he mentioned taking over the world, he meant taking over the record charts.

PAUL McCARTNEY: He could've asked first. It would've been nice to have some time to mentally prepare. All John had to do was say, "Wanna live forever, mate?" I probably would've said yes.

LAWRENCE CARROLL: And then Paul let out this high-pitched, falsetto moan, which got the schnauzer in a lather again. Then John moaned even higher, and they held it for a good long while. It was almost hypnotic. The next time I heard that beautiful sound was when the two of them harmonized the second *please* in the first chorus of "Please Please Me."

PAUL McCARTNEY: My family wasn't too keen on having an undead boy at their breakfast nook, y'know, but they said I could keep on living at home, so long as I didn't slurp out anybody's brains in the middle of the night. I told them they had themselves a deal.

⬩

*A*s he's a man who has gone through numerous physical, metaphysical, and spiritual transformations, it's little surprise that any conversation with George Harrison runs the emotional gamut. One minute, he's waxing poetic about the joys of sitting atop a peak in the Zaskar Range, studying transcendental meditation with a translucent guru named Kamadeva Kartikeya (which, for those of you keeping score, translates to "God of Love/God of War"), then the next, he's waxing sarcastic about his years as a Beatle, a period that he repeatedly—and, at times, grouchily—refers to as the Mania.

That said, George is nearly as honest as John Lennon, albeit he's less chatty and has a significantly lower level of angst. Another similarity he has to John: George made me jump through a few hoops before he deigned to chat on the record . . . except his hoops were—hmmm, how does one put this accurately?—sadistic. And I mean sadistic to the tune of making me drop a poker-chip-size tab of acid, then meditate while standing on my head for twenty-four hours straight while reciting the mantra, "Chiffons to hell, hell to the Chiffons."

Fortunately, I passed George's drug-and-meditation test, so in August 2006, he invited me to spend three weeks at Friar Park, his one-hundred-plus-room Victorian mansion near Henley-on-Thames. Unfortunately, for the majority of my stay, Harrison was off in India doing that whole head-cleansing thing, so I was able to get only about six hours of on-the-record material. Luckily, George had fallen off the vegetarian wagon and had recently feasted on the brain of two Bengal tigers and one Bengal fox, and with all that protein floating through his system, the aptly named Quiet Beatle was focused and energetic.

It should be noted that while I didn't suffer any violence at the hand of Mr. Harrison, I was stabbed on three separate occasions by three separate intruders. (Apparently, knife-wielding intruders had been a problem at Friar Park since 1999.) My injuries were minimal, as I was able to retaliate with some ninja stars I'd recently been given as a gift. I've said it before, and I'll say it again: Thank you, Ringo!

GEORGE HARRISON: For me, the Mania started fast. One day, I'm talking to Paul McCartney about how I'd learned to play the tune

"Raunchy" by Bill Justis, and the next, he's blowing brain fluid into the conical stump where my big toe used to be, and I'm in the Quarrymen.

PAUL McCARTNEY: It seemed strange that John didn't want to transform George, y'know. He knew George was a great guitarist, better than anybody else he'd played with, myself included. He also looked good onstage and was a nice bloke, but, erm, John wanted nothing to do with killing him. And he never really gave me a satisfactory explanation.

JOHN LENNON: George was too young. Plain and simple. After I reanimated Paul, I vowed never to transform anybody under the age of seventeen again. I was almost twenty at that point, and killing somebody in their teens felt wrong. Even if they asked for it.

And Georgie asked for it again and again and again.

GEORGE HARRISON: Yeah, I guess you could say I pestered John about it. My usual line was, "You killed lots of other people. Why can't you kill me?" After a few months, I gave up and went to Paul.

PAUL McCARTNEY: I was happy to oblige George, and would've dropped everything I was doing to make it happen sooner than later . . . but I'd never transformed anybody. Never even considered doing it, y'know.

At that point, I was ambivalent about my undead situation. On one hand, the thought of being in a band with John until the end of time sounded cool, an' that, but on the other, I rarely used what John liked to call my "zombie powers," so I sometimes felt like there was no point to any of this. Oh, sure, I hypnotized a bird or two, but only girls who I knew wanted to be with me in the first place; it was more about speeding things along than taking advantage.

GEORGE HARRISON: Paul transformed me in my bedroom, and it was awkward, to say the least. It was like being on a blind date, complete with stilted conversation and elliptical innuendo.

He said, "So."

Then I said, "So."

Then he said, "So."

Then I said, "So."

That went on for, I dunno, five minutes or something, then I said, "Erm, d'you think we could get started?"

Paul said, "Starting would be a good thing to do. How would you like to begin?"

I said, "Well, Paul, I'm new at this sort of thing. How would *you* like to begin?"

He said, "Dunno. I'm new at this sort of thing, myself, y'know."

That went on for *another* five minutes. At no point did either of us say the words *zombie* or *undead*.

Finally I said, "Come on, Paul, just bloody bite me already."

He went after my neck first. He was very gentle. I barely felt it, and when I didn't say, "Ouch" or anything, he said, "D'you think it took?"

I said, "No clue, mate." I felt dizzy and strange, but that could've been from the blood loss.

He said, "I don't want to take any chances, so I'm gonna try something."

PAUL McCARTNEY: John may have told me about the toe thing, but there's also the chance it came to me in one of my many dreams about scrambled eggs.

GEORGE HARRISON: The world started closing in on me, and the last thing I recall before I woke up undead was Paulie saying, "Take off your shoe, mate."

PAUL McCARTNEY: By the time I began work on George's big toe, he was at least *somewhat* undead, because it came off in my mouth like it was a Mars bar—and when I compare George Harrison's toe to a Mars bar, I'm only referring to the consistency, not the taste. Taste-wise, it wasn't anything close to nougat and caramel. Fact is, a half-zombified toe tastes like a combination of rancid sweat socks, burnt asafetida powder, and, naturally, rotting human corpse.

In the end, it all came out fine—as everybody knows, George became a great zombie, an' that—but I never again bit off a toe, zombie or otherwise.

GEORGE HARRISON: Nobody was shocked when I turned up undead, and everybody assumed John did it, because all of Liverpool thought of him as the kind of guy who'd kill and reanimate his bandmates at the drop of a hat. I didn't dissuade anybody of that notion, and neither did John. Even then we realized the value of mystique.

For a few weeks, I had the same problems every zombie guitarist has immediately after transformation—randomly detaching fingers. I'd switch from an E-minor to an A-major, and next thing I know, *plunk,* my left ring finger's lying at my feet. I'd take a tricky solo, and *plop,* off'd come my right thumb and index finger, still clutching my plectrum. It took some messing about, but I got it mostly under control; still, once in a while, I'd forget myself and strum a hard chord, and my whole hand would take a swan dive. That happens even today. Old habits are hard to break. Clapton has the same problem.

For the most part, things went on as they always did: school, friends, family, music. Yeah, I ate a few folks here and there—I had no choice; brains were the only thing that filled the raging, burning hole in my belly—but trust me, I didn't kill anybody who didn't deserve to be killed.

*

In 1958, John entered his second unhappy year at the Liverpool College of Art. He was frustrated because his band wasn't taking off as quickly as he would have liked, and the LCA faculty and student body were less than thrilled with his state of being. It was a rough time for John, but, resourceful as always, he made the best of it.

In July 1998, former classmate William Norman and ex-painting instructor Dr. Forrest Stephens discussed with me Lennon's hardships with understandable sympathy.

WILLIAM NORMAN: It wasn't like we weren't fully aware he was undead. Hell, the bloke wore his zombieness on his sleeve, shuffling and moaning about the campus like he was William Baskin or Robert Cherry. We all knew full well he could speak normally and walk quickly, but he insisted on rubbing it in our faces. It was almost like he wanted us to be scared of him.

John was a skilled illustrator, but his choice of subject matter was a bit on the limited side. Most everything he drew was morbid: cemeteries with elaborate headstones, mutilated corpses, human heads with insect bodies, and the like. Once in a while he'd doodle a music- or history-oriented picture, and I seem to recall him slapping together a comic book of some sort, but the majority of his work was gruesome, simply gruesome.

DR. FORREST STEPHENS: When it came to painting, young Lennon had more talent in his little gray finger than 95 percent of my students, but he had difficulty focusing. During class, he had a tendency to go off into the ozone for minutes at a time. I have a distinct memory of him standing motionless in front of an easel, staring out the window, and still holding his wet brush, with red paint splattering on his shoes: drip, drip, drip, drip, drip. It was such a brilliant tableau that I wondered if he was pretending.

JOHN LENNON: Of course I was pretending. Each and every one of those ponces at school was a racist. They all grew up in nice neighborhoods, in nice houses, with nice parents, and nice friends, and nice bank accounts, and heaven forbid they socialize with the likes of me. Heaven forbid they get their hands a little bit dirty. I was different. I was the other. I was an alien, and you can't forget that *alien* is the first half of the word *alienated*. So yeah, I spent most of my four years at that fookin' school all by myself.

The only good thing that came out of the entire experience was meeting Stu.

•

Lennon's college chum Stuart Sutcliffe died in 1962 of a brain hemorrhage. Or did he?

Considering how much the two budding artists respected and—let's just go ahead and say it—loved each other, and considering John Lennon's habit of murdering and reanimating those closest to him, it's little surprise that Beatleologists worldwide have long theorized Sutcliffe continued to shuffle about this immortal coil post-1962. Unfortunately, none of them had the wherewithal, connections, or financial means to do the legwork. That's where I came in.

Lennon was uncharacteristically evasive when I asked if Sutcliffe was still around, saying, "No comment, mate. You're on your own with that one." When I pressed the issue, John gave me a backhand to the noggin that sent me flying across his living room. After I wiped the blood from my face and sloppily taped up my broken nose, I changed the subject and made a mental note to never again mention Sutcliffe in Lennon's presence.

So in the fall of 1999, it was off to Germany for the first of my three meetings with Astrid Kirchherr, photographer/stylist/early Beatles worshipper, and Sutcliffe's fiancée at the time of his supposed death. When the talk turned to Stu's current, shall we say, situation, Astrid was polite but vague; she insinuated that there was a possibility he was still around but provided no concrete leads. Realizing Lennon was right—that I was on my own with this one—I followed a hunch and made what some might construe as a questionable decision: I flew to Liverpool, bought myself the biggest shovel I could find, took a taxi out to the Huyton Parish Church cemetery, and dug up Stu's grave.

Turned out my hunch was on target: Stuart Sutcliffe's death was a nondeath, an elaborate piece of performance art. His casket was empty, save for an index card that said, "Probably in Ibiza, living the eternal nightlife. Ta-ra!" Based on the two-sentence note, my gut told me that Stu had been turned into a vampire; after what I'd seen over the previous several years, somebody Stokerizing Sutcliffe seemed like a logical conclusion. My gut, it turned out, was right.

The vampire community in Ibiza is downright cordial—hell, if you got to spend eternity partying in paradise each night from dusk to dawn, you'd probably be pretty darn cheery yourself—and I had no problem finding Mr Sutcliffe. After offering a succinct, sarcastic, and patently false story about how he was transformed from human to bloodsucker ("John knew a guy who knew a guy") and snidely ex-

plaining why he'd gone underground ("I was trying to avoid journal-
ists—you know, like you"), Stu bought me one of the best meals I'd
ever eaten—the so-called blood martini was a little creepy, but when
in Ibiza, do as the Ibizans—then spoke until sunrise about his brief
tenure with John's merry band of misfit zombies.

STUART SUTCLIFFE: I couldn't play a damn bit of bass, and it drove
Paul "Mr. Perfectionist" McCartney nuts. Yeah, I sometimes played
a half step out of key, but so what? Where's it written that just because everybody else is playing in E, the bassist can't play in E-flat?
Nowhere, that's where. Okay, I'm having a laugh here. I couldn't play
for shite, but John's attitude was, you look good, you dress cool, and,
frankly, we can't find anybody else we can stand, so climb aboard.

Sometimes after we finished up a rehearsal, I'd hang out in the
doorway and listen to John and Paul have these endless arguments
about me. John would say things like, "Band unity, mate. All for
zombies, and zombies for all. Toppermost of the Poppermost."

Paul would say, "What the bloody hell is 'Poppermost'?"

John'd say, "Don't worry about it. So listen, I'm transforming
Stu."

Then Paul'd say, "No. Don't. We need *somebody* in our group who
has blood coursing through his veins. The audience has to have one
person onstage—just *one*—who they won't be afraid of, y'know."

John'd then say, "Stu's a pussycat. Nobody's gonna be scared of
him, dead or alive." Frankly, he was right about that one. Nobody
was *ever* scared of me. Even now, even when I'm trying to suck the
blood out of some poor soul, they're like, "Oi, Stu, lookin' good,
mate! Properly pale, an' that! Talk to Johnny Moondog lately?" Why
do you think I always wear shades? It adds mystique, brother . . .
and maybe a tinge of fear.

And then one day—it was a Sunday afternoon, I recall—Paul let his true feelings out: "The man can't play, John. If you zombify him, we're stuck with him, y'know. Forever." Obviously they didn't know I was eavesdropping.

John said, all quietlike, "I don't have a problem with that, mate. He's the kind of guy I'd *like* to have around forever."

Paul said, "Yeah, he's a decent bloke, I suppose, but if you want this band to make it—if you honestly, honestly want to take over the world like you're always bloody saying—we need to keep our options open. If he's undead, he's with us for eternity, y'know. If he's alive, we can sack him whenever we want."

I couldn't listen to any more, so I tiptoed out of the house and headed home. Music wasn't my true artistic love—I was a painter first and a bass player second, or maybe even third—and Paul wasn't exactly my best mate in the world, so I wasn't particularly concerned what he thought about me. But I did respect him, and hearing him say that hurt.

And by the way, that particular Lennon/McCartney discussion led to a, ehm, physical altercation that left Paul with a cracked guitar, and John with a missing ear . . . which George discovered when he slipped on it at rehearsal the next day.

GEORGE HARRISON: I tried my best to stay out of the arguments. John wanted Stu in the band, and Paul didn't, and I kept my opinion to myself. As a matter of fact, I'm *still* keeping my opinion to myself.

They argued about everything, those two. After the blokes from Quarry left the band, John wanted us to be called Johnny and the Maggots. Paul said no way, and if John wanted it to be Johnny and the Something-or-others, it would have to be Johnny and the Moondogs, because he'd heard that *moondog* was an American slang term for "oversize zombie pecker." I actually spoke up that time and took Paulie's side.

STUART SUTCLIFFE: I should note that Paul fancied me enough to keep me around for the Larry Parnes thing. Man, witnessing that cock-up was worth the price of admission.

A well-known English club owner and music impresario who shaped the careers of pseudonymous teen sensations such as Duffy Power, Lance Fortune, and Dickie Pride, Larry Parnes allowed John, Paul, George, and Stu to audition for him in 1960—not, however, as an entity unto themselves, but rather as backing band to one Ronald William Wycherley, aka, Billy Fury.

The audition was held at the Blue Angel, a Liverpool club owned by Allan Williams, a local music heavy who'd taken on the position of manager for the artists temporarily known as the Moondogs. Several Liverpool bands and a whole bunch of hangers-on were at the Angel that day, but only one was able to speak about the audition on the record. Neither Lennon, McCartney, Harrison, nor Sutcliffe wished to discuss what went down that afternoon, and Parnes and Fury had both been dead for decades, and who the hell knew where all those other bands disappeared to. So, in December 2003, after dozens of unreturned phone calls, letters, and emails, I had no choice but to invite myself over to Allan Williams's house in Liverpool.

Williams greeted me at the door with a big smile on his face and a bigger shotgun pointed at my schnozz. Knowing he was a rabid jazz fan, I came armed with a copy of Hard Bop Academy, my biography of jazz drummer Art Blakey, which had been published back in 2001. His smile expanding by the second, Williams took the gift, tossed it into the air, pulled the trigger of his Remington Express Super Mag, and blew my book to confetti; it was literary skeet shooting at its *finest. He then invited me in, prepared me a cup of tea, and told me exactly what happened on May 5, 1960.*

ALLAN WILLIAMS: The boys'd played a few shows at the Jacaranda in Liverpool, but nobody paid them much mind—nobody except me, of course, because I was the only bastard in the whole city who had any ears. John and Paul were frustrated with the less-than-enthusiastic response, so a week or three before the audition for Parnesy, I suspect in order to bolster their confidence, they did a few gigs at a place in Caversham called Fox and Hounds. Since it was just the two of them, they didn't want it to be a Moondogs gig, so John suggested they call themselves the Rotting Oozing Fetid Corpses. Fortunately for everybody, Paul convinced him that the Rotting Oozing Fetid Corpses was a tad too long for the marquee, and he suggested they call themselves the Nerk Twins, NERK being an acronym for Never Eat Road Kill. They both found that hilarious, but I didn't get it. Zombies have an odd sense of humor, I've found.

They played all right for Parnesy at the Blue Angel, the four of 'em did. I don't remember what they started out with—probably some Buddy Holly song or some blues tune or another—but it sounded fine, just fine. They weren't world beaters yet, but anybody with even an iota of musical know-how—like me, thank you very much—could tell they had *something*. Little Billy Fury, however, didn't even crack a smile, but I don't think the boys were particularly concerned with his opinion. I know I wasn't, because the bloke was, at best, semitalented. No, Parnesy was the one we wanted to impress. He had a proven track record, and if he got behind the boys, he'd be able to get them some gigs and some dosh. And that'd make me look good, damn good.

So they finish up the second song, and Parnesy doesn't move a muscle. No nod, no smile, no thumbs-up, no clapping, no comment

about Stuart playing with his back to the crowd, no nothing. All you could hear was crickets, and I don't mean crickets of the Buddy Holly variety. Paul looked over John, then back at Larry, then he gulped and said, all dodgily, "Er, wouldja like to hear something else, Mr. Parnes?" That was the first and last time I ever heard Paul McCartney sound nervous.

Before Larry could answer, I stood up and said, "Hold on, lads," then I ran over to John and Paul—the zombie brains of the outfit, at that point—and gently led them into a back corner. I told them, "As your manager, I'd like to make a business suggestion. I recommend that you put down your instruments and do that hypnotizing thing you always talk about. *Make* him give you the gig. You deserve it. Shit, *we* deserve it."

John glared at me, and for a minute, I thought he was gonna tear my head off. He said, "Listen, Allan, we will never, ever, *ever* use fookin' hypnosis to get a gig. I'll take a job only if we're hired on merit. If Parnes likes us, great, and if he doesn't, sod him, we'll find somebody who does."

I told him if that's the way he feels, I was behind him 100 percent. I'd seen what an angry zombie could do, and even though I wanted to earn a few bob off these blokes, I didn't want to die doing it.

So we all went back to our proper places, then Paul counted off "Bye Bye Love," and despite the fact that Stu flubbed note after note after note, they were spot-on; in comparison, the Everly Brothers sounded like rotting oozing fetid corpses themselves. Billy Fury clapped for a bit, until he noticed that Parnesy still wasn't moving, at which point he folded his hands on the table and said, "That was all right, I suppose." Billy Fury wasn't one to cheese off the boss.

Parnesy walked over to the bandstand and said, "Boys, boys, boys, I don't hear it, I don't feel it, and I don't want it." He pointed at

John and said, "You can sing a little." Then he pointed at Paul and George and said, "And you two can play a little." Then he pointed at Stu and said, "As for you, well, I don't know what the hell you're doing, mate. If I were you, I'd take off those shades, cut my hair, throw that bass in the river, and apply for a job down at the local chemist."

Now even at that early date, there was no love lost between Paul and Stu, but seeing one of his bandmates get blasted set Paulie right off. He dropped his guitar and said, "Excuse me, Mr. Parnes? Can you repeat that?"

Parnesy shook his head. "Not necessary. You heard what I said, mate. Loud and clear."

John put down his guitar, very calmly—too calmly, as far as I was concerned—strolled up to Parnes, grabbed his earlobe between his thumb and index finger, and lifted him off the ground, then said, "Paulie asked you to repeat what you said, *mate*. If you do, maybe I'll let you live. Maybe."

Parnes was a soft cunt who probably hadn't been in a fight of any kind since primary school, and he was pissing his pants. Literally. George pointed at the front of Parnesy's trousers and said, "Looky, looky, Parnesy went wee-wee." Back then, George generally kept quiet in public, and he was rarely snarky, so for him to have opened his mouth, you know he was cheesed.

John then did something I'll never forgive him for: he let go of Larry's ear, dropped him on the floor, grabbed him by his wrist, picked him up, twirled him over his head—around and around and around, like he was a football hooligan waving an Arsenal banner— then he threw him across the club, right into the bar, breaking every bottle of booze in the place. That cost me about three hundred pounds, which, in 1960, was a fookload of dosh. Like I said, unfor- givable. But if violence was what my boys wanted, I was all for it.

Back then, I stupidly supported all their decisions. If I knew then what I know now, I might've tossed those cunts out right then and there.

And then Paul, in what seemed like three steps, bounded across the room, grabbed Parnesy by the ankle, and did the same thing John had done: Arsenal banner spins, then a toss. John caught Larry, and for the next few minutes, Lennon and McCartney alternately kicked and threw Larry Parnes across the Blue Angel. I yelled at them to watch the furniture, and they were somewhat respectful. I asked them if they wanted any help, and they just laughed. Cunts.

Parnesy screamed and screamed and screamed, and, finally, after Paul accidentally-on-purpose dropped him on his arse, Parnesy said, "Okay, okay, you're hired, you're hired. My boys are going on a Scottish tour. Get a drummer, pick a better name, and you can back up Billy Fury."

Fury said, "Mr. Parnes, with all due respect, there's no fookin' way they're backin' me up. I don't want to fookin' die."

Parnesy picked himself up, dusted himself off, and shot a long look at Fury. After a moment, he said, "Understood," turned to the lads, and said, "You'll back up Johnny Gentle." Johnny Gentle was another singing mediocrite who I wouldn't have hired to wipe my bum.

John said, "Brilliant. So you're hiring us on merit, right?"

Parnes said, "Fook, no. I'm hiring you because you'll kill me if I don't."

John grabbed his guitar from the bandstand and brandished it over Larry's head as if it were a mallet, then said, "I asked you, You're . . . hiring . . . us . . . on . . . merit. Right?"

Parnes cringed and said, "Of course I'm hiring you on merit, Mr. Lennon. Of course."

John put down his guitar, smiled, and said, "Great! We'll take it."

GEORGE HARRISON: Picking a name for our band was a contentious struggle, and I wanted no part of it. It was a powder-keg topic, and in those early days, I didn't offer up an opinion unless I was asked, and even then, I was as noncommittal as possible. You never knew what would set off John or Paul. And if they disagreed with something you said while they were hungry, forget it.

The day after the Blue Angel audition, John showed up to rehearsal with a *long* list of name suggestions, and I remember each and every one of them: the Deads-men, the Deadmen, the Undeads-men, the Undeadmen, the Rots, the Rotters, the Dirts, the Dirty Ones, the Grayboys, the Eaten Brains, the Eating Brains, the Mersey Beaters, the Mersey Beaten, the Bloodless, the Graves, the Head-stones, and the Liverpools of Blood.

Paul ripped off John's right arm and used it to slap John across the face, then he said, "Those're horrible, mate, just horrible, y'know."

John took back his arm, bit off the pinkie, spit it toward Paul's gut—apparently Johnny didn't take too kindly to being slapped, especially with his own hand—and said, "I had this dream last night—"

Stu interrupted him. "Brilliant. Here we go again with the dreams."

STUART SUTCLIFFE: It seemed like every fookin' evening, like at three in the fookin' morning, John would ring me to tell me about some fookin' dream he'd had. One night he'd dream about being in heaven and talking with Robert Johnson about the Devil, then the next, he'd dream about being in hell, talking to the Devil about Robert Johnson. Even if it was a good dream, he'd be upset, and I was happy to try and calm him down, but, well, shite, he could've called Paulie once in a while.

GEORGE HARRISON: I ignored Stu and asked John what his dream was about. If nothing else, it would be an entertaining story.

He said, "Right, then. So I'm sitting on a canoe in the middle of the Thames, floating about without a paddle, and the sky is fookin' orange, and I see some girl in another canoe, and she's got two paddles. She's got these eyes that're shining like silver or diamonds, and she says, 'John Winston Lennon, d'you want to eat a piece of pie?'

"I say, 'I don't want any pie, I want one of your fookin' paddles. This river smells like shite, and I wanna get back to Liverpool.'

"She says, 'What if I set the pie on fire, John Winston Lennon? What if the pie has flames shooting out of it? Tasty, tasty flames.'

"I say, 'It'll probably improve the scent around here, but I don't want any pie. If you wanna feed me something, get me some fookin' brains.'

"She says, 'So I can't interest you in a flaming pie, John Winston Lennon?'

"I say, 'No, you can't interest me in a flaming pie, you sparkle-eyed wench.'

"She says, 'You know what? You're a right cunt, John Winston Lennon. Can I interest you in flaming *hell*?' Then she sets me on fire, whacks me on me head with her paddle, and turns into a giant silver bug.

"I jump into the water so as not to burn, then I say, 'What's this Kafka shite, then?'

"She says, 'I'm not a cockroach, idiot. I'm a beetle. And you're going to die a real death. Unless you call your band the Beatles. And that's Beatles with an *a*.'

"I say, 'What d'you mean Beatles with an *a*? Are you talking B-E-A-T-L-E-S or B-A-E-T-L-E-S or B-E-E-A-T-L-E-S or A-B-E-E-T-L-E-S or—'

"She says, 'Figure it out for yourself, cunt. Figure it out for yourself.'"

John ran his hand through his hair—which was getting a bit shaggy, I should note—and said, "And then I woke up."

See? Entertaining.

PAUL McCARTNEY: I was tired of arguing, y'know. By then, I didn't care if it was the Deads-men or the Deadmen or the Undeads-men or the Undeadmen or the Rots or the Rotters or the Dirts or the Dirty Ones or the Grayboys or the Eaten Brains or the Eating Brains or the Mersey Beaters or the Mersey Beaten or the Bloodless or the Graves or the Headstones or the Liverpools of Blood or B-E-A-T-L-E-S or B-A-E-T-L-E-S or B-E-E-A-T-L-E-S or A-B-E-E-T-L-E-S or A-B-C-D-E-F-G. If Johnny wanted to let a giant dream bug dictate our name, that was his prerogative.

He declared we would be the Silver B-E-A-T-L-E-S, and I gave it a thumbs-up, because I needed to focus my energy elsewhere. Y'see, I was having some issues with a certain percussionist.

•

Sacked just before the Beatles exploded onto the international scene, Pete Best is the unluckiest footnote in rock 'n' roll history. A solid if not unspectacular drummer and a notorious grump, Pete joined John, Paul, et al. in 1960, right after the Scotland tour with Johnny Gentle, a tour that left the boys miserable and broke. Pete was a classically attractive young man, and, almost immediately, a goodly portion of the band's ever-growing female fan base took to him like flies to a corpse.

Pete, who still resides in Liverpool, has mixed feelings about his twenty-four months as a Beatle (or, more accurately, his one month as a Silver Beatle and his twenty-three months as a regular Beatle), and

during our five-hour, increasingly drunken chat at Le Bateau over on Liverpool's tony Duke Street during the summer of 1997, his emotional conflict was always evident, and I couldn't help but feel bad for the guy. But Pete Best doesn't want you to feel sorry for him. He just wants you to listen.

PETE BEST: Except for George, who was a couple of years younger than us, we were all about the same age, but John and Paul were clearly the bosses. You know how sometimes when you have a boss who's really charismatic and mysterious, you spend a lot of time with your coworkers trying to analyze him? Well, that was what it was like with Stu and me. We used to talk about John and Paul all the time: *Did John like my snare fill on "Be-Bop-A-Lula"? Did Paul notice that Stu'd dropped a couple of notes on "Long Tall Sally"? Did they mind that I'd scooped that blond bird who was off to the side of the stage, shaking her big titties at us? Were they going to kill me and turn me into a zombie without any advance notice?* It was always a head game with Lennon and McCartney, and what with their habit of murdering at the drop of a hat, the stakes were high.

Two weeks after they brought me aboard, we went to Hamburg to play what seemed like five hundred shows at a sleazy joint called the Indra Club, run by this dodgy bloke named Bruno Koschmider. Bruno ran us ragged: we played seven nights a week, and some nights we're talking six hours straight. It got to the point we were eating uppers like they were sweets.

You could always gauge how many uppers John, Paul, and George had taken by their skin tone: If they took four pills or less, they turned green—like as green as a lawn in the middle of the summer. Anything beyond that, they turned bright fookin' yellow, so yellow that they glowed in the dark. Green and yellow complexions are the best advertisements for undeadness, so everybody knew what we were about. But even with the stench of death that permeated the club, the crowds packed the joint night after night after night.

PAUL McCARTNEY: Pete wanted nothing to do with death or undeath. I told him over and over that I wouldn't hurt him and that he should ask George how simple and painless it was. Of course, I talked to him about it only when John was, erm, out of earshot. Sometimes I just had to throw John's "all for zombies, and zombies for all" precept right out the window. Sometimes I had to make a decision for the band all by myself, y'know.

PETE BEST: The one thing that almost convinced me to let Paul do his thing to me was the birds. No matter how unhealthy looking those zombies' faces may have been, and no matter how many times their fingers fell off during guitar solos, those blokes had the girls drooling over them, and drooling girls looked pretty fookin' good to me. The thought of that dustmen shite shooting out of my plonker wasn't very appetizing, however, but having the ability to hypnotize twin sisters into bed, well, that was kind of appealing. Not that they *did* hypnotize twin sisters into bed, but knowing the ability was there was greatly comforting and greatly exciting.

*

S*ix months before this book was to go to press, I received a scary-as-hell email from a certain German-born, Spain-based photographer-cum-artist-cum-vampire who'd been all but invisible for almost three decades.*

Jürgen Vollmer and his pals Astrid Kirchherr and local artist/ musician Klaus Voormann were a tight-knit clique who dubbed them-selves the Exis, and that's "exi" in honor of their pet philosophy, existentialism. (Jürgen cheerfully admits the Exis were a tad on the pretentious side.) The threesome discovered the Beatles when the band was relocated from the Indra to another Bruno Koschmider–run venue called the Kaiserkeller. With their ever-increasing musical con-fidence and ability to simultaneously entertain and scare the crap out of their growing audiences, the five Liverpudlians knocked the three Hamburgers on their collective hindquarters. The smitten Exis imme-diately latched onto the undead quintet and held on for dear life.

By all accounts, Jürgen was the quietest of the Exis, and his near si-lence came about because he simply didn't have enough energy to talk; turned out, the poor guy was always starving. After all, what with the scurvied prostitutes and drunks clogging up the streets surrounding the Kaiserkeller—streets that were home to Hamburg's red-light dis-trict—it was difficult for a young vampire to find quality blood with-out drawing attention to himself. So it was either scurvy-flavored hookers and gin-soaked alkies, or nothing at all.

In the summer of 2009, Jürgen stumbled onto my website, where he read one of the many blog entries in which I bitched about Stuart Sut-cliffe's reticence to divulge the specifics of his transformation from meat eater to bloodsucker. Jürgen sent me an email:

> MR. GOLDSHER, I WISH TO DISCUSS MR. SUTCLIFFE WITH YOU! MEET ME AT CA L'ISIDRE IN BARCELONA ON AUGUST 15 AT EXACTLY MIDNIGHT! SHOW UP AFTER 12:01, AND I'LL BE LONG GONE! SHOW UP AT OR BEFORE 11:59, AND I WILL KILL YOU IN A HIDEOUS FASHION! I'LL BE THE ONE WEARING THE PRETENTIOUS BLACK CAPE ☺! YOURS ALWAYS, MR. JÜRGEN VOLLMER.

*What with the formality, the capital letters, the numerous excla-
mation marks, the incongruous smiley face emoticon, and the threat
of a painful death, how could I refuse?*

*Despite the menacing tone of his missive, Mr. Vollmer—like his
fellow vampire, Mr. Sutcliffe—is as gracious a dinner partner as one
could hope for. Better yet, he's painfully honest and has a fine memory
of his brief period as a Beatles-worshipping Exi.*

JÜRGEN VOLLMER: We fancied all five of the boys, but we fancied Stu
the best because he was the most interested in what the Exis were
all about. He and I had long talks in the Kaiserkeller's piddling little
dressing room about Sartre, and Heidegger, and Jaspers, and
Stoker . . . although he didn't know I was a vampire, so my lengthy
forays into the hidden meaning of *Dracula* probably confused the
hell out of him.

I knew he was at ease with the otherworldly beings—if you're
with John Lennon and Paul McCartney twenty-five hours a day,
eight days a week, you'd *better* be comfortable with the inhuman—
but I still didn't want to spring my vampire life on him. I mean, if
your bandmates are zombies, you might be hesitant to become a
friend to a Child of Osiris, because, let's face it, how much inhu-
manity can one person take? But that all changed when Stu started
falling for Astrid.

I'll freely admit it: I was jealous; I was the odd man out, so how
could I not be? John and Paul gravitated toward Klaus because he
had an aptitude for music, and Astrid was trying to seduce Stu, and
Pete was always trying to score with girls, and George was off doing
whatever a zombie who'd taken too many amphetamines does at
three in the morning, so I didn't have a Beatle to call my own. I
tried to ingratiate myself, believe me, but outside of Stu, they simply
weren't all that interested. In retrospect, I feel it had a lot to do with

the fact that I was too quiet, but I couldn't help it. I was exhausted, as good blood was at a premium.

One night while Stu and Astrid were kissing in the corner of the club, I got fed up with the whole situation, so I grabbed Stuart by the collar of his leather jacket and hauled him back to the dressing room. I carried him like he weighed nothing, and I could tell he was taken aback by how strong I was. I held him against the wall by his neck and gave him a brief history of vampires, everything from revenants of the twelfth century to good old Vlad Tepes to the falsitude of bat transformation to the enlightened vampire colony that was already forming in Ibiza. I purposely didn't mention what is going to happen in Swaziland in 2028, because a prophecy of vampire-based genocide would likely have soured him on the concept of me giving him a nibble on the neck, wouldn't you say?

After I released him and he crashed to the floor, he told me the thought of immortality was suddenly appealing now that he'd met the girl of his dreams. He told me that John and Paul weren't going to zombify him because he wasn't a good enough bass player. He told me that at first, the thought of living forever sounded kind of daunting, but now with Astrid in the picture, it sounded farkin' good.

I said, "I'm glad to hear that, Stuart, just thrilled." Then I asked him if he wanted to share my life.

Stu looked at his hands and asked, "How do you think Astrid will feel about the whole thing?"

I told him that never once in the years we'd known each other did she say anything disparaging about vampirism, and that she was an all-embracing woman who would spend time with Negros, Orientals, Christians, Jews, vampires, zombies, or werewolves, so long as they brought something interesting to the table.

He asked me, "So let me get this straight: with this vampire thing, unless somebody jabs a stake into your chest, you're immortal?"

I told him that was more or less the case.

He stood up and gently kicked Paul's guitar case. "To tell you the truth, mate, I don't know if I'm long for this band. Paulie doesn't like having me around. John loves me, but he doesn't like having me around as a musician. And I miss painting. And I love Astrid. I love her a lot, mate."

I told him she loved him a lot, too.

We spent the next few minutes talking about vampire logistics, then Koschmider poked his head in the door and said, "Sutcliffe, get onstage, *mach schnell, mach schnell!*"

Stu looked at me and said, "Okay, Jürgen. Let's do it. Tomorrow at sundown."

I couldn't have been more pleased. Stu was going to be my friend for life.

STUART SUTCLIFFE: The choice was simple, really. I loved Astrid, and Astrid loved me. Jürgen was a good, kind man, and as much as I loved John, well, let's just say, if he was a moody cunt in 1960, imagine what he'd be like in 2060 or 2160 or 2260. So Jürgen did his thing, and here I am.

Paul and Pete were deported that December. The cover story we came up with was that they got sent back home because they set fire to a johnny-hat in the Kaiserkeller dressing room, then were thrown in jail. The real reason they went home was that John Q. Law got wind of John W. Lennon's plot to go to Magdeburg and dig up Hitler's brain as a laugh. (The cops watched our every move, and who could blame them? At the time, Germany had the smallest per capita zombie population in the world, so they didn't know *what* John, Paul, or George might do.) After Jürgen turned me out, Astrid

and I went underground for a while; then in '62, when the Hamburg cops decided they wanted to rid the city of vampires, Astrid and I staged my funeral, and it was off to the Spanish islands.

Jürgen spends his winters here in Ibiza, and his summers in Munich, and he's still my best mate, and when he's in town, we're inseparable. As for Astrid, I get to see her maybe six or seven weeks out of the year. See, she had to continue her life in Germany as if I was dead, so in '67, she married a nice bloke named Gibson Kemp. I'd bet most of your readers won't know that he's the drummer who replaced Ringo in Rory's band.

Like I said, Gibson's a nice bloke, but I'm sure when they were together he touched Astrid in places where I'd prefer she not be touched by anybody but me. That being the case, given the opportunity, I'd fookin' suck him dry in a heartbeat.

●

A *quick backtrack:*

In the months before German law enforcement officers sent the Beatles back to the UK, the lads made an interesting discovery: Rory Storm was a Fifth Level Ninja Lord.

A Liverpudlian singer who had a head of hair to die for, Storm (who was born Alan Caldwell and passed away in 1972, found dead next to his equally dead mother; some say they were both mistakenly killed by a confused low-level yakuza lackey) always had an affinity for the world beyond the world, so much so that in 1958, he named his first band Dracula and the Werewolves. Rory considered the Quarrymen as rivals, and even though he would've been thrilled to be undead, he refused to approach Lennon or McCartney with his zombification request, telling anybody who'd listen, "Fook the Quarryboys. I want to have me own bag."

Enter 忍の者乱破.

A *Sixty-sixth Level Ninja Lord,* 忍の者乱破—*which loosely translates to Badass Ninjutsu Dude—relocated to Liverpool in 1955, partly because he was fed up with the bureaucracy of the Iga Ueno Ninja scene, and partly because he had an inexplicable affinity for drab cities and lousy restaurants.*

In 1958, 忍の者乱破 *quietly opened up a secret-but-not-as-secretas-a-Ninja-should-be dojo on Molyneux Road, right by the Mersey River. He didn't do any advertising, per se, and how Rory Storm heard about it is anybody's guess. But hear about it he did, and Rory became* 忍の者乱破's *first British student.*

Aside from evolving into a solid but unspectacular Ninja Lord, Caldwell was a marketing genius, and when he realized his band, Rory Storm and the Hurricanes, simply didn't have the firepower of Lennon and McCartney's crew, he decided to sprinkle some Japanese flavor into his skiffle stew. But we're not talking a tinge of Japanese music—that would've been tough, as kotos, biwas, and samisens weren't easy to come by in Liverpool—but rather a sampling of Ninja demonstrations in between songs.

忍の者乱破 *was less than pleased with his disciple, taking the understandable stance that Ninjas and rock 'n' roll shouldn't share the same stage. The old hurts are still there, a fact that was made abundantly clear when I spoke with the then-305-year-old warrior at his home near the top of Mount Omoto in February 2004.*

忍の者乱破**:** Alan Caldwell was a great disappointment to me. His skills: solid yet unspectacular. His demeanor: courteous yet envious. His discipline level: sizeable yet inconsistent. His ultimate life goals: unsatisfactory. He wanted to be an artist—specifically, a musician. Now, I have the utmost respect for music makers, but what Alan Caldwell never realized is that Ninja warriors are just as artistic as the best singer or guitar player or drummer . . . if not more so. He was quite vocal in his opposition to *my* opposition to modern music.

This is not to say I dismissed Alan Caldwell's goals entirely. As a matter of fact, I thrice watched Alan Caldwell and his band perform. (I refuse to refer to him as Rory Storm; that is a ridiculous name for a Ninja Lord, and no matter what I thought of his skills, Alan Caldwell *was* a Ninja Lord.) Had Alan Caldwell's Ninja moves been more than merely solid, and had his band's music been less derivative, I might not have been so saddened by his choice to merge the worlds of Ninja and rock 'n' roll. Besides, there was already one Lonnie Donegan walking the Earth, and even to my unenlightened ears, one Lonnie Donegan was more than enough.

Most galling to me was that he taught the members of his band numerous Ninja moves . . . and he taught them sloppily. Double spins became half spins. Graceful cat somersaults became clumsy dog rolls. Please do not get me started about their abominable work with the shuriken, as my stomach becomes pained when I think about it.

However, there was one gentleman in the band for whom there was hope, who had a glimmer of talent. With regular training, with hard work, and with proper discipline, young Richard Starkey— who became known to the world as Ringo Starr, a pseudonym that was far more palatable to me than the silly stage name Rory Storm—had the potential to become Great Britain's first true Ninja Lord.

*

*R*ingo Starr is happy to talk to you. He'll tell you stories, he'll crack some jokes, he'll laugh, he'll cry, and he'll drink you under the table. Thing is, you have to find him first, and good luck with that one.

Lennon thought he was somewhere in China, studying kung fu with a rogue group of former Shaolin monks. I wasted ten days and almost ten grand on that tip.

McCartney said he hadn't spoken with Ringo in several years, but added that one of his mates told another one of his mates that Starr was in Los Angeles, holed up with a swimsuit model. Wrong-o.

Harrison didn't have a clue, but he had a gut hunch that the drummer was in South America, possibly Brazil. All I got out of that trip was sun poisoning and the knowledge that I look horrible in a Speedo swimsuit.

If the rest of the Beatles didn't even know where Ringo spent his time, how the hell was one little journalist from Chicago supposed to track him down?

Ultimately, 忍の者乱破 pointed me in the right direction, explaining that after the Beatles' demise, Ringo made it his goal to move up fifteen levels on the Ninja Lord scale, and the only way to make that happen is to practice your Ninja art in the coldest place on Earth. So, since 2001, Ringo has been bopping between London, the North Pole, and the South Pole.

In December 2005, before I'd fully healed from the various beatings John Lennon imparted upon my body, I went to my friendly neighborhood camping supplies store, bought nearly three thousand dollars' worth of cold weather gear, and boarded a plane to Bumfuck, Antarctica, where, for twelve days, I drank a whole lot of piping-hot miso egg-drop soup with good ol' Richie Starkey.

RINGO STARR: The Hurricanes only did three Ninja/rock shows in Liverpool. Rory wanted to keep the Ninja stuff secret until we got it just right, and, man, talk about secret—outside our families and our Ninja master, he didn't tell anybody about the gig. Our audience consisted of Rory's sister, 忍の者乱破, and two of 忍の者乱破's disciples. Not an auspicious way to start a new trend, eh?

But Rory's goal wasn't to start a trend; all he was concerned about was, as he so inelegantly put it, "kicking some fookin' Quarrymen arse." Nobody was beating down my door with an invitation to join their band, so I stuck with Rory, even though I didn't want to kick *anybody's* fookin' arse. Personally, I thought John, Paul, and George were fine fellows, spot-on musicians, and a credit to the living and undead alike.

The Hurricanes had already been playing at the Kaiserkeller for a good long while when the Beatles were unceremoniously dumped into the club, and I've gotta tell you, the audiences that saw both bands play were treated to one helluva show. The Beatles'd go on first, roar through fifteen or twenty songs in forty-five minutes, then John would pick three girls from the crowd, bring them up onto the stage, and juggle them, while the other guys played circus music in the background. I still have no idea how he was able to do that without hurting anybody.

Then it was our turn. Rory liked to structure our sets so we'd play two songs, then give five minutes of Ninja demo, then two more songs, then more demo, and so on. Musically speaking, we weren't too bad, and our Ninja moves improved more every day, especially those of Johnny "Guitar" Byrne, who got to the point where he could open a bottle of beer with a Ninja star from ten meters away. Bruno probably could've charged more than a three-deutsche-mark cover—today, it's a common triple bill, but in 1960, no club in the world could deliver a Ninja/zombie/music trifecta—but Mr. Koschmider wasn't exactly the brightest star in the Hamburg sky.

I thought Pete Best was one helluva drummer, and aside from that one Wednesday night when George broke a guitar over his head, hauled him up with one hand, and threw him all the way across the club, I saw no indication that any of the other Beatles were dissatisfied with his drumming. I jammed with them every so often, and though they always liked my playing, they never came close to asking me to join. And I was cool with that. I knew if I left the 'Canes and neglected my Ninja studies, 忍の者乱破 would be pissed. And 忍の者乱破 is the last person in the world you want to piss off. So I treaded water and waited to see what would happen next.

JOHN LENNON: It was the day after Crimbo, 1960. Paul, some bird that Paul'd picked up, and I were at a party at Paul's mate Neil Aspinall's flat. Right before midnight, I dragged Paul into Neil's bedroom—I accidentally ripped off his right hand, but he slapped it right back on, so that's neither here nor there—then threw him onto Neil's bed and asked him, "What the hell're we doing, mate?"

He said, "I dunno about you, but I'm repositioning my hand, which you just ripped the hell off. And I'm drinking, y'know."

I said, "I don't mean here, I mean *here*."

Paul said, "Umm, you lost me."

I said, "What're we doing with the band? What's the point?"

He gave me a funny look, then said, "I thought the point of being in a band was that there's no point. We play a few tunes, we drink a few drinks, we have a few laughs. That's enough for me. Who needs a point? It'd be nice to have some dosh in our pockets, and maybe make a record someday, but if we keep going the way we're going, I think that'll come."

I said, "That's not enough for me."

He said, "Well then, what do you want?"

I said, "You have to remember, Paul, we're different from any other band in the world. Nobody's got what we got."

He said, "What's that?"

I said, "We're on this planet forever. For fookin' ever."

Paul said, "Yeah. I'm well aware of that, y'know. What does that have to do with our band?"

I said, "Ten years from now, do you want to be some sad cunt cranking out Chuck Berry tunes at the Cavern Club for ten shillings and two pints?"

He said, "Erm, I suppose not."

I said, "Ten years from now, do you want to be playing at, I dunno, Wembley Stadium in front of tens of thousands of people?"

He said, "That sounds good."

I said, "Yeah, but here's something that sounds better: ten years from now, do you want to rule the world?"

PAUL McCARTNEY: I laughed so hard that I almost chundred my champagne. I asked him, "Okay, mate, you've been talking this shite for years, y'know. What the fook do you mean, 'rule the world'?"

He said, "Just like it sounds. Do you want to rule the world?"

Now, one of the things I've always loved most about John is that he thinks big, an' that. I was happy making slow moves, taking baby steps: play for a few people at a little party, play for a few more people at a big club, make a record, play at a *bigger* club, get on the radio, play an even *bigger* club. Up the ladder one rung at a time, y'know. John, on the other hand, apparently wanted to go immediately from the Kaiserkeller to the moon. After I got my laughter under control, I readjusted my hand, which I'd done a lousy job of reattaching, and asked him, "Erm, why, Johnny? Why d'you want to rule the world?"

He said, "We're a bunch of yobbos from Liverpool. It'll be a laugh. Plus, those Hammer movies are pretty cool, and if we get big, maybe they'd make one about us: *The Curse of the Beatles* or something."

I said, "Erm, okay. Not the best reasons, but I'll accept it. And how exactly do you intend to take over the world?"

He kneeled down on the floor, gave me a huge grin, and said,

"First of all, we have to get to the Toppermost of the Poppermost."

Again with the Poppermost. I said, "Give me a straight answer, Johnny: what the bloody hell is the Poppermost?"

He got a dreamy look in his eyes, then said, "The *Poppermost* is the *Toppermost*, man, the *top*, the summit of the mountain, the place where we can do *whatever* we want, *whenever* we want. In the Poppermost, if we feel like starting a zombie colony in Glastonbury where the undead can roam free without fear of being popped with a diamond slug, we can. Or if we want to draw and quarter Cliff Richard, then cook his cortex for supper, we can. If we want to zombify Spike Milligan and Peter Sellers so *The Goon Show* can live on forever, we can. *Whatever* we want, *whenever* we want."

I said, "That sounds brilliant. But again, how do you plan to do it?"

He asked me, "What do we do best?"

I said, "I suppose we're good at being a nice little rock 'n' roll band."

He said, "Right. Now we have to figure out how to become a nice *big* rock 'n' roll band. First, we have to start writing more of our own songs. Fook playing covers. That isn't gonna get us out of the small clubs."

I wasn't sure what writing tunes had to do with world domination, but in terms of advancing the Beatles, that made solid sense. I said, "Right. I can get behind that. What else?"

He said, "We tour and tour and tour and tour, and we try not to cause any trouble . . . or, at least, not get caught. I know we have to eat—and sometimes we have to eat a lot—but no obvious murders, no public decapitations, no castrations just for the fook of it, kill only those who deserve to be killed, no sex slaves . . ."

I said, "I haven't made any sex slaves."

He said, "Yeah. Right. Sure. And neither have I. Wouldn't even consider it." He said that in his famous John Lennon sarcastic tone, which made me certain he *had* created a few sex slaves. But I'd never know for sure, because there's an unwritten zombie code: keep your sex life to yourself. You could talk about drinking the postman's brain fluid all you wanted, but a discussion about how big of a dustmen pile you blew on some bird's bum is a no-no.

I said, "Right, then. No sex slaves, an' that. Next?"

He stood up and scratched his head, then said, "I haven't quite gotten that far yet. I'll figure it out when we get there."

I got up, then clapped him on the shoulder, and told him, "Sounds like a plan, mate. Let's get rolling on this next year, cool?"

He said, "Cool. But this being the holiday season and all, I don't think we need to put our plan into effect until January second. So what d'you say we go and cause some trouble?"

I said, "Absolutely." And then, right after midnight, John and I snuck down Neil's back stairs, went down to the Mersey River, and feasted. Over many glasses of champagne and many handfuls of fresh, firm, warm brains, we decided that 1961 was going to be a big year.

✦

The year 1961 saw a major change for the infrastructure of Liverpool's soon-to-be-finest: with Stu Sutcliffe back in Hamburg guzzling down all the German blood he could get his fangs on, the quintet became a quartet, forever and ever, amen. They booked dozens and dozens of shows throughout the UK and soon realized that driving the van and hauling their gear themselves put a crimp in their style, so they asked Paul and George's childhood pal Neil Aspinall to become their roadie. A loyal, hardworking sort, Aspinall stayed with the band until the end, becoming one of the many so-called Fifth Beatles.

Nobody knows for certain if John, Paul, or George jammed their respective tongues into Aspinall's neck and gave him eternal life, because nobody could ever tell whether or not Aspinall was a zombie. He's always sported that gray English pallor, but that could be credited to living in Liverpool. He has an ageless look about him—he could be forty or ninety or anywhere in between—but that might be due to, I don't know, cigarettes or something. He refuses to discuss whether or not he's a living being, but any other topic is fair game, as I learned when I spoke with him in January 2006, two years before he either passed away or relocated to the Liverpudlian sewers.

NEIL ASPINALL: I couldn't tell you exactly how many concert dates we did in '61. I'd say as few as one hundred and as many as two-fifty. It became a blur.

John told me right after I was hired that they were going to be good lads, or, at least, as good as they could be, and his definition of being good meant no deaths—or, at least, no *obvious* ones. Like all Liverpool zombies, the boys ate people food for enjoyment, but they had to eat brains to survive, so they had no choice but to, ehm, take care of their business every once in a while. I can't blame them. If you crave a fried Mars bar, you go and get a fried Mars bar. If you crave a brain, you go and get a brain. End of story.

As far as I know, nobody died in '61 at the hands of Lennon, McCartney, or Harrison, but that's not to say they didn't feed—trust me, they fed. That somehow didn't hurt the development of their loyal fan base. I'd suspect that if you loved a zombie band, you'd be thrilled to have one or both of their lead singers murder you.

But John and Paul didn't do all the killing. George took on his

fair share, and the interesting thing about that was, all the folks George reanimated that year became virtuoso guitarists.

GEORGE HARRISON: Back then, the thing I lived for the most was music, and I figured if *I* thought that way, then *everybody* should think that way. So whenever I had a brain craving, I'd pack up my trusty Gretsch 6128 Duo Jet and head over to the trendiest part of whatever town we were gigging in. I'd look for a cool-looking guy or girl in their late teens or early twenties who was carrying a guitar; if they recognized me, so much the better. Then I'd invite them for a walk, and if they needed a little nudge, I'd look into their eyes and bend their will, but thanks to either my Beatle status or the fact that I was carrying a cool guitar, most came willingly. I'd ask them if they wanted to go back to their place and jam on some Leadbelly; if they said no, I'd move on, but if they said yes, it was off to their flat.

Once there, after a few tunes, I'd put them to sleep, then, after a quick cuppa cuppa, I'd take the traditional zombie chomp right beneath their earlobe, then, after I did the brain fluid switch, I'd jam the fretboard of my Gretsch into the wound and circle it around for a bit, like for thirty-one seconds, then I'd replace the divot, seal it shut with my tongue, and voila, an undead teenager who could play the hell out of their axe.

I purposely never found out any of their names, so it's possible that some of them became stars. If I were to venture a guess about who I turned into an undead fretman, I'd go with Dave Davies. I mean, just *look* at the bloke. Those're some zombie eyes if I've ever seen 'em.

Arguably the Beatles' most important moment of 1961 went down at the end of June, when the boys took to producer Bert Kaempfert's studio to record a backing track for UK rock crooner Tony Sheridan. Sheridan, who refused numerous invitations to speak with me, was going to have his name front and center on the record sleeve; for that matter, there was the possibility the Beatles moniker wouldn't appear on the cover at all, a fact that either wasn't communicated to or understood by the Beatles.

GEORGE HARRISON: I left the studio before most of the bad stuff went down at the Sheridan session, and what I did see was a bit of a blur. But I think Pete was the instigator.

PETE BEST: I was a troublemaker, but my trouble was mostly juvenile shite—you know, messing about with girls I probably shouldn't have messed with and playing practical jokes, that sort of thing. I wasn't into destruction for destruction's sake.

No matter what anybody says, I had nothing to do with what happened to Bert's studio. Seriously, how could I? I was a regular living human being and didn't have anywhere near the strength necessary to cause such a ruckus. But they tried to pin it on me, John and Paul did, and I think for yours truly, that was the beginning of the end, although the end wound up being quite a ways away.

Besides, I know for a fact that Paul started it. I saw it with me own two eyes.

PAUL McCARTNEY: I didn't start it, y'know. I mean, you've seen the pictures of Pete's drum kit, right? It was *obvious* that he started it.

John and I might've finished it, though.

JOHN LENNON: That hour or two is a little hazy, but I'm pretty certain it wasn't Pete or Paul. I think I cast the first stone. I think I threw the first amp. But I refuse to accept the entire blame. I was bad, and Paul was bad, but Pete was worse.

PETE BEST: Here's what really happened, and if any of those undead fookers tell you differently, they're feeding you more shite than you'd find in the sewers.

So we run through the arrangement a few times, and once Bert and the engineer are pleased with the mix, they give us the go-ahead, and we rock out for forty-five minutes. Bert says he's happy with the material, and thanks for coming, then John puts down his guitar, walks right up to Kaempfert, and says, "That's it?"

Bert says, "Yes, that's it, Mr. Lennon. Were you expecting something else?"

John says, "I was under the impression we'd get to do a couple tunes of our own." I don't know where he got that impression from.

Bert says, "Ehm, no, I'm afraid not. This was always Tony's session, and Tony's session alone."

John says, "That's not what Tony told us." Truth is, Tony didn't tell us fook-all. We had, maybe, five words with the bloke.

Bert says, "Well, that's between you gentlemen. You have thirty minutes to pack up. Please turn the lights out when you leave." And then he splits.

And then John throws his Fender Deluxe amplifier at the wall across the room.

GEORGE HARRISON: Pete did or said something to Bert, and Bert looked pissed, and I was ready to go to bat for Pete. All for zombies, and zombies for all, and yeah, Pete wasn't a zombie, but he was still one of us. But the second John's Fender whizzed by my head—and missed knocking off my nose by only a couple of millimeters, I should note—I packed up and cleared the hell out. I wasn't gonna let Johnny lay a finger on my GA-40 Les Paul, that's for damn sure.

PAUL McCARTNEY: From the beginning of the band, John was the idea man, and most of his ideas were good ones. So I figured, if he thought destroying the studio was a wise move, I was game.

Problem was, my Selmer Truvoice Stadium was a solid piece of equipment, y'know, and seemed like it was built to survive a nuclear holocaust. Now, what with my so-called zombie powers, I'm a strong bloke, but it took me three chucks to turn that baby into sawdust. John, however, trashed his Fender in one toss.

JOHN LENNON: There was a method behind my mad amp-toss. I'd had my Rickenbacker 325 for three years, and I wasn't about to turn my beloved guitar into firewood, so I did the next best thing.

PETE BEST: Man, I loved my Premier drum kit. The cymbals were cherry, the toms rang across the room, and my snare head was to that point where it was broken in but not *too* broken in. Needless to say, I was livid when John started going to town on it, just fookin' livid.

JOHN LENNON: The first thing I did after my amp went to the great Fender factory in the sky was take off Pete's ride cymbal and sharpen it on my teeth. I gave that thing a razor's edge so sharp it could've decapitated a fookin' elephant. Then I threw it like a Frisbee toward Bert's recording setup . . . and I put some quality spin on it, so it did maximum damage. The reel-to-reel machine was in tatters, and the mixing board had sparks shooting out of it.

That felt good, but it wasn't enough. I was hungry, you see, and that's the kind of thing that happens when I don't have access to sustenance.

I retrieved the cymbal, flung it at the wall, flicking my wrist just so. It cut through like a chain saw, and it moved so fast that it started smoking. The smoke turned to a campfire, and the campfire turned to a forest fire. We grabbed our gear—broken and unbroken alike—and got the fook out of there. For some reason, the story never made the paper.

Good thing Bert took the master tapes with him, or else the world wouldn't have been treated to our first real record, a cover of "My Bonnie," which wasn't released under the Quarrymen or the Silver Beatles or the Beatles or the Maggots, but rather Tony Sheridan and the Beat Brothers. The whole thing was ridiculous, but I suppose you've gotta start somewhere.

●

*O*ne afternoon while I was at the Dakota, out of nowhere, Lennon turned to me and said, "Eppy's still around, you know."

I almost dropped my cup of Kopi. "Bullshit. Quit fucking with me, Lennon," I said. As far as I knew, Eppy—John's nickname for the Beatles' brilliant manager Brian Epstein—died of a drug overdose in 1967. Whether or not it was a suicide has always been up for debate.

"Not fucking with you, mate. It's true," Lennon said. "Dunno where he's at, though. Aspinall probably knows."

Neil Aspinall was the de facto Beatles gatekeeper, and it was his job to know that sort of thing . . . and to keep it quiet. Turned out John was right on both counts. Eppy was still around, and Aspinall knew his whereabouts—specifically, Edinburgh. (It also turned out that this was the one and only time John blatantly lied to me; he knew exactly where Brian Epstein was.)

I wasn't comfortable approaching Epstein myself, but Neil kindly
offered to set up the meeting. Much to my pleasure, Brian agreed to
see me immediately, which was a shock, as I assumed he wasn't the
kind of guy who'd speak to the likes of yours truly. I'm certain the only
reason he okayed the meeting is because of Neil's endorsement.

Brian's wheelchair-friendly house—it's a mansion, really—is set so
far back from any road in Edinburgh that if you didn't know it's there,
you wouldn't *know it's there . . . and that's just the way Eppy wants it.*
Courteous and affable as one would hope, if not somewhat guarded,
Brian insisted on discussing his personal, more recent backstory first,
before he launched into the back-backstory.

BRIAN EPSTEIN: It doesn't matter whether or not I committed suicide.
It doesn't change the story *before,* and it doesn't change the story
after. I was unhappy, I took a lot of drugs, and I died. The end.

John was off in Lennonland for most of '66 and '67, but he sensed
my state of mind, even though I thought I was doing a fine job of
keeping up appearances; he's always been good like that, John has.
One afternoon, he asked me if I wanted him to turn me, claiming
that a transformation might brighten my mood.

I said, "No way. My life will end when it's time for it to end. I
don't want to be around five hundred years from now. I don't even
want to be around *fifty* years from now. Life is meant to be lived fi-
nitely."

He said, "I'm infinite, and I'm doing okay."

I said, "Well, John, you're you, and I'm me. So don't reanimate
me. Ever. Don't try to sneak up on me when I'm asleep or hypnotize
me or pull any of that bollocks you pull when you kill a stranger." I
made him promise. And he kept his promise. For seven years.

In 1974, John Lennon and Yoko Ono dug up my grave, and John
reanimated me. Initially I was livid, but when he apologized and

said he did it because he was lonely, well, I had to forgive him, didn't I? He bought me this house and made arrangements so I'd have enough money to be solvent until the end of time. In 2001, he said, "I'm glad I set you up with the dosh, Eppy. Imagine if you had to go back to work. You might get stuck managing some sad cunts like those fookin' Gallagher brothers."

The problem is, since I'd been dead for so long, John was able to reanimate only my head. My body, as you can see, is mostly paralyzed. I can move my neck, and my hands are fine, and I have some slight movement in my arms, but my legs are useless. I have live-in help, and John made sure that will always be the case. John Lennon has murdered God knows how many thousands of people, but he's a good man.

I'm blathering on. You didn't come here to talk about me. You want to hear about the lads.

I saw them perform for the first time at the Cavern Club, and I knew right away they had *something*. I didn't know anything about the undead—after all, there weren't any zombies on tony old Rodney Street, where I grew up—and I wasn't sure whether I should expect a murderous rampage for an encore, or what. Turned out the lads could keep it under control . . . most of the time. But only most of the time. Once in a while, they went off the rails. I assume you're familiar with the Shea Stadium show.

In any event, our business marriage happened fast. After that wonderful Cavern performance, I told John that they needed a manager. He immediately agreed and asked where he should sign. The rest, as they say, is history.

PAUL McCARTNEY: Some folks say the Beatles' story began after that Quarrymen show at St. Peter's, y'know. Some say it was when we went off to play in Hamburg. Some say it was when Stu went vampire on us, and I took over on bass. Some say it was when we started our residency at the Cavern Club. Me, I point to the day we brought Brian Epstein aboard . . . and we restrained ourselves from zombifying him.

That's when I realized John might be right. Maybe we could do it. Maybe the Beatles could take over the whole world. And our first step toward world domination took place at the Decca Records studio, way out in bloody West Hampstead.

CHAPTER TWO

1962

BRIAN EPSTEIN: One of the first things I did when I took on the band was to make certain they developed some semblance of onstage decorum. They were a rough lot, those lads, and it showed before, during, and after their performances, and it needed to stop. It was all fine and good for them to wrap a bar stool around a heckler's neck in Hamburg, but not in the UK. They had to learn to look, and somewhat act, the part.

The first problem was their hair. The Exis got them in the habit of wearing what I suppose you could call a pompadour, and to my mind, that didn't sit well with their overall look. I felt that having their 'dos stick up in the air *emphasized* what should have been *de*-emphasized. That said, God knows I didn't want them to cut it; they needed as much cover on their heads as possible, because John and George periodically broke out in festering skull sores, and long hair covered the evidence. More or less.

Problem number two: their attire. They often wore leather, and to me, that made them look, erm, aggressive. Granted, they *were* ag-

gressive—they were undead, for goodness sake, and you couldn't expect anything less—but I felt like a change of costume would tone things down without sacrificing their innate zombieness, something John was quite concerned about, because, as he famously told *Mersey Beat*, "Until the end of time, I intend to stay as true to my zombie roots as possible."

So I suggested they try wearing matching suits, with the proviso being the suits were always a dark color. If they wore a lighter tone, any blood or brain fluid that spilled between sets would stain and be easily seen, whereas with black, nobody would be the wiser. I took them shopping, and they looked smashing.

I firmly believed that a spiffy look would lead to a spiffy record deal. A logical thought, but at first, I was very, very wrong. Not a single label wanted to touch us. I didn't know why, and I couldn't figure out how to rectify it. Aside from the afternoon that George overturned a city bus, the boys handled the constant rejection well, but I could tell that John was reaching his boiling point.

*Z*ombies *have been a familiar entity throughout the world for many decades now, and though the majority of them look somewhat grotesque, most of us have seen enough of the undead that we're rarely fazed in their presence. A lumpy, gray face? So what else is new? Oddly positioned limbs? No biggie. Scars, permanent dried blood, scars, festering sores, and more scars? Who cares?*

On the other hand, few have seen a Midpointer up close and personal; thus, Midpointers tend to elicit a more noticeable reaction: they don't cause a panic, but if you encounter one, you'll likely be, at the very least, taken aback. It has nothing to do with the Midpointer attitude—demeanor-wise, they're a perfectly nice lot, if not a little de-

pressed—but rather their physicality. I can report that an up-close encounter with a Midpointer will disconcert even the most jaded zombie enthusiast.

Midpointers are partly alive, partly dead, and partly undead, but unfortunately for them, they take on the worst physical characteristics of all three states of being. Immediately after their zombie-to-Midpointer transformation, their skin tone changes from typical undead gray to an almost translucent white, so translucent that in the correct light, their body's infrastructure is visible. Making matters worse for the passerby, the infrastructure is inevitably severely damaged, so if you catch a glimpse of a Midpointer with his shirt off, you might be treated to a view of a lacerated liver or a punctured lung or a squashed heart. That being the case, Midpointers tend to wear extra layers of clothing, so, for the most part, you'll only be treated to the sight of a chip in the skull or a sheared cornea. The clarity of the skin makes any scars and bloodstains stand out in sharp relief, which doesn't exactly sweeten the view.

And lest we forget, Midpointers float. That may not sound like a big deal, but try spending a few hours chatting with a blood-covered, ghost-skinned, bummed-out, deadish man who's constantly hovering several inches off the ground. No matter how tough you think you are, your brain isn't wired to be at ease in the presence of an odoriferous, gored-out floater.

It takes a whole lot of physical trauma for a Liverpool zombie to become a Midpointer, and the vast majority of them are the by-products of horrible accidents, oftentimes involving high levels of heat; e.g., a bomb, a fiery car wreck, or a fall from a great height. Purposefully turning a zombie into a Midpointer is a difficult proposition, and for the transformation to occur, you have to hurt them badly. Very few humans have the strength or wherewithal to produce a Midpointer; thus most Midpointers are created by other zombies.

All of which brings us to Dick Rowe.

A legendary A&R man for Decca Records, Rowe was cited as being responsible for discovering and/or signing such acts as the Rolling Stones, Tom Jones, and Van Morrison's first band, Them. After seeing the Beatles tear up Cavern both musically and physically, Rowe had Decca invite them into the studio for a New Year's Eve session that would serve as their audition for the label. John, Paul, George, and Pete laid down a whopping fifteen tunes in an hour, and most Beatles fans justifiably think the quartet sounded damn good. Believing guitar bands were on their way out, and zombie bands would never find their way in, Rowe disagreed, and a couple of weeks after the session, Brian Epstein received the unfortunate verdict.

BRIAN EPSTEIN: The boys felt terrific about their studio performance for Decca, and I knew they'd be heartbroken not to get offered a deal. I decided to deliver the news to John face-to-face, as it's easier to console somebody in person than over the phone. It was the right thing to do . . . or, at least, that's what I thought until I found myself lying on my arse in the middle of the street outside his flat.

JOHN LENNON: Never meant to hurt Eppy. Couldn't be helped. Strictly reflexes.

BRIAN EPSTEIN: John wanted to speak to Rowe personally, and I thought that was simply an atrocious idea. The English record industry was tiny and insular—everybody knew everybody—and if John went after Rowe, word would get around, and it would make landing a deal even more difficult. I pointed out that we'd already been rejected by almost every label in town, and if he went after Rowe, nobody else would give them an audition, let alone a contract.

He ignored me. He's a bullheaded one. But that's what makes John John.

JOHN LENNON: I called Paulie and told him to put on his best gear, because we were gonna have a little palaver with Mr. Rowe.

He said, "Do you think that's a good idea? I've been on the receiving end of your *palavers,* and I barely survived, and I'm a bloody zombie, y'know."

I said, "We're just gonna talk to the man. That's why I want you to wear your nicest outfit. I dunno about you, but I wouldn't want to get my finest finery all fooked-up with blood and brains. If we look nice, we'll be more apt to act nice."

He said, "What time did you make the appointment for?"

"I didn't," I said. "The appointment is when I say it is."

*

*A*nother *piece of the Beatles puzzle who I had to sweet-talk into speaking with me on the record, Dick Rowe, is a classic Midpointer: clear skin covered with seeming buckets of fresh-looking blood, incessant floating, eyes overflowing with blue tears. He's made the best of his undead/dead situation, creating a comfortable, if not solitary, life for himself, a life lived in a small, nondescript London flat, surrounded by tens of thousands of albums, cassette tapes, eight-tracks, and compact discs. The blue tears that dot Dick Rowe's cheeks mask the fact that he's a quietly content individual—for a Midpointer, that is.*

Rowe rarely enters John Lennon's or Paul McCartney's thoughts, but conversely—and perhaps unsurprisingly—Lennon and McCartney are almost always on the former Decca maven's brain, as he told me in August 2005.

DICK ROWE: Was it a cock-up not to sign them? Yes. Would I do it differently if I had it to do over again? Musically speaking, no, I wouldn't. The band wasn't ready. The potential was there, but I wasn't about potential. I didn't have time to hold a band's hand until they got their sound together. I needed hits, and I needed them fast. Sure, I was upper-level management, but I still had to answer to the moneymen, and for the boys on the eighteenth floor, failure was not an option.

In terms of how it all affected me personally, well, let's just say I might've made some different choices.

The day after we let Brian Epstein know we were passing on the band, Lennon and McCartney burst into my office, without an appointment, wearing tuxedos. I'd met them briefly after one of their performances at the Cavern Club, but I didn't know how simultaneously gruesome and charismatic they were until I saw them in the light of day. They were gorgeous and appalling, all at once.

I stood up, offered my hand, and said, "Gentlemen. This is unexpected."

Lennon slapped my hand away. Fortunately he held back; if he had hit me with full strength, my entire arm would've flown through the closed window, across the city, and into the Thames. He said, "You're right, mate. It *is* unexpected. Matter of fact, this whole *situation* is unexpected. I mean, what the fook d'you want from us?" After I asked him what he meant, he said, "Our tape. What was wrong with our tape?"

I said, "Nothing was *wrong* with it, Mr. Lennon. You gents have a ton of potential. It was . . . nice. That's all. Just nice."

In an eyeblink, Lennon was standing behind me. He whispered into my ear, "One thing the Beatles are not, Mr. Rowe, is nice."

PAUL McCARTNEY: Right then, right when Johnny zoomed behind Rowe, I was certain that one of two things was gonna happen: John was going to hypnotize Rowe into giving us a recording contract, or he was gonna chuck him across the room.

The answer: number two.

JOHN LENNON: No chance I'd hypnotize him. Remember, I made that promise to the cosmos: no hypnotizing my way into a gig.

DICK ROWE: I never saw it coming. For that matter, I still don't even know what *it* was. A punch? A kick? Something telekinetic? Who knows? One second I was standing in front of my desk, and the next, I was on the other side of the room, on the floor, curled against the wall, with a framed photo of me and Jimmy Young on my lap.

PAUL McCARTNEY: I grabbed John's shoulder and asked him, "What the fook are you doing, mate? I thought we were gonna lay low, y'know. I thought we were gonna keep our monkey suits clean."

He said, "Yeah, well, I got caught up in the moment."

I said, "What *moment*? He offered to shake your hand. That's not a *moment*. That's a bloody pleasantry."

He said, "So *you* say. *I* say that we need to send a message to the music industry. We've gotta make an example of this Rowe bloke. Let everybody know they can't mess with Lennon and McCartney."

I said, "What kind of example are you thinking of?"

DICK ROWE: I've since been told by experts that Liverpool zombies have the ability to make their attacks painless for their victims, both mentally and physically. For me, Lennon was merciful, which I've heard wasn't always the case. I'm sure my transformation was horrific, but I don't remember a single thing.

JOHN LENNON: The only reason I didn't torture Dick Rowe was because Paul asked me not to. And when Paulie gives you those sad puppy-dog eyes, well, it's hard to refuse him . . . and it has nothing to do with hypnosis. There's a reason people call him the Cute fookin' Beatle.

PAUL McCARTNEY: Johnny's attacks were always intense, y'know, but this one was an Olympic-level performance. After he threw Rowe against the wall, he picked him up by his hair and zombified him in twelve seconds flat . . . and yes, I counted. But he did a sloppy job, because he knew he was going to kill him only moments later.

John then unceremoniously dropped Rowe on the floor, ran to the other side of the office, and opened the window. Before Rowe even knew he was a zombie, John grabbed him by the waist, wound up like a cricket player, and underhanded him out the window onto the sidewalk thirty meters below.

JOHN LENNON: In my defense, I took the time to look down at the street and make sure I wasn't throwing Dickie onto any pedestrians, because I knew I was gonna throw him so hard that if he'd have landed on somebody, they would've been dead instantly. Killing somebody without eating them was pointless. At least I thought so then.

I'd never purposely Midpointed anybody, and I wasn't sure if it would work. But this was a ten-story drop, and I was comfortable thinking that that would end it, especially if he was falling at fifty kilometers per hour. If it didn't work, I was prepared to go downstairs and set his body on fire.

DICK ROWE: When I came to, I was in my own bed. Wait, check that: I was hovering over my own bed. I wasn't in pain, but I wasn't *not* in pain, and I think the only way you'd understand what I mean by that is if you get Midpointed, and I hope to God that never happens to you.

JOHN LENNON: I'll never let Dick Rowe become a zombie. No diamond bullets in the noggin for him. He's a Midpointer for life and death. And whenever one of those blue tears drips onto his slacks, I want him to remember the names John Lennon and Paul McCartney.

DICK ROWE: None of the Midpoint characteristics kept me from being able to do my job—frankly, all the Midpoint symptoms are more of a nuisance than anything else—so I kept right on working.

Sometimes being the way I am has worked in my favor: Like Tom Jones said he signed with us instead of Vee-Jay, because he thought my floating was, as he put it, "far out, baby."

On the other hand, it almost hurt me with the Rolling Stones, as Mick had issues with zombies of any sort. But that's another story.

*

W*e now interrupt our narrative for a digression about zombie sex slaves. Everybody asks.*

John, Paul, and George had similar reactions when I raised the topic of sex slaves: brief silence and a frightening glare, followed by the threat of a painful death without reanimation. No confirmations. No denials. Just really, really scary warnings. Thus, nobody can say for sure if the three undead Beatles used their zombie powers to create minions of women who would fulfill their every sexual desire.

There is, nonetheless, some compelling evidence that points toward . . . something.

LYMAN COSGROVE: I've been told that the most controversial chapter of *Under the Canal* is chapter nine, the section about the sex life of beings who have undergone the Liverpool Process. And saying that's the most controversial is quite a statement, because both zombologists and casual undead watchers alike have made it clear that they believe the entire book to be *exceedingly* controversial. I've never shied away from controversy, however, and I never will.

L*yman told me that he hasn't made any new zombie sex discoveries since the original publication of* Under the Canal, *so rather than discuss something he's discussed time and again, he prefers I pull the information verbatim from his book, so as to avoid any possible inconsistencies.*

FROM CHAPTER NINE OF LYMAN COSGROVE AND ELLINGTON WORTHSON'S *UNDER THE CANAL: THE UNDEAD OF ABYSSINIA CLOSE AND THE BIRTH OF THE LIVERPOOL PROCESS:*

There are precious few studies on the sex life of the Homo Coprophagus Somnambulus, as many zombies are unable or unwilling to engage in the act at all. Female zombies find it difficult, if not impossible, to naturally lubricate, and male zombies suffer from a plethora of obstacles, running the gamut from an inability to produce and/or maintain an erection to penile detachment.

For the fortunate zombies born via the Liverpool Process, sex is a realistic possibility, but fully satisfying sex, less so. For females, the chance of reaching orgasm is infinitesimal. Of the 7,153 female undead I questioned, only one has experienced a post-Process climax, and the veracity of her claim is questionable, as the person who reanimated her left the poor woman with only 89 percent of the brain fluid necessary to enjoy a satisfying undeath.

Males, however, are far luckier. They can easily achieve multiple orgasms, as many as ten an hour. (One gentleman claimed that he ejaculated 214 times in a twenty-four-hour period.) On the downside, the orgasms are less than fulfilling. Dustmen particles do not create the same sensation as seminal fluid, possibly because dust is not a singular entity and is not able to create the proper traffic flow down the vas deferens highway. (We speculate that the vas deferens is one of the body's internal components not affected by the Process; we may never know why, as no male zombie has been willing to donate his penis and/or testicles for study.)

Which begs the question, if their climaxes are mediocre at best, why are the handful of male zombies who are interested in intercourse so obsessed with the act? Simple: *power*. Even though Liverpool Processers are a strong bunch, they suffer from the same downfall as all zombies: they are, for all practical purposes, dead. A living being has far more spiritual power than a dead one. And as the living are aware, spirituality generally plays a large role in sex. So one could argue that it is the zombie's lack of spirituality—its missing soul—that explains why male Processors insist on creating minions of sex slaves.

Creating a female slave is simple enough: at the exact moment of penile insertion, the zombie looks directly into the female's eyes and yells the four-word phrase ᎤᎶ! ᎣᎣᏦᎬ! ᏆᏘᏒ! ᏏᏏ! (We are not at liberty to divulge the pronunciation, because as far as we know, no living being has ever said the phrase aloud, and the results could be disastrous.) The indoctrination is said to be pleasurable and comfortable, but the enslavement itself, although mostly enjoyable, is apparently oftentimes frustrating, as the woman's sexual desire is sharp and constant. When she is within two hundred kilometers of her master, all thought leaves her mind, and the only thing that matters is how soon and how often she can have intercourse.

The enslavement spell is easily reversed. The male zombie looks in the female's eyes after ejaculation, sprinkles her lips with dustmen, and recites the aforementioned four-word phrase backward. Like most English zombies, male Liverpool Processers are relatively polite and very rarely enslave a female for more than several months.

Impregnation is, of course, impossible.

PETE BEST: Yeah, I knew that Liverpool zombies could make sex slaves, but I have no clue if my bandmates were doing any of that. I should point out that we always had a goodly number of female unmentionables piled up in our van—bras, panties, and the like. Take that as you will.

NEIL ASPINALL: I never saw them enslave a single girl, but I made a point of staying out of that particular arena. I did, however, notice

that they never pursued women, which to my mind means they were either totally uninterested or totally satisfied.

BRIAN EPSTEIN: The only thing I ever told them about their offstage cavorting was to imagine that every move they made was being filmed. I'm not sure whether that encouraged or deterred them from creating slaves. But regardless of what they were doing, no ladies ever complained, so I let it be.

In Under the Canal, Cosgrove and Worthson contend that mortal women remember nothing of their enslavement, and when it comes to the UK undead, Cosgrove and Worthson know of what they speak, and I trust their word implicitly. So when notorious zombie groupie Janette Wallace tracked me down and told me about her encounter with a nameless Brit rocker, I took it with a grain of salt. She might not have been telling the truth, but she delivered one helluva story, and even if it was a tad on the Harlequinish side, it's worth recounting here.

JANETTE WALLACE: When a boy zombie decides he wants to wrap you around his finger—and around his brain, and around his cock—the first time with him is dreamy. The, ehm, subject we're talking about in this particular instance broke my zombie cherry, and it couldn't have been sweeter. He touched me in ways I've never been touched, either before or since. I didn't care that his finger detached and plunked in between my breasts or that he smelled like dirt or that two of his teeth snapped off in my mouth during our first encounter—and that he stopped to put them back in right before I was about to orgasm. None of that mattered, because my first experience with zombie love was so fun, so fun, so very, very fun.

The enslavement itself is magical. When I was under his spell, every time he looked me in the eyes, I quivered all over and nothing else mattered. My being at his beck and call made things difficult at work, especially when his band went on tour and I couldn't get my dustmen fix, but it was worth it . . . even when my boss told me to take a leave of absence until I, quote, got my shite together, unquote. What a heartless, soulless bastard he was. He didn't understand zombie love. Poor him.

I followed my undead lover all over Europe: Hamburg, Liverpool, Elgin, Dingwall, Aberdeen, Manchester, Stoke-on-Trent, Sunderland, Croydon, *everywhere*. I ran out of money, and I got arrested twice, and after he released me from the spell, I was so out of sorts that I got thrown out of my apartment and had to move back in with my parents for a couple of months. But it was worth it.

So for all you girls out there, if you ever have the opportunity to fook a zombie, fook him, and fook him good.

＊

PETE BEST: The writing had been on the wall since Paul gave me his "all for zombies, and zombies for all" talk right after I'd been hired. If I'd have let them zombify me, they might've kept me around. But I didn't. So they didn't.

Brian sacked me in August. He was polite about it—Eppy was polite about *everything*—but I almost would've rather had John and Paul do the do. Yeah, I might've reacted angrily, and yeah, an angry reaction on my part might've led to my death or undeath, but at least there would've been closure. As it was, for the next eight years, I watched their shenanigans from the audience, just like everybody else in the fookin' world.

I suppose there's really nothing else to say, is there?

RINGO STARR: I honestly don't remember who officially asked me to join the band. But I remember exactly what happened the day after the invite.

GEORGE HARRISON: We'd all known Ringo for a good long while, and we all liked him, and he was one helluva drummer, so of course none of us wanted to hurt him. But we had to make sure that he was one of us.

PAUL McCARTNEY: It wasn't like we were hazing him, y'know. The Beatles weren't a fraternity. The Beatles were a rock band. Still, it seemed like the right thing to do at the time.

JOHN LENNON: Ringo was a good bloke, but with a new guy, you never know. What if we were playing in, say, Scotland somewhere, and some marksman plugged George with a diamond bullet? Paul and me aren't gonna want to immediately go after the guy—we've gotta save our own hides, and we're talking about a marksman, after all—so we needed to find out whether Ringo had the skills necessary to defend both himself and the rest of the band, should the need arise.

RINGO STARR: They took me down to the Cavern for a celebratory pint, and for, I dunno, three or four hours, we talked music, because music is what we all loved the most: Chuck Berry, Carl Perkins, the Shadows, Eddie Cochran, Buddy Holly, Motown, and, of course, Elvis. John was saying how we were gonna take over the world and kept talking about Poppermost, whatever the hell that meant. Eventually, as always seems to be the case when someone's first getting to know me, the conversation turned to Ninja.

John was especially inquisitive, and he asked me in ten different ways what skills I possessed. I explained to him that I'd just become a Seventh Level Ninja Lord, and, as an example, I told him that one of the skills all Seventh Levels have to develop is virtual invisibility.

George said, "Virtual invisibility? What level do you have to reach to be *really* invisible?"

I said, "Fifty-second."

He said, "I was kidding, mate. People can't become really invisible."

I said, "I *wasn't* kidding. And yes, they can."

GEORGE HARRISON: And then the little fellow disappeared. Hell if I know how. One second, he's sucking down some Guinness, then the next, his mug is empty . . . and so is his chair. Then, before any of us could say anything about anything, boom, he's back.

I said, "Bloody hell. If that's virtual invisibility, what does the real thing look like?"

He said, "Believe me, mate, you don't want to be in a situation where that would be an issue."

RINGO STARR: I could tell John was impressed. He asked me what else I could do.

I told him, "Well, there's the obvious Ninja stuff, like the ability to move in utter silence without displacing air; or to hit a target with a shuriken from fifty meters; or to climb walls like a spider, then hang on to the ceiling with your fingertips; or to know thirty-six different ways to kill a human being in under thirty seconds without leaving a single mark. You know, that sort of thing."

John said, "What about physical confrontation? How do you fight?"

I said, "Anticipation is the key. That's a big deal for me right now, anticipation, because if I want to become Eighth Level, I'll have to pass a number of anticipation tests."

Paul said, "What the bloody hell are you talking about, Richie?" He looked to be three sheets, which surprised me, because I didn't know zombies could get pissed.

I said, "In a battle, I know what you're gonna do three steps before you do it. I know where you're gonna move before you do."

George said, "How do you take a test for that?"

I said, "Dunno, really. You just do."

Then John guzzled half a pint in one swallow and said, "How'd you like to test us, Ringo, m'lad?"

JOHN LENNON: I guess you could call it an initiation. The thought of an initiation was ridiculous, but it had to be done.

Back when I wanted to kill and reanimate Stuart Sutcliffe, Paul would tell me time and again, "We need *somebody* in our group who has blood coursing through his veins." I didn't agree with him at the time, but I'd come around to his way of thinking. He convinced me that not everybody in the world could get behind an all-shuffler band.

Also, we couldn't have somebody in the drum chair who couldn't handle himself, so we had to make sure.

PAUL McCARTNEY: That night, around three in the morning, we all met up at Calderstones Park. It was empty, which was just how we wanted it.

GEORGE HARRISON: John and Paul wouldn't let me participate. John's reason was the same as it always was: "You're too young." So I watched.

RINGO STARR: There's no such thing as a Ninja uniform. Everybody thinks it's that all-black deal with the hood and the mask, but the truth is, that comes from Kabuki. Modern Ninjas will wear anything from a white karate suit to a pair of blue jeans. Just for the fun of it, my first teacher, 忍の者乱破, sometimes wore a double-breasted suit to class. But that night, just for the fun of it, I wore my all-black deal.

JOHN LENNON: Ringo is the least scary-looking person you'll ever meet. He's always smiling and cheerful and utterly nonthreatening. That is, until he puts on that Ninja suit. All of a sudden, Mr. Starkey transforms into a cat you don't want to mess with.

PAUL McCARTNEY: I'd seen John have hundreds of punch-ups—hell, I'd fought him at least two dozen times myself—but I'd never seen him as nervous as he was when Ringo appeared out of nowhere.

GEORGE HARRISON: I wish I could've videotaped the battle. The whole thing took about three minutes, and it happened so fast that I missed all of the details. It'd be nice to go back and watch it frame by frame.

JOHN LENNON: It was two against one, but it may as well have been two against fifty, because Ringo used the trees as his defenders. He'd hide behind one, then when we'd spot him, he'd be behind another before we even had a chance to touch him. And then when he jumped up into the branches of this big oak tree and started leaping from one tree to another like Tarzan without a vine, forget it. We'd never seen that sort of skill, and we had no fookin' chance.

PAUL McCARTNEY: While Ringo was whizzing about from tree to tree, I said to John, "We have to separate, y'know. We have to spread out. And we have to anticipate. Forget this zombie shite—it's time to start thinking like a Ninja."

John said, "What do you mean, 'think like a Ninja'? How in Jesus' name do you think like a Ninja?"

I said, "No clue. Let's just get this little cunt. I haven't stayed up this late since our last gig at the Kaiserkeller, and I'm knackered."

RINGO STARR: They never laid a finger on me, and I never laid a finger on them. 忍の者乱破 made his philosophy very clear to me: never hurt a being—zombie or otherwise—in anger or jest, only in defense.

Nonetheless, before we called it a night, while I was hiding at the top of the tallest tree in Calderstones, I zipped a shuriken at each of them and cut off their pants at the waist.

GEORGE HARRISON: That was—and still is—the funniest thing I've ever seen. There's Lennon and McCartney, in full attack mode, going nuts trying to find this little Ninja, and then *zzzzzip*, there's Lennon and McCartney, standing in the middle of the park with their trousers and briefs around their ankles and their plonkers flapping about for the world to see.

At that point, I yelled out, "Oi, Johnny, who's too young to fight now?"

JOHN LENNON: So I'm standing there with my pants on the ground, with my member shriveling up in the cold morning air. I looked over at Paul and said, "Well, I guess we've got ourselves a new drummer."

Rod Argent may not be a Ninja, but he is nonetheless a true warrior, a gent who's been making music professionally since 1959, and when I spoke with him in August 2002, he showed no sign of slowing down.

Back during the British Invasion's halcyon years, Argent tasted a small dose of international success—not nearly as healthy a dose as fellow Invasioneers like the Rolling Stones, the Kinks, and the Who, but he did okay for himself and his quintet. Some would say his band was just as interesting as any of the aforementioned units, and some might question why they never reached such dizzying heights, but as all rock fans know, it's a crapshoot. Bad bands sometimes go platinum, and great bands sometimes never even get a record deal.

Rod isn't bitter—as noted, he's a warrior, content to fight the good fight and take life one gig at a time—but there's one topic that gets his dander up big-time, that topic being the zombification of the Beatles.

You see, Rod Argent is the cofounder of the Zombies.

ROD ARGENT: Everybody thinks we called ourselves the Zombies so we could ride the Beatles' coattails, but for your information, we were the Zombies well before we ever heard of the Beatles. We'd been around since '59, and since we were from St. Albans, those Liverpool brats wanted bugger-all to do with us, and that was fine. They had their thing, and we had ours. Still, there probably wouldn't have been any problems between us if it wasn't for that sodding article by sodding Bill Harry in sodding *Mersey Beat*.

Bill Harry was one of Lennon's school chums from that pretentious art school, and he started up an entire paper to follow the English music scene . . . such as it was. It was all very pro-Beatles, and he all but ignored every other up-and-coming band outside of Liverpool.

I remember that sodding article word for word.

The article of which Argent speaks was published in a September 1962 issue of Mersey Beat. Harry printed a limited number, so limited I couldn't find a copy or find anybody who had a copy or find anybody who knew anybody who had a copy. So we'll have to take Argent's word for it. Rod's recount of the article reflects MB's typically breathless writing style, so Rod's memory is probably solid.

FAKE ZOMBIES VS. REAL ZOMBIES!!!
The Beatles Go to Battle

The Beatles, our beloved boys from Liverpool, are in the midst of the biggest controversy of their young career. It just so happens that a band from St. Albans has named themselves the Zombies, and, as anybody who has ever heard or seen them will tell you, *they are not zombies*!!! They are regular blokes who do not sound like the Beatles or look like the Beatles, and it is our belief that the Zombies christened themselves the Zombies to capitalize on the inevitable success of Liverpool's favorite rockers.

Not a single Zombie would comment. However, John Lennon told *Mersey Beat*, "If I ever run into one of those fake Zombies, I'm going to hurt him, and hurt him bad. Believe me, they'll know what it's like to deal with a *real* zombie!"

JOHN LENNON: I never said that. I didn't want to hurt Argent. Besides, if I did, I certainly wouldn't have announced it in the press . . . and you can thank Ringo for that. From the minute he joined the band, Ringo spent a lot of time preaching to us about the element of surprise.

ROD ARGENT: That entire article was patently bullshit. The worst part of it was that Bill sodding Harry never tried to reach any of us; I'll wager he didn't even know any of our names.

We were still struggling along when the Beatles started playing regularly at the Cavern Club. My bandmate Colin Blunstone and I would check them out every once in a while. The guys played the hell out of their instruments, and their vocal harmonies were mind-blowing, so we couldn't deny their greatness, but from our perspective, it looked like they were using their zombie powers to build a base. In other words, they were either *scaring* people into liking them or *hypnotizing* people into liking them. That being the case, we felt they were giving zombies a bad name, thus they were giving the Zombies a bad name.

We'd go play venues like the Playhouse in Manchester or the Tower Ballroom in New Brighton or the Palais Ballroom in Aldershot, places that the Beatles had wreaked havoc upon at some point in the past couple of years, and the cats at these clubs would be frightened of us, because they thought we were honest-to-sodding-God zombies. Can you blame them? Imagine you're working at a place where one of the guys in the zombie band that'd played there the week before gets mad at the soundman, but then murders the doorman. (That never made much sense to me, by the way; if you're pissed at the soundman, kill the sodding soundman.) From then on, whenever you heard the word *zombies*, you'd probably want to pack it in. Until we proved to the world that we

didn't have the ability or desire to mangle our audience, getting work was a bitch.

I got some measure of revenge, but that wouldn't come for another six sodding years.

●

As alluded to earlier, the list of those who have been thought of as the Fifth Beatle is endless: Aspinall and Epstein top the heap, of course, but journalist and eventual press officer Derek Taylor, New York–based radio jock Murray the K, roadie Mal Evans, and even boxer Muhammad Ali are among the many who have had the spurious title bestowed upon them. But none were as integral to the Fab Four's story as the real Fifth Beatle, George Martin.

A versatile composer, arranger, and engineer, Martin eventually produced all but one of the Beatles' albums and was oftentimes as integral to the sound of the band as any of the lads themselves. That being the case, Beatleologists have wondered for decades why Martin was never made undead.

By the time the band auditioned for Martin at the end of 1962, Lennon had established his MO of giving immortal life/death to those he loved and respected; as Martin quickly became a beloved father figure, he appeared a logical candidate for the Liverpool Process. Neither Lennon, McCartney, Harrison, Starr, nor Martin himself would discuss why George was allowed to live, and as of this writing, it remains one of the great mysteries of Beatledom.

On the plus side, Martin is a hale and hearty gent and comes across in conversation as immortal, the kind of guy who'll be here for the long haul. When we spoke in April 2007 on the rooftop of Abbey Road Studios, the then-eighty-one-year-old Knight Bachelor looked like he could give even the most powerful monster a run for his money.

GEORGE MARTIN: The first question everybody asks me is, "Were you frightened? When they walked into the studio for the first time, did they scare you?"

The short answer: yes.

I spent my formative years living in Highgate, which, as I'm sure you know, is a zombie-free zone. Looking back on it, I realize how prejudiced and small-minded that was, but as a child, you don't know any better. As an English boy in the 1940s, if your parents told you the undead were awful, then the undead were awful. You didn't ask questions.

When I moved to London in 1950, I saw a few shufflers here and there, but always from a distance. As I never encountered one face-to-face, the fear remained. No matter how enlightened I became, my trepidation was deep-seated, but in the grand scheme of things, it didn't seem to matter, because I worked in the classical music department for EMI. You don't meet too many zombie orchestra conductors, so I figured my attitude toward the undead would never be an issue.

By the time the lads auditioned for me at Abbey Road Studios in June 1962, I'd been to several parties that counted zombies among the guests but was always too nervous to engage with any of them. That experience of being in close proximity to them got me used to their look and smell, so at least I wasn't put off by the Beatles' physicality. Another plus for me was that I was polished and professional enough to the point that I could sublimate my fear. I acted so cool and calm that nobody had a clue I was quaking in my loafers.

As soon as they started playing, any fear, any trepidation, went out the window. After they finished their first tune, I viewed them as moneymakers—some scruffy undead boys from Liverpool who had the potential to make our label, Parlaphone, a load of dosh. But

then, after the second tune—and after we discussed music and shared some jokes—I began to see them as the warm, talented, caring, intelligent death merchants that they were. I thought, *I could work with these lads.*

RINGO STARR: For our first honest-to-goodness session, George brought in a vampire from Glasgow named Andy White to cover the traps. George claims he hired Andy because he was concerned I might not be able to cut it in the studio. Neil and I always theorized that it was because George believed that a band should either be all dead or all alive. But George grew up in Highgate, and everybody knows how those Highgaters think.

He's since said he was sorry. Numerous times. And all the apologies were completely unprompted. It wasn't like I had to use my big toe to break his collarbone or anything.

PAUL McCARTNEY: John and I spent the week leading up to our first real, honest-to-goodness recording session talking. And talking. And talking. And the topic of discussion: mind control.

I firmly disagreed with John's stance about not wanting to, as he put it, *force* anybody to buy our records. His line was, "If we have to fookin' hypnotize someone into liking us, that's not the kind of person we'd want buying our records anyhow."

I'd tell him, "I don't care who buys our record, just as long as they buy it, y'know. And it's not like they'll be *permanently* under our power." Actually, I didn't know that for certain. I wasn't even certain we'd be able to get hypnosis onto wax. And if we could, I had no idea of the effects. It was dangerous, unknown territory. It could've blown up in our faces. It could've ended the world as we knew it. But I wanted to give it a shot. Why bloody not?

JOHN LENNON: The morning before the session, ~~we were all at a res-~~ taurant, and Paul was blathering on about mind control, mind control, mind control. He was driving me mad, so instead of agreeing to disagree, then closing the topic, then finishing off breakfast, then heading off to the studio to cut our first record, I ripped his lips off.

RINGO STARR: I wouldn't have chosen to tear up Paulie's face mere hours before he had to sing into a microphone for several hours, but that's me.

PAUL McCARTNEY: Ripping off my lips was one thing, but tossing them over to George was another.

GEORGE HARRISON: We weren't being malicious. We were just having a bit of fun. I mean, what's a few rounds of keep-away between mates?

PAUL McCARTNEY: When George accidentally threw my lips over John's head and into a bowl of porridge belonging to the poor bloke at the next table over, that's when I, erm, lost it.

RINGO STARR: Paul yanked off John's left ring and index fingers, right there at the breakfast table. Before it could escalate, I threw a shuriken toward Paul's wrist and pinned his shirt to the table. I gave John his fingers back, then I retrieved Paul's lips from the poor soul who'd gotten splashed with oatmeal—and I picked up his check, of course—and said, "Okay, lads, let's go record ourselves a number one hit! Let's go to the Toppermost of the Poppermost!"

John used his detached fingers to poke me in my eyes, then said, "What the fook do you know about the Poppermost, Ninja?" Then he tore off his leg below the knee and used it to clout me on my forehead.

At that moment, as I wiped away the blood that was dripping into my right eye, I knew in my heart and soul that the Beatles were ready.

CHAPTER THREE

1963–1964

Mick Jagger has a diamond shard embedded in his upper right incisor, and the general belief among the rock cognoscenti is that he put it there for one reason, and one reason only: because it's really fucking cool.

Wrong. Truth is, the sinewy frontman of the Rolling Stones wants that diamond easily accessible in case he needs to launch it into an errant zombie.

You see, Mick Jagger, while he digs the musical stylings of Messrs. Lennon and McCartney, despises the undead. He always has and always will, and he refuses to discuss why. Some have theorized that his mother, Eva, survived an undead attack in her teens, and he wants to do some avenging, while others believe Mick was bullied in preschool by either a zombie or a schoolmate pretending to be a zombie. Regardless of the backstory, Jagger has dedicated his life to three things: making music, having as much sex with as many of the planet's most beautiful women as possible, and ridding the galaxy of the undead.

Which is why it was curious that in the spring of 1963, he struck up a friendship with the Beatles. Needless to say, the first thing I asked Mick when I spoke with him in Sapporo, Japan, in March 2006—in the midst of yet another Stones world tour—was, why did he make nicey-nice with a band of zombies?

MICK JAGGER: When we first met, the Beatles had no idea about my stance on the undead; all they saw was my sincere enthusiasm about their work. No way they could've known how I felt about zombies, really. I kept it under wraps because, if I was gonna get close to them, I had to earn their trust, mate. If they thought I had it out for them and I came with a frontal attack, I'd have been a dead man. And if one of the three zombies didn't get me, the Ninja certainly would've.

I never discussed my zombie hate in public. Nobody outside of my inner circle knew how I felt, and I thought nobody ever would, because at that point, there weren't any journos digging into my past. And it's a good thing nobody was digging, because I had a few secrets I wanted to keep buried for a while. For instance, rock fans didn't need to know about Norbert.

*E*nglish zombies, *in contrast to the majority of the undead men and women who inhabit our fine planet, are a relatively docile group, feeding only when hungry, and, for the most part, getting physical only when defending themselves. Thus, unlike in North America—where you can't throw a stone without hitting a zombie exterminator's storefront—British zombie hunters are few and far between.*

It was even more difficult to find one in 1955, the year that a young Mick Jagger started looking for somebody to mentor him in the ways of zombie extermination. After months of searching, Mick finally found his guru; serendipitously, the guy lived in Kent, almost right around the corner from the Jagger family's prim middle-class abode.

Norbert Eliot didn't advertise his services and was surprised when the skinny, thick-lipped thirteen-year-old undead-hater showed up on his doorstep with dreams of zombie butchery dancing through his head. For the next three years, six days out of the week, two hours each day, Mick went to Eliot's cramped house and trained with the veteran zombie hunter, eventually surpassing his teacher in strength and knowledge.

Eliot has a soft spot in his heart for his most famous student and still speaks of him with an affection that borders on love. The sad irony of it all is that in 2000, Norbert, after a six-day battle, was beaten by a four-hundred-plus-pound Irish zombie, who, rather than finish him off, decided—you guessed it—to make him undead. Eliot, who still lives in Kent, has come to terms with his state of being, and, in December 2008, spoke with me about his years teaching the man that some call Lips.

NORBERT ELIOT: Some young men came to me full of spit and vinegar, without a milligram of discipline. Others had a heap of physical aptitude but not a single iota of mental acumen. But Mick Jagger, well, that boy had the whole package: fire, desire, a sense of purpose, and a set of lips I knew would serve him well.

He was such a slight lad that the first thing I did was get him into shape. We spent three or four months on a handful of exercises that combined yoga, martial arts, and ballet. His favorite move was a pelvic thrust and a strut, something that he used to fine effect as both a zombie hunter and, eventually, a rock performer. I still find it amusing that for eleven years, Mick pretended he couldn't dance; I taught him well, and the bollocks story about

him learning his more sensual moves from Tina Turner cracks me
up to this day.

I wouldn't let Mick near an honest-to-goodness zombie for a full
year, which frustrated him to no end. He wanted to kick some
undead arse, and he wanted to kick it *immediately,* but he simply
wasn't ready. Even if he were ready, it wouldn't have mattered, because *none* of my students were allowed to spar until they'd been
with me for a year, and I wasn't going to make an exception for
Mick just because he was more skilled than my other lads and lass-
ies.

I staged my sparring sessions in my basement. My house is tiny,
and one might think that a fight between a husky, plus-size zombie
and a teenage apprentice zombie hunter in a room that could fit
only a bridge table and four folding chairs wouldn't be very useful
for the youngster; I mean, how many fifteen-year-olds can handle
themselves against an undead individual who's been there, done
that, and killed everybody, let alone in such a tiny area? Not many.
So to an outsider, that wouldn't seem logical. But when you saw
how my kids moved once they got into the heat of a real battle,
you'd agree that it made a lot of sense.

For most of our second year together, Mick would get his arse
handed to him five days a week, but in year three, he started holding his own in the basement, and when it came time to fight in the
real world, Mick was *ready.*

He never knew that I arranged his first battle. He thought he'd
stumbled onto a zombie robbing a young woman in Godmersham
Park, but in reality, I planned the whole thing. I watched from
behind a nearby tree and was so proud of my Mick, the way he
knocked the zombie to the ground with a mere twitch of his hips.
But the pièce de résistance was when he pinned the zombie to a
tree, then kissed him on the chest with those lips of his, which res-

urrected the zombie's heart, making him mortal and, thus, killable. I had to run over and intervene, or else the one zombie in the world that I actually liked would've been a goner.

Mick left me when the Stones began gigging regularly; he told me there was nothing else I'd be able to teach him that he couldn't figure out for himself. He came to me for one more lesson in 1963, however, and I taught him a few more things that I'd been saving for the perfect occasion.

MICK JAGGER: Norbert showed me a blocking spell that would cloud zombies' minds a tiny bit, just enough so they'd never have a clue of either my abilities or my burning hatred. So John, Paul, and George had no idea what I was about. They liked me, even. They thought I was just another singer from just another band who dug their tunes, and whose tunes they dug. I think Ringo might've been suspicious, but I can't be sure.

RINGO STARR: When we first met Mick Jagger, I thought he had zombie exterminator written all over him, but I kept it from the other lads. He seemed like a nice enough bloke, plus I figured fellow musicians—especially those he respected—would be exempt from any attacks. Shows what I knew.

◆

Nobody can say for sure what Roy Orbison is. A zombie? A vampire? A regenerated Frankenstein-like monster? A deity? An alien? A scientific experiment gone horribly awry? No clue. And Roy ain't sayin'.

All we know for sure is that if you search really hard, you can find him, and if you manage to find him, he'll talk to you, as long as you

give a literal blood oath that you'll never tell anybody where he is or
how you tracked him down or what he smells like. Honorable journalist that I am, my lips and nose are sealed. Plus the guy scared me shit-
less, and I truly believe that if I spill the beans, he'll come after me.
And he won't show any mercy.

In 1963, the Beatles went on a tour of the UK with Orbison, Gerry
and the Pacemakers, Tony Marsh, and a handful of other Brit acts. As
Orbison was a veteran whom the lads believed could offer them some
pointers about tunes and touring, they followed Roy around like
puppy dogs. They were so impressed with him that they never noticed
that something was a bit off with the man.

Unlike the Beatles, who wore their zombieness on their sleeves, Orbison kept his otherworldliness under wraps; he was so good at hiding
it that even fanatics like Lennon and McCartney had no idea what
Orbison was. But on the way to a gig in Sheffield, damned if they
didn't get a good idea.

ROY ORBISON: They were good men in those days, the Beatles were.
I think the press painted them all wrong in the later years—yeah, I
suppose journalists had it out for them after they offed that Tyler
guy from *New Musical Express*, but in '63, they were okay with me.
They caused a little trouble, but they were twenty-ish-year-old zombies, and if you think twenty-ish-year-old zombies are always gonna
behave themselves, you're not exactly in touch with reality.

PAUL McCARTNEY: I wanted something to remember this tour by,
and a mere autograph wouldn't suffice—I needed a real souvenir,
something special. I mean, we're talking about Roy bloody Orbison, y'know. We didn't know where the Beatles were headed, and
who knew if we'd ever be in close proximity to such a fine musician ever again? If I'd have gotten nailed with a diamond bullet

and gone to my grave without having taken the opportunity to liberate a treasure from Roy bloody Orbison, I'd never have forgiven myself.

ROY ORBISON: That Paul McCartney was awfully grabby, and I'm certain he thought he was being subtle. He thinks I didn't know he ripped off about twenty of my guitar picks, and that I didn't see him snatching a couple of my broken guitar strings off the stage. But when he filched my shades, well, that was a problem.

GEORGE HARRISON: He should've gotten Ringo to do it. That would've saved us all a lot of nightmares.

PAUL McCARTNEY: Roy's sunglasses were the big prize, y'know, but he always had them on. *Always.* Before the shows, during the shows, after the shows, in the hotel, at restaurants, going for strolls, while he was catching Zs, all the bloody time. A couple of weeks into the tour, I realized the only chance I'd have to get them would be while he was asleep in the tour bus. I knew it wouldn't be easy, but I'd be damned if I wasn't gonna try.

JOHN LENNON: I told him, "No way you're gonna get those glasses off his face while he's asleep, mate. You're a zombie, and zombies aren't good tiptoers."

He said, "I can do it, y'know. I can be subtle. I can be quiet."

I said, "Right. But what happens if you manage to be subtle? What if you somehow get the shades? What're you gonna do with them? It's not like you can wear them around and about."

He said, "Haven't planned that far ahead yet."

I said, "Maybe you should."

PAUL McCARTNEY: My thinking was, What's the worst that could happen? If he wakes up, I'll tell him I was playing a practical joke, just, erm, having a laugh.

So it's the second week into the tour, and we're in the tour bus on the way to Sheffield, and it's two or three in the morning, and I'm the only one who's awake, and I think to myself, *Right, Macca, if you're gonna do it, do it now.*

Ringo and I were in the back of the bus, George and John were in the middle, and Roy was up in the front. I tiptoed up the gangway and realized that John was right: it's rough for a zombie to keep quiet. This was a job for a Ninja, but I'd never even considered asking Ringo to get involved; I didn't think it was fair to drag the new guy into it.

I did the best I could to get up front without rousing anybody, an' that, and my best was good enough—nobody even stirred. So I'm standing over Roy, moving my hands as slowly as possible, hoping that we don't hit a bump that'd have me falling on top of him. I get close to the glasses, and closer and closer; then, when I'm, erm, five millimeters away, Roy lets out a loud snuffle, and I almost shit my knickers.

He stirs for a moment but doesn't wake up. I give it another go: closer to his face, closer, closer. Finally, after what seems like an hour, I pull those glasses right on off, and the guy doesn't notice a thing. It took all my restraint to keep from running back to my seat, but I kept it cool, y'know, and kept tiptoeing. And I didn't awaken a soul.

RINGO STARR: Of course Paul woke me up. Zombies aren't exactly Ninjas now, are they?

PAUL McCARTNEY: I sat down and stared at my prize. All I could think was, *I nicked Roy bloody Orbison's bloody shades, I nicked Roy*

bloody Orbison's bloody shades, over and over. The only thing that would've been better is if I'd have gotten Carl Perkins's blue suede shoes.

The lenses were a bit on the dirty side, so I gave them a quick wipe on my shirt, and then put them on.

And that's when things went off the rails.

RINGO STARR: Something started rumbling. I couldn't tell if it originated from inside the bus or from outside on the highway or from the middle of my gut. All I knew was that one second I was on the verge of falling back asleep, and the next, it was as if we were in the middle of an earthquake.

And the smell was indescribable.

PAUL McCARTNEY: The second the glasses were on, they took on a life of their own, y'know. A stream of red smoke poured out of the stems, and the lenses cracked, then repaired themselves, then cracked, then repaired themselves. The frames went up in flames, and then, just as quickly, extinguished themselves. My face blistered, and my nose hairs got singed.

Then came the bad part.

RINGO STARR: The rumbling got far worse, and people started waking up. Everybody was yelling and screaming and holding on to their seats for dear life. Interestingly enough, Roy slept through the whole thing.

PAUL McCARTNEY: And then a laser beam shot out of each lens, right at poor Gerry Mardsen. All I'll say about that is, it's a good thing he wasn't wearing a pacemaker, if you catch my drift.

JOHN LENNON: I wake up, and the bus is bouncing around like a roller coaster. I look around, and Gerry's rolling on the floor, trying to put out the flame that's lapping up his pajama bottoms, and Ringo's hitting himself on the head with a pillow—I think his hair got ignited—and Roy Orbison's fookin' sunglasses are floating in the air, above everybody's head, and they drift down to the front of the bus and rest themselves gently on Roy's face. As soon as they're back in their proper place, the rumbling stops and all the fires die.

PAUL McCARTNEY: I could tell Roy knew it was me who'd started the whole mess, and he also knew that I knew that he knew, but neither of us ever mentioned it. And, erm, after that tour, we never spoke again.

ROY ORBISON: All I can say is, never touch another man's sunglasses.

The Cavern Club is only slightly bigger than a rent-controlled apartment on New York City's Lower East Side, but come August 3, 1963—with Beatles songs clogging up the European airwaves and climbing up the British charts—Beatles fanatics were more than happy to wedge themselves into the tiny joint in order to get a glimpse of the on-the-rise rockers . . . especially since this was to be their final appearance in the tiny Liverpool haunt.

It was one of those "I was there" kind of nights; the club held only several hundred, but apparently everybody in the Western world attended the show. But there's one simple way to tell if somebody's fibbing: if they were at the gig, they've been through the Liverpool Process.

There's little doubt that Carol Jennings, Lee Reynolds, Morry "Moto" McGee, and a gentleman who goes by the moniker of Elvis Beethoven IV experienced John, Paul, George, and Ringo's Cavern Club swan song. Their gray pallor and neck scars say it all.

CAROL JENNINGS: I'd seen them play the Cav over twenty times, and as happy as I was that they became stars, I wished they'd play there every week, for the rest of time. But that last show was magical, and they gave us something to remember them by.

LEE REYNOLDS: I was with my girlfriend and two of my mates. We showed up at the club four or five hours before they were gonna go on, and we managed to nab a spot in the front, right by the stage. I'd never been that close to *any* undead before, and I didn't realize how powerful and, erm, pungent they are.

MOTO MCGEE: I dunno if the Beatles planned what happened, or if it was a spur-of-the-moment deal. Considering how methodical the whole thing was, I'd venture to say it was the former, although I've always suspected that those unruly fans who started screaming, "Ringo never, Pete Best forever!" were the catalyst.

ELVIS BEETHOVEN IV: I was off to the side, stage right, about three meters away from George. I was so wrapped up in the moment and the music and the vibe that I didn't know what happened until it happened.

LEE REYNOLDS: We were the first ones attacked, and it was John who did the attacking. That was kind of an honor, because he was the guy who started the whole modern zombie thing in Liverpool. He was in a rush, so it hurt like hell.

CAROL JENNINGS: Paul did me, and he was lovely about it. I think he thought I was attractive, because he first kissed me on the cheek, then whispered something in my ear that I will not discuss—it was very personal—then launched right into the Liverpool Process. I know he was especially gentle with me, because my friend Olivia said that when he did her, it hurt more than when she gave birth.

MOTO MCGEE: What surprised me more than anything was the speed of their attack. I was in the back of the room, and they'd transformed everybody in front of me within five or ten minutes.

I was especially impressed by George's work. I know he was the last Beatle to be turned—there was a big article about it in *Mersey Beat* the week before—but in terms of sheer numbers, he seemed to be keeping up with John and possibly surpassing Paul.

I could've run, you know. I was standing right by the door and was one of the few who had a chance to escape. But I was indecisive, and back in the early sixties, when it came to the Beatles and transformation, indecision was not an option.

So George finished me off, and here I am, a shuffler forever. I don't blame George. It's his nature. He's hungry. He's vindictive. He can't help it. He doesn't *want* to help it. Now that I am what he is, I understand. It's impossible not to kill once in a while. Does that make me a bad person? I'd like to think not. But I suspect the families of the ninety-eight people I've turned undead might disagree.

I've spoken to a number of people who were at the Cavern Club show, and they were thrilled about how things turned out, but not me. My zombie powers don't seem to be as strong as others', and I'm not a very good-looking man, so I haven't been able to find love. Plus, the undead aren't in great demand in the job market, so it's been a tough life. If I had to do it over, I'd have run.

ELVIS BEETHOVEN IV: After John, Paul, and George jumped out into the audience and went on their rampage, I jumped up onstage and chatted with Ringo. I said, "Oi, mate, what do you think of all this?"

He kinda shrugged and said, "It's their thing. It's what they do. Who am I to argue?" And then he started in with a groove on his tom-toms. It sounded African, almost tribal; it was like he was giving their attack a soundtrack. Then he told me, "You know, you can avoid this whole mess. There's a rear exit. You can go. I won't tell anybody."

I said, "Are you fookin' kidding me, Rings-Baby? I *want* in!" And then I stepped offstage, danced my way through the writhing bodies strewn on the sticky, booze- and blood-coated floor, caught up to Paul, and tapped him on the shoulder. When he turned around, I pointed at the magic spot under my ear and said, "Go to town, Mr. McCartney! Go to fookin' town!" And it's been zombie bliss ever since.

I love everything about being a Liverpool zombie; the limb removal alone is fantastic. And call me a perv, but I might be the only being in the world that prefers shooting dustmen over semen. The birds don't like it, but that's life. Or death.

ROD ARGENT: Yeah, I was at the Cavern that night. The vibe was weird. I sensed what was gonna happen before it happened, and I didn't want any part of it, so I snuck outside the club and stayed there until John, Paul, and George were done. Nobody'd reanimated by the time I went into the place, which is what I was hoping for, because I wanted to do a head count.

I was able to navigate my way through the puddles of blood and get an accurate number: 277 Beatles fans were made undead. And it made me sick. And I knew for damn sure that the Cavern Club was now done with zombies, which meant they were now done with *the*

Zombies. Another club we couldn't play in, thanks to those gits John, Paul, George, and Ringo.

MICK JAGGER: For almost seventy-two hours after the Cavern show, I stood across the street, hidden behind a lamppost, and watched every last one of those newly made undead leave the club. I wanted to take them all down—this wasn't personal; even today, I want to take down virtually all zombies, no matter how innocent they may be—but for that moment, well, that wouldn't have been fair. After all, they were just fans following their heroes.

That said, I took mental pictures of all those fookers, and if *any* of them started getting out of hand at *any* point, I was gonna wiggle my hips, kiss their chests, and then kill them dead.

I bided my time until October. I probably should've bided some more.

✱

GEORGE MARTIN: The boys and I were in the studio, working out the harmonies on a record-label-mandated rendition of "Rudolph the Red-Nosed Reindeer," when Mick Jagger burst in. I'd met Mick a few times and thought he was a lovely man . . . but he certainly wasn't that day.

He came into the control room, shoved me off my stool, and commandeered the talkback mic. He turned the volume all the way up—even then he knew his way around a mixing board—then yelled, "Zommmmmmmmmbieeeees musssssssssssst dieeeeeeeeeeeeeeeeeeeeeeeeee!!!" It felt like the building shook. He was a passionate man, that Mick Jagger.

Then he dived headfirst through the window separating the control room from the recording area and landed face-first on the pile of newly broken glass. He stood up, dusted himself off, and wiped the blood dripping from the gash in his forehead. Then, very quietly, he said, "Good afternoon, gentlemen. How are we all doing today?" Mick wasn't only a passionate bloke; he was also polite.

Ringo said, "Afternoon, Mick. What brings you here, mate?" I think he was trying to stall him so John, Paul, and George could sneak out the back should they so choose.

Mick said, "Oh, you know, I'm in a zombies-must-die bag. Nothing personal. Love your records. Hate your race."

Ringo said, "What about us Ninja types? Must we die, too?"

Mick said, "No, you're a big bit of all right." He pointed at John, Paul, and George. "But I need to rid the world of these buggers." Then Mick looked at his watch, clapped his hands once, and said, "Right, then. I'm meeting Wyman for dinner in an hour. Shall we get started?"

MICK JAGGER: That was my first time attacking the Beatles in closed quarters, and I wasn't expecting the sheer speed and ferocity of their defense-turned-offense. There's nothing Norbert Eliot could've shown me that would've prepared me for that onslaught.

GEORGE MARTIN: Like most every Beatles battle I've witnessed, it was over in under three minutes.

Mick gave it a go, but how is one inexperienced zombie hunter supposed to emerge victorious against three seasoned undead lads? (Ringo wanted nothing to do with it, and he joined me in the control room.) I mean, John threw a piano at the poor man—I think he missed Mick on purpose, but I could be wrong—then Paul picked up an amplifier in each hand and tried to clap Mick's head in between them. Mick managed to do a drop-roll out of that one.

After Harrison nearly decapitated Jagger with Ringo's hi-hat, Ringo got on the talkback and yelled, "Oi, lay off my gear, you yobbos! If you don't cut it out, I'm sending George Martin in there!"

RINGO STARR: The thought of George Martin going into battle was hilarious, and I thought some laughter might cut the tension. I was wrong.

MICK JAGGER: I was exhausted from rolling about the studio and dizzy from blood loss, but I had one last rush in me. I picked up the cymbal that George'd thrown and threw it right back at him. I knew I didn't have the arm strength to cause any real damage, but I thought I might be able to distract him . . . and I was right.

George dived to the ground, but I was already there, lying on my back, waiting for him, my lips pursed for the kiss of life. If he'd have fallen on me chest-first, he'd have been dead. As it was, he fell on me arse-first . . . then he broke wind on my face.

Norbert Eliot never mentioned anything about the effect of zombie farts.

The next thing I remember, it's three days later, and I'm passed out in Keith Richards's bathtub—right next to Keith Richards, who, as was often the case, was *also* passed out in Keith Richards's bathtub. As Keith snored his booze breath into my face, I thought, *I've gotta come up with a new strategy.*

BRIAN EPSTEIN: We managed to keep both the Cavern attack and the blowout with Mick under wraps; neither story made it into a single newspaper. Sure, there were whispers on the street, but since the lads had never done battle with a musical peer—and since they gave no public indications that they ever would—nobody really took it

seriously. Think about it: if word had gotten out, Lord knows there's no way they would've been invited to play at the Royal Variety Performance in November.

I was nervous about it, frankly. Things were going great for us, and the last thing we needed was for John to get cheeky in front of the Queen.

JOHN LENNON: Eppy had reservations, which was fine with me, because I didn't want to do the gig anyhow. I'm not a fan of the monarchy, and I didn't know whether I'd be able to keep my temper under control in Her Royal Highness's presence. I mean, what if I slipped and said something sarcastic?

PAUL McCARTNEY: John was exaggerating about his temper. He could stay cool when he needed to stay cool, y'know. Like there were dozens of times he wanted to murder Bruno Koschmider— hell, we *all* wanted to murder Bruno Koschmider—but John kept his teeth to himself. If he'd avoided eating Bruno, I was confident he could avoid eating and/or saying something inappropriate to the Queen.

JOHN LENNON: In the end, Ringo was the one who convinced me it would be okay. He swore he would stop me from doing anything to the old biddy. I wasn't sure *how* he'd stop me, but he seemed confident.

RINGO STARR: Oh, I could stop John. Easily. I knew John's typical mode of attack better than he did. I don't even think he realized that he used the same game plan over, and over and over again.

When John went after somebody, the speed of his first step toward the victim was astounding. Sometimes I had no idea how he got from point A to point B, no idea at all; for that brief moment, he was as fast, if not faster, than 忍の者乱破. But if the victim was more than three or four meters away, John could be cut off at the pass—at least, by a Ninja—because his second step was considerably slower. Also, he always faked right, then went left, *always*. So my thinking was, if he decided to take a trip up to the balcony and pay a visit to the Queen, I'd be able to at least slow him down enough so that the Queen's guards could hustle her away.

GEORGE HARRISON: Me, I was ambivalent. The international Mania hadn't kicked in yet, but it was getting there, and if we got in good with Her Highness, who knew where it would lead? To more Mania, probably.

Part of me wanted to sabotage the show, but I didn't bother, because I figured Johnny would take care of that in his own inimitable style.

JOHN LENNON: Oh, I had plans, all right. I thought about yanking off my shoe-covered foot and hurling it up into the second balcony—not at the Queen, mind you, but in her general direction. I also considered hypnotizing the rich people in the crowd and commanding them to flip HRH the bird, just for a laugh, but the problem with that was I'd never put more than one person at a time under my spell, so I wasn't sure I could make a mass hypnosis come together, and if it didn't work, I'd be standing onstage with my plonker in my hand—figuratively, of course—and we couldn't have that, now, could we? So I decided to cut them with my wit rather than my teeth.

PAUL McCARTNEY: Erm, I suppose it was kind of amusing.

GEORGE HARRISON: Frankly, John's come up with better material.

RINGO STARR: Let's just say he wasn't exactly Peter Cook *or* Dudley Moore.

BRIAN EPSTEIN: At that point, I, like most mortals, didn't understand zombie humor.

JOHN LENNON: Right before we played our closing number, I gave them what I thought was my scariest look, then said, "Those of you in the cheaper seats, tear your neighbor limb from limb. And those of you in the more expensive seats . . . *do the same fookin' thing.*"

In retrospect, I dunno why everybody made such a huge to-do about it. Only one person actually followed my instructions, and from what I was told, his victim had it coming anyhow.

GEORGE HARRISON: Some may point to the Royal Variety Performance as when the Mania started, but I think it got out of hand when we first went to America, specifically when we landed at John F. Kennedy Airport in New York at the beginning of '64. That was a bad time for me, our first American appearance. It was a maniacal blur. Mania here, Mania there, Mania, Mania, and more Mania. I dunno, this whole line of questioning makes me hungry. Probably best for your health and your sanity if you drop this and ask Paul what he thinks.

PAUL McCARTNEY: When did the Mania begin? New York, y'know. At least, that's what I think. Ask Ringo.

RINGO STARR: New York. It was beautiful, man. At least, that's what I think. Ask John.

JOHN LENNON: Fookin' New York, of course. It's one of the two centers of the Earth. Hell's the other. Hmm, speaking of hell, maybe you should ask the Devil when the Mania started. That cunt'll know better than anybody.

And then there was my extensive, expensive Devil hunt. If you read my blog, you know I met with a prophet, a soul rebel, a Rastaman, an herbsman, a wild man, a natural mystic man, a lady's man, an island man, a family man, Rita's man, a soccer man, a showman, a shaman, a human, and a Jamaican, and then, $25,162 later, in April 2007, I found myself sitting in Mephistopheles's tasteful, well-air-conditioned office down in the Sixth Ring, chatting amiably about where Beatlemania really began.

THE DEVIL: Oh, yes, it was New York, my pretty little journalist. *Bwah hah hah hah hah hah hah hah!* Now piss off, you twat.

Unfortunately, after spending $25,162 to find the guy, the Devil gave me only twelve seconds of his time. And I'm the twat?

GEORGE HARRISON: I hated New York. That city scared my bollocks off.

RINGO STARR: George's line has always been "That city scared my bollocks off," but what most people don't know is he means that literally. At that particular moment—the moment things got tetchy at the JFK terminal, and the undead contingency of our traveling

circus got a little freaked out—I was glad not to be a zombie. But on the other hand, if I *had* been a zombie, I would've freaked out, too, which means I wouldn't have had to . . . had to . . . ehh . . . oh, bloody hell, I can't even bring myself to discuss it.

LYMAN COSGROVE: A little-known fact about the Liverpudlian undead: unlike other zombies, their adrenal glands are fully active, and when overstimulated, they produce a shocking amount of adrenaline. And when a Liverpool Processer's system is flooded with adrenaline, the genitalia is the most affected area of the body.

I could go on endlessly about my scientific theory of the reaction, but, to make a long story short, when a Liverpool zombie gets overly excited, his franks and beans fall off.

JOHN LENNON: So there we are, going into the terminal, on the way to the press conference. Everywhere we turn, there're girls, girls, girls, and all these screamin' blokes are closing in on us, and we'd already decided we couldn't get physical with them because killing dozens of young men in front of telly cameras wouldn't have been a good way to introduce ourselves to America, so we were a bit at their mercy. For the first time in my life, I felt completely helpless. Right when we got inside, I felt an odd sensation in the pit of my stomach, and the next thing I know, my bollocks are rolling down the hallway.

GEORGE HARRISON: As I watched my nuts bounce into John's, I said to Paul, "Tell you what, mate, I didn't sign up for this."

PAUL McCARTNEY: So, erm, there're six Beatle bollocks rolling all over the floor, y'know, and John, George, and I are quietly freaking out. I mean, there were reporters stomping everywhere, and I was picturing somebody coming down hard with his loafer on my left testicle. Thing is, we couldn't bend over to pick up our marbles, because our plonkers would've fallen right down our trouser legs and onto the ground, and that would've attracted some real attention.

So how did we solve this little problem without causing a ruckus? All I can say is, we were lucky to have a Ninja in the band.

BRIAN EPSTEIN: Ringo didn't want to pick up John's, Paul's, and George's testes, and I can't blame him. God knows I wouldn't have done it. It's no secret that I'm gay, but that didn't mean I had any urge to handle half a dozen zombie kerbangers. I told him, "Listen, Rings, just do your virtual invisibility. Nobody'll be the wiser."

He said, "Eppy, I don't care if anybody sees me doing it. I just don't want to touch the bloody things. Handling undead marbles can't be sanitary, d'you know what I mean?" He pointed at the throng and said, "Also, it doesn't look like it'll be possible for me to slip away and wash my hands after I give the boys their balls back, now, does it?"

I said, "Don't you remember, Ringo?: All for zombies, and zombies for all!"

He said, "I'm not a zombie."

I realized I was going to have to get forceful with him. I said, "Yes, but you're a *Beatle*. So get invisible, get on your knees, and collect Lennon's, McCartney's, and Harrison's testicles."

He sighed and disappeared. He was always a good, loyal lad, Ringo was.

JOHN LENNON: I'm not at all convinced the nuts Ringo gave me were both mine. I mean, it's not like I'd recognize them—I'd never spent much time checking out my bollocks, and I certainly never in-

scribed them with my initials, because losing your softies is not an event you prepare for.

GEORGE HARRISON: Who cares if I've got one or both of John's or Paul's nuts? It's not like I'm having kids anyhow. The fact of the matter is, having a bit of Lennon and/or McCartney in my sack probably helped make me a better songwriter.

PAUL McCARTNEY: Listen, I've got one plonker and two bollocks, and it all works fine, so I'm not gonna worry about it.

*

*J*ulie Proust's face is riddled with S-shaped scars. The bruises on her arms are a veritable rainbow: along with the standard black and purple, we're talking red, orange, yellow, green, and sky blue. Her nose has been broken and reset so many times that it's less triangular than octagonal.

But man, what a rack.

A former Miss New York, Julie was killed, then reanimated in 1955 by the pageant's third runner-up; her reign as pageant queen lasted a grand total of three hours.

A rabid music fanatic, Julie has the temperament and vibe of a true American zombie girl: sassy, headstrong, opinionated, and, dare I say it, sexy. I don't know whether she cast some sort of spell on me, but when I spoke with her in April 2008, I couldn't stop staring at her astounding cleavage. Aside from the constant litany of "Hey, sailor boy, eyes up here," our chat was enlightening and revealing, and she readily offered up the truth behind what happened during the band's ride from JFK Airport to Manhattan, a ride that, up until now, was one of the greatest Beatles mysteries of our time: The Case of the Missing Limousine.

JULIE PROUST: After plowing through two or three issues of *Mersey Beat,* I decided the Beatles were exploiting their zombieness for the sake of their own success. Now, I had no real moral problem with that—shit, I would've done the same thing to revive my pageant career if I could've figured out how—but there was one aspect that bothered me:

The girls.

According to that silly little paper, hundreds of little English teenyboppers screamed at Beatles shows until they were hoarse. Apparently these girls also ran after them in the street—which, when you think about it, was a farce; I mean, we're talking three zombies and a Ninja, all of whom could run like the wind, and if they didn't want these girls chasing them, they'd have sped the hell up. I also heard rumors of sexual enslavement, and yeah, those were never proven, but still.

It's not like I was this staunch feminist or anything, but something about the whole deal made me want to give all these girls a big slap. "These guys are just zombie musicians, for cryin' out loud," I'd tell them. "They're a good band, but jeez Louise, have some dignity."

When I found out the Beatles were coming to the States, I decided to do something about it. I rounded up as many young female zombies as I could—a grand total of nineteen—and formed a little group: BEATLES (Brain Eaters and Tongue Lovers Ending Sexism). We didn't really think the Beatles were sexist, but it was a pretty cute little acronym, right?

I knew that if my little group of American zombie girls pooled our powers, we'd be able to cause some serious damage. *Serious.*

JOHN LENNON: So we're in the limo on the way to the hotel, going slowly because the streets were clogged with fans, when all of a

sudden we screech to a halt. I look out the window and see a bunch of gorgeous zombie girls trying to lift the car. Check that: they weren't *trying* to lift it; they *were* lifting it. Then one of them opened the door, pulled Ringo and Eppy out, and threw them into the crowd.

PAUL McCARTNEY: I still dunno how they did it, y'know, but once they had us full in the air, time stopped and the living people froze, yet we undead zombies remained awake and mobile. That was fortunate for Brian and Ringo, who would've been torn to pieces had they hit the mob before being suspended in midair.

JULIE PROUST: How did we stop the clock? Simple: *girl power*. It involves synching menstrual cycles and realigning the moon and . . . well, I'm not going to tell you any more, because I'm working on a book of my own.

GEORGE HARRISON: The girls, those BEATLES, carried our limo through the unmoving bodies, and they were moving *quick*. We were at their lair in three minutes flat, and from what I gathered, we covered several kilometers getting there. My geography was a bit hazy at the time, but I knew we weren't in Manhattan anymore.

JULIE PROUST: Our lair was a shabby coach house in Yonkers—even back then, the rents in Manhattan were too damn high for us, and we weren't exactly well funded.

We named it the Lair of Love and Death, and we filled it with water beds and medical supplies. We were shooting for sexy and scary, but we ended up with silly and clichéd. Still, it served its purpose.

JOHN LENNON: Those birds had it all planned out, man. They dropped the limo right by the front door of what they called the Lair of Love and Death or some shite, then opened the car doors and pulled us in like we weighed nothing. They somehow blocked our zombie powers, so we couldn't fight back. Which, as it turned out, wasn't such a terrible thing.

PAUL McCARTNEY: Right after they stripped us naked and bolted us to the operating tables, they stripped *themselves* naked, y'know. John turned to me while one of the zombie girls gently whipped him with her bra, and said, "I bet Ringo would've loved this."

RINGO STARR: Hell yeah, I would've loved it!

JOHN LENNON: One of the birds looked closely at my bollocks and said, "Looks like you've had some recent damage down there, Mr. Lennon. Adrenaline problems?" Those zombie ladies knew the score.

GEORGE HARRISON: I don't quite know what they were trying to prove. They kidnapped us, they tied us down, they showed off their bodies, and then they untied us and bounced us from water bed to water bed. What was the point?

JULIE PROUST: Our whole point was to show these boys that we girls weren't playthings, that we had feelings and shouldn't be taken for granted. Thing is, they were pretty cute and *very* charismatic, and some of us got distracted, so, as the politicos say, we went off-message. How off-message? Let's say that by the time we put them back in the limo, the Lair of Love and Death was a dust-men repository.

BRIAN EPSTEIN: After John and George loaded me and Ringo back into the limo, they told me what happened, and I had no choice but to believe it. How else could you explain a car that was there one second, then gone the next, then back the next after that? How else could you explain me losing a full ninety minutes of my life?

At the end of the day, the lads were happy and safe, and that's all that mattered. Well, that's not exactly *all* that mattered: I needed them to be ready for Sullivan.

*

*E*ver *since talk show host David Letterman and his crew began broadcasting their late-night gabfest from New York's Ed Sullivan Theater in 1993, many on Letterman's staff believe that Mr. Sullivan's ghost still haunts the venue that was home to his beloved variety show for more than three decades.*

Guess what? They're right.

The theories as to why Ed is all ghosted-up are myriad: maybe he was bitten by Anna the Juggling Bear after her less-than-successful 1959 appearance on Ed's show, maybe he inhaled too much Brylcreem, maybe he ate a bad hot dog in the green room. However it went down, Ed is conflicted about his ghostly status: on one hand, his pre-ghost life was pretty good, but on the other, if he's going to be stuck somewhere for all eternity, where better than a place that holds so many rrrrrreally big memories . . . memories that the specter is always ready to share.

As Ed's ghost told me in January 2002, one of his favorite moments as host of arguably the most revered variety show in television history was the night that the Beatles conquered the United States . . . almost.

ED SULLIVAN: No matter what anybody tells you, deep down, John, Paul, George, and Ringo were nice boys. I always felt that all the talk about *total* world domination was for show. Think about it: if three artistically creative zombies and a talented Ninja don't make a token effort to rule all the heavens and the Earth, they have no credibility. At the end of the day, I think they would've been happy to rule the charts, as well as a handful of key metropolises in the UK and the USA.

You might not have appreciated their music, and you might not have liked the length of their hair, and you might not have cared for their predilection for murder and mayhem, but you can't deny that the Beatles were professionals. Music was both their life and their job, and they took it very seriously. They came to my studio with a plan, and they executed it to perfection. If the plan had worked, the world as we know it would've been quite a different place.

They called me into the dressing room after the afternoon dress rehearsal. John told me, "Listen, Ed, we're not gonna be your normal guests."

I said, "Oh, I know that. America's going to remember this one."

George quietly said, "Not if we have something to say about it."

I asked, "What do you mean by that."

Paul stood up, put his arm around me, and said, "Listen, mate, we like you. But most important, we respect you, and we don't want any harm to come to you, y'know. So here's a bit of advice: when we start singing 'All My Loving,' cover your ears."

I said, "Why in God's name would I do that? That's a wonderful song, just wonderful."

John said, "Thanks, Ed. We appreciate that. But trust us: You. Don't. Want. To. Listen. To. That. Song."

JOHN LENNON: I *thought* we'd be able to make it come to fruition, but I wasn't sure. See, it's not the kind of thing you can practice, so we wouldn't know until we knew. Or didn't know. Whichever came first.

GEORGE HARRISON: If you were to point the finger—and I'm not pointing, mind you—but if you were to point, you'd have to point at Paul. After all, John and I had the background harmonies down.

PAUL McCARTNEY: It wasn't anybody's fault. We tried, and it didn't work. Sod it. Lesson learned. Move on.

RINGO STARR: Whenever John, Paul, and George did something a bit off, they always blamed it on their zombie nature. Like, "Oh, we couldn't help killing everybody at the Cavern Club; it was our zombie nature." Or, "Oh, we didn't mean to destroy EMI Studios; it was our zombie nature." They had plenty of free will; they just didn't use it all the time. So when they try and play off the Sullivan thing like it was their zombie nature, well, that's utterly ridiculous.

PAUL McCARTNEY: The plan was simple. When we got to the bridge, John and George's descending "Ooh's" would meld with my lead vocal and create a frequency that would allow us to control the minds of each and every listener. And, erm, it worked. For exactly thirteen seconds.

ED SULLIVAN: When they stopped singing, I uncovered my ears and yelled, "Boys, what's going on? Keep playing, keep playing!" Then I noticed that everybody in the room was staring at the four of them with a glazed look on their face, not moving a muscle.

John called over, "Oi, Eddie, keep it down. We've got some work to do!" Then he said into the microphone, "Concentrate on my voice. Heed my command. You have three tasks, and you will follow them to completion. Task one, buy our latest record. Task two . . ."

And before he could continue, everybody snapped out of it and started screaming.

RINGO STARR: When the studio audience awoke, they were scared like you wouldn't believe. Just check out the pictures. The look of horror on their faces was chilling.

JOHN LENNON: I was having a laugh with that first task. I always said I wouldn't sell records by hypnosis, and I meant it. I thought the boys would get a kick out of it. They didn't.

I'm not gonna tell you what the other two tasks were. See, I might pull them out at some point down the line, and like Ringo says, "The element of surprise is your friend." But trust me, they're good ones. Really, really good ones.

PAUL McCARTNEY: That was the last time we tried to control the minds of a telly-viewing audience. Electronic hypnosis accomplished very little and, frankly, was a pain in the arse, y'know.

JOHN LENNON: We tried to take over the United States that night, and all we ended up with was another number one single.

BRIAN EPSTEIN: They played Sullivan's show again the following week; this time it originated from Miami Beach, rather than New York. All they talked about in the two days leading up to it was mind control, mind control, mind control, and I wasn't thrilled. I begged them to forget hypnosis and just play their tunes, but they were insistent. John said, "America could forget all about us next week. Think about it: coming over here didn't help the other Brit acts, so we have to do *what* we can, *when* we can."

I asked him, "Why do you have to do it?"

John said, "It's our zombie nature."

GEORGE HARRISON: We scaled it down considerably, intending to own the minds and bend the wills of just the people attending the concert at the Deauville Beach Resort. Since hypnosis hadn't worked when Paul was singing lead, we opted to use "This Boy" as our launching point. Most of the song was sung in three-part harmony, but there was a moment right before the bridge where John did a "Whoa, whoa, whoa" bit, and that was the spot.

RINGO STARR: Man, that was a disaster. If I were undead, I'd have been embarrassed for all zombiekind. As it was, I was embarrassed to be a Beatle.

JOHN LENNON: Nothing ventured, nothing gained, I always say.

PAUL McCARTNEY: We got to the bridge of the song, and we did our hypnotize-with-harmony thing, and *nothing*. Nobody froze, and nobody yelled their heads off in horror. The whole crowd just sat there and watched while the lenses of all four television cameras shattered. The cameramen were dead before we even had a chance to reanimate them.

Yeah, we sold a whole bunch of records, and yeah, we earned a whole bunch of loyal fans, but to us, our first trip to the States was a failure. We didn't kill a single person, except for those cameramen, but they don't count, because we didn't *really* kill them, an' that. They just died on our watch.

Nobody said much of anything on the plane ride home. Right before we landed at Heathrow, I leaned over to Johnny and said, "Listen, we did the best we could, and that's all we could do. We'll get 'em next time."

He said, "If there *is* a next time."

•

When *film director Richard Lester—Dick to his friends—was hired to helm the Beatles' film debut,* A Hard Day's Night, *he'd had only limited experience working with otherwordly beings: the assistant director on his 1963 outing* The Mouse on the Moon *was a reformed mole man, and his regular collaborator the Brit comic legend Spike Milligan was rumored to have modest telekinetic abilities. So, as Lester told me over too many bottles of wine in March 2005, he was a bit on edge when filming started in the spring of 1964.*

RICHARD LESTER: Three questions gnawed at me from the beginning: How do you *film* zombies? How do you *direct* zombies? And are zombies even *directable*? I had no clue. I had nobody to ask. So I dived in. Brian Epstein swore to me up and down that nobody in the band would harm me, so what was the worst that could happen? I'd lose a few shillings for the studio. It wouldn't be the end of the world.

Aside from the one overnight setup when Paul took too many pep pills and turned neon green, the first week of the shoot was a breeze. Word went around the set that George had had some sort of dust-up with a zombie townie, but I chose not to get involved. Georgie's business was Georgie's business.

It all went to shit eight days in. We had about half of the film in the can, and the entire cast and crew felt great about the whole thing, just great . . . until we all sat down to watch the first batch of dailies.

To this day, nobody knows exactly how it happened. There was no precedent for it. But then again, nobody had shot a feature film that gave zombies any significant screen time, so how *could* there be?

BRIAN EPSTEIN: Ringo looked marvelous. Wilfred Brambell, the actor playing Paul's grandfather, was genius. Lester's visual style was original and arresting, full of quirky angles and madcap energy. There was one teeny, tiny little problem:

No zombies.

RICHARD LESTER: The studio was putting a lot of pressure on me to finish on time and under budget, so when neither John, nor Paul, nor George showed up on the screen, my first thought was, *We pissed away half of our budget: 250K, right out the window.* And then I got curious: *Is a zombie not showing up on film the same principle as a vampire not showing up in a mirror? How come you could see them perfectly well when filmed with television cameras, but not with movie ones? How come their clothes also became invisible?* Then I went into problem-solving mode: *How can I make this work? How do I get these boys to be seen on the screen?*

And then the answer dawned on me. Two words: Claude Rains.

JOHN LENNON: Dick took Paul and me aside and said, "Do you guys want to make this movie work?"

I said, "Fook, yeah. If Elvis can get people in the theaters, we have to at least *try*."

He said, "This is a major problem. Are you willing to do anything to make it work?"

Paul said, "Absolutely."

Dick said, *"Anything?"*

I said, "Yes, *anything*. What're you thinking?"

And then he showed us a roll of duct tape.

RICHARD LESTER: In the 1933 version of *The Invisible Man,* when Claude Rains wanted to be seen, he wrapped himself in gauze. There wasn't any gauze on the set of *A Hard Day's Night*—and based on what we'd learned to that point, soft material became invisible on camera when it was resting on an undead body, which I eventually learned was due to the noxious gasses that emanated from the Fab Four's rotting, pus-covered, nausea-inducing skin.

The good news was, we had plenty of duct tape.

I told the guys, "Get into your trailers, get naked, and get Ringo to cover your entire body with this stuff."

They stared at the tape for a bit, then Paul said, "Dick, that'll look ridiculous."

I said, "It's better than nothing, Paulie. And if you don't do that, that's exactly what this damn movie will be: *nothing.*"

RINGO STARR: Maybe it was because I was the last one to join the group, or maybe it was because I wasn't a zombie, but I sometimes felt like the band's whipping boy. Think about it: If I'm not picking up their fallen testicles, I'm wrapping duct tape around their naked bodies. And how many songs do they let me sing per album? One, that's how many.

On the plus side, that was the last time I ever had to handle Lennon's and McCartney's boy parts.

GEORGE HARRISON: Ringo was very thorough. He didn't miss a spot. I'm not necessarily convinced he needed to stick any tape on that little area between our bollocks and our arseholes, but he claimed he was following Dick Lester's orders.

PAUL McCARTNEY: Me, I liked having tape up in that particular vicinity. Still stick some on there once in a while, y'know.

RICHARD LESTER: I never, ever, ever told Ringo Starr to put duct tape on the area between John Lennon's, Paul McCartney's, and George Harrison's respective zombie scrotums and anuses. Even if I wanted or needed tape there, I wouldn't have broached the subject; yes, I was from the States, but I'd worked in the UK long enough to know that that little spot of body isn't the kind of thing you bring up in conversation.

But considering how nicely *A Hard Day's Night* came out, it was worth it.

GEORGE HARRISON: I refuse to discuss the removal of the duct tape. I'm not going to tell you who did it. I'm not going to tell you how it was done. I'm not going to tell you the aftermath. There are some things better left unsaid, and some memories better left unremembered.

◆

*I*rvine Paris had just turned twenty when he landed a job as the arts critic for the *Liverpool Herald in 1960. A staunch Beatles fanatic, he wrote lovingly about the band for his entire fifteen-year tenure with the newspaper. Every record write-up or concert report or hard news story was glowing. Never an ill word was written.*

Except for two teeny-tiny negative write-ups. And the first was a critique that almost ended in a Liverpool-style fatwa.

John's first book of verse, In His Own Write, *was published on March 23, and Paris's review, which ran the following day, wasn't exactly what you would call glowing.*

JOHN LENNON IN HIS OWN WRONG
Farcical Poetry or Poetical Farce?
By Irvine Paris

March 24, 1964

For the last thirteen months, Beatles cofounder John Lennon has been Liverpool's darling. He can do no wrong. His group's music is scintillating. His public demeanor has been exemplary. He is a credit to our city, to rock 'n' roll musicians, and to the undead. However, you cannot expect perfection. John Lennon is going to have a long career, and there will be missteps along the way. Beatle John's first misstep was a big one.

Considering its amateurishness, one wonders if *In His Own Write,* Lennon's collection of simplistic poems and pointless stories, is a joke on fans of the Beatles. This gentleman who, along with his partner Paul McCartney, cocomposed some of the most memorable pop ditties in recent music history, has presented a pile of dung that could be enjoyed only by a six-year-old zombie of dubious intelligence.

Consider, if you will, the opening two verses of the piece entitled "I Eat Salami":

> *I eat salami mixed with brains*
> *Sitting in the winter rain*
> *Song on my lips, chunks in my teeth*
> *My favorite Scottish town is Leith*
>
> *Googly moogly bombity bombie*
> *I'm a gray and rancid zombie*

Bombity bombie your blood is red
You are alive, I am undead

Upon a cursory read, one would assume that the sole message Lennon attempted to get across in "I Eat Salami" is that he's lonely. One would also assume that since Lennon is Lennon, such is merely a surface message and a deeper meaning is hidden beneath. After four or five reads, one realizes that this is not the case. The remainder of the poem consists of nonsense words similar to "googly moogly" and off-putting imagery similar to that in line three. That sort of imagery—descriptions of death, dismemberment, and oozing innards—grows tiresome.

So please, please, Beatle John, please, please go back to the guitar. We love you, yeah, yeah, yeah . . . but only when you are singing, strumming, or talking. Leave the verse to the experts.

JOHN LENNON: If you like my book, you like my book. If you don't, you don't, sod you, it's your loss. Irvine Paris? The little git didn't bother me a bit.

NEIL ASPINALL: Irvine Paris bothered John quite a bit.

We all knew what happened when John *really* lost his temper—lunchtime killing sprees, ripping off his own left leg and tossing it out a hotel window, eating all the live pigeons he could get his hands on, that sort of thing—but he always managed to regain control of himself within a few hours. However, when he saw Paris's review, he crossed over to what George began calling "Johnny's dark place."

BRIAN EPSTEIN: John walked through the door of my flat—literally walked through it; he broke the thing to smithereens—holding the newspaper an arm's length away from his body, between his thumb and index finger, as if it were a fish that had been dead for a week. He yelled, "Oi, Eppy, did you see this?"

I hadn't. It was unquestionably a grim review, and I can understand why he was so upset: up until then, nobody had ever written an ill word about him or the band, and as anybody in the arts field knows, that first bad review is tough to swallow.

I sat him down, gave him some tea, and said, "Listen, John, people will say what they'll say. Sometimes they'll like you, but sometimes they'll want to tear you down. What someone says about you shouldn't change you or your vision or your dreams. Keep writing your poetry. Keep writing your songs. Be the best John Lennon you can be."

He calmly said, "Right, then. I understand, Brian, I understand. Not every word written about us can be a good word. Writers have their opinions, and they're allowed to write them. I believe in artistic freedom. I believe in individuality. I believe in the right of every man to look at the rest of world from his own perspective and to share that perspective with the rest of world. And now I'm going to the *Herald* offices to Midpoint Irvine Paris's arse." Then he stood up, smiled, gave me a little pat on the shoulder, and went on his merry way.

Still not sure why he crashed through my picture window rather than walking through the hole in the door he'd created five minutes before. But that was John Lennon for you.

Fortunately for Irvine Paris, John was so upset that he got lost on the way to the *Herald* offices. He somehow ended up in Everton, and his car ran out of gas in the middle of nowhere, and he didn't have any money with him. Paulie found him three days later, in the

Everton Cemetery over on Long Lane, curled up under the threshold of a small mausoleum. John claimed it was the only comfortable place he could find to sleep, but I think he settled there so that when he was found, it would look more dramatic. I think he was pretending.

JOHN LENNON: Of course I was pretending.

BRIAN EPSTEIN: Irvine Paris wisely went underground for a while. John did too, but in his case, underground meant two weeks in the Liverpool sewers. We had a tour coming up, but neither Paul nor George would go down there to get him out, so it was up to me, and as much as the thought of it repulsed me, I did it because that's what managers do.

Seeing how those zombies lived, all I can say is, no wonder they're so grouchy.

*

Thanks to his laconic wit, his cuddly demeanor, and the fact that he was the Beatle least likely to launch an unprovoked physical attack that could lead to a crushed larynx or a dislocated kneecap, Ringo Starr had developed a little following of his own. As a matter of fact, the Queen herself believed that he was actually the band's founder and leader.

Which put Jimmy Nicol in an awkward position.

A solid journeyman traps-man, Jimmy was hired to replace Ringo on a brief tour of Europe, China, and Australia when the world's favorite Ninja took ill with tonsillitis—or so the newspapers were told. As Jimmy explained when I spoke with him at his London home in October 2000, the tonsil story was just that, a story.

JIMMY NICOL: When Brian Epstein called to invite me on tour, the first thing I asked was, "Can I get speak with Ringo before I decide? I'd like to get his blessing." He told me the same thing he told everybody else: Ringo was sick and in the hospital and, because of his tonsils, unable to talk. That sounded odd to me, but I didn't dwell on it. The most important thing was to learn the material.

After a couple of shows, I more or less forgot about the Ringo situation, but on the plane ride from Amsterdam to Hong Kong, Paul came by my seat and said, "Listen, mate, you've played great over the last week, so I'm going to tell you something that only six or seven other people in the world know about, but you have to promise not to discuss this with anybody other than John, George, and me. If you open your yap to the outside world, there could be dire consequences, y'know."

I said, "My yap is sealed." Of course my yap was sealed. I knew what'd happened at the Cavern Club back in '62 and was well aware what "dire consequences" meant.

Paul said, "Ringo's not sick."

He stared at me like he wanted a response, but I kept quiet, for fear of saying something that could lead to pain. Finally, once I realized he wasn't gonna open up his mouth until I said something, I asked, "Did Ringo shove off, then?"

He nodded, then said, "He sort of did, Jimmy. He sort of did." Then he kind of sighed all sadly and said, "See, Ringo is a Seventh Level Ninja Lord, y'know, and to reach Level Eight, he has to complete the Shu Shen Shwa Triumvirate to the satisfaction of Mistress Sbagw N'phszyz Xi, who happens to be the world's only living Twenty-Sixth Level Ninja Lord, and she's in bloody Greenland. We can't let anybody know about it, because if people know Ringo feels the need to jump a Ninja Lord Level, they might think of him as vulnerable, and that could lead to an attack, and, really, who needs that sort of malarkey? The thing is, Ringo could've hopped a taxi to the West End to study with a Twenty-Fifth Level, but he had to go to sodding Qaqortoq, Greenland. D'you know what I mean? That Ninja lot is completely mental."

We stared at each other for a bit, then I said, "What the bloody fook are you goin' on about?"

Paul said, "Don't worry about it. Just tell everybody Ringo has a sore throat, and he'll be back soon."

I said, "*Will* he be back soon?"

Paul said, "Dunno, mate. That's why I'm discussing this with you. You play some mean drums, and you're a nice bloke, so if Ringo refuses to leave Greenland after he's Level Eight, would you be interested in joining us permanently? Or at least semipermanently?"

Obviously I was flattered, but I wondered exactly what "joining us permanently" meant. Did it mean I'd be a drummer or a zombie or a zombie drummer? I wasn't too keen on the last two. I'd been known to faint at the sight of blood, and the thought of eating brains was, well, let's just say that eating English food was more appealing, and anybody who's shoved down English faire, circa 1964, knows that's saying something. I didn't want to close off the idea, but I didn't necessarily want to keep it open, so I told Paul, "Let's see what happens."

He smiled and said, "Sounds good, Jimmy." Then he leaned over, touched me right below my earlobe, smelled my neck, and said, "Sounds good indeed."

I suddenly got dizzy and felt cold all over. Ringo couldn't get back fast enough.

PAUL McCARTNEY: If Ringo had gotten stuck in Qaqortoq, we'd have killed Jimmy in a heartbeat, y'know. That cat could play.

JIMMY NICOL: It wasn't like I could up and quit. I couldn't come across as scared, either—I think they can smell fear, and they don't like it—so I did my best to go about my business without making any waves. But it's hard to act normal when you've got people holding up RINGO FOREVER, JIMMY NEVER signs, or when John Lennon leaves both his thumbs in your hotel room's sink for a laugh, or when gorgeous young sex slaves beg to taste your dustmen, whatever that is.

So I went about my business and didn't make any waves. And when Ringo showed up in Melbourne, I smooched him on the lips, then asked Eppy to get me on the next plane back to England.

When I got off the plane at Heathrow, I kissed the ground. Never had an airport floor tasted so sweet.

RINGO STARR: I didn't pass my Ninja Lord exam. Mistress Sbagw N'phszyz Xi was a very political animal, and she exemplified all that was bad about Ninja bureaucracy. And as I learned in Greenland, the jump from Level Seven to Level Eight was less about skills and more about arse-kissing, and I wasn't going to kiss anybody's arse for anything.

However, she did give me a lovely I ❤ QAQORTOQ T-shirt, so it wasn't a complete loss.

•

BRIAN EPSTEIN: The band's first real US tour in the fall of '64 was defined by one thing, and one thing only: *screaming*. The press played it off like it was fabulous, but really, it was horrific.

The lads didn't mind the screaming in and of itself—for that matter, John and Paul seemed to get a certain thrill out of the whole thing, especially when a man sitting in the front row at the second Hollywood Bowl show yelled so intensely that blood gushed from his eyes, nose, and mouth and spurted all the way onto Ringo's hi-hat—but it was difficult to hear what was happening onstage.

GEORGE HARRISON: Touring was a blur. Going from town to town, from city to city, from country to country without a minute to breathe was hard enough. But when you add Mick Jagger to the equation, well, talk about Mania.

RINGO STARR: We were in Chicago for a gig at the International Amphitheater, and after we finished up our sound check, Brian and the four of us went back to the limo, and there he is, Mick Jagger himself, waiting for us in the backseat, his massive lips fashioned into a puffy sneer, or maybe a smile—it was always hard to tell with him. No clue how he got past security. No clue how the limo driver didn't notice him. It was Ninja-like behavior, and I couldn't help being impressed and flattered that a fine singer such as Mick would go to all that trouble just to see us.

Mick picked up Eppy by his collar and said, "Brian, if it's okay with you, I'd like to chat with my favorite Liverpudlians. I need to pick their brains . . . that is, before they pick mine." A pretty good line for a bloke from Kent, I thought. Mick kicked open the door and threw Eppy out onto the concrete, then, in a dead-on Lennon voice, told the driver to take us to the William Green Homes.

John said, "What the fook are the William Green Homes?"

Mick said, "Never you mind, Johnny. Just sit back and enjoy the trip." Nobody said a thing during the fifteen-minute ride to what turned out to be a low-income housing development parked right next to a big, empty field—if you could call it a field. Mick told the limo driver to piss off, that we'd find our own way back to the hotel—if we made it back to the hotel. While the driver sprinted away, Mick said, "Okay, lads, out."

We stumbled out of the car. The sidewalk was cracked, and there was broken glass everywhere. George whispered to me, "Aren't you gonna do something, Rings? Get invisible, mate. Save the day."

I whispered, "You got it." I might not have made Eighth Level, but I still had a few tricks up my sleeve. Right as I was about to blend into the scenery, a van screeched into the lot and ran over the escaping driver, then plowed smack into the limo.

And out jumped a Zombie.

ROD ARGENT: My bandmates weren't too keen on tracking down the Beatles; they made it quite clear that they found my little grudge to be pointless. They also thought that any combination of John, Paul, George, and Ringo would easily kill us all, but I don't think they gave our collective fighting skills enough credit. I personally thought that at least one of us could've survived a full-blown Beatles versus Zombies clash.

Having said that, I understood where my fellow Zombies were coming from. The Beatles had killed thousands, and the Zombies hadn't made one single person so much as bleed. Nonetheless, that left me in the lurch, as I stood no chance of competing with the Beatles as a solo act, even if I'd had ten thousand machine guns and fifty thousand diamond bullets. So once I heard Mick was on the case, I started following him, and he never had a clue. Besides, even if Jagger realized I was on his trail, he probably wouldn't have known who the fook I was anyhow. The Zombies didn't exactly travel in the same circles as the Rolling Stones, d'you know what I mean?

Anyhow, there're John, Paul, and George all huddled together in a desolate Chicago field, and there's Ringo going in and out of focus—Ninja Lords drive me nuts with the disappearing—and there's Jagger giving them a *look*. I said, "I'm here, Mick! Let's do this!"

MICK JAGGER: My first thought: *Who the fook is this?*

ROD ARGENT: I was right. The cheeky bastard didn't recognize me.

MICK JAGGER: My second thought: *I might be able to use this guy.* I said to him, "State your business, mortal!" There was no need for me to call him "mortal," or to speak like a sixteenth-century knight. It just sounded cool.

He held up his hands and said, "I'm here to offer you aid, O great hunter Jagger."

Again, I said, "State your name!"

"I am Rod Argent, co-leader of the rock band the Zombies."

I said, "I am vaguely familiar with your band, but I need proof you are who you say you are. Recite your discography, mortal!"

He said, "Our first single has just been released, O great hunter. 'She's Not There,' backed with 'You Make Me Feel Good'!"

I said, "State the label and catalog number!"

He said, "Decca F11940!"

I said, "I am familiar! You may join the hunt!" Of course, I was talking out of my arse. He could've told me his first single was called "Wankity Wank Wank" for the Wank label, and I wouldn't have known any better.

He said, "Thank you, O great hunter! What would you like me to do?"

I said, "You can clean up the mess after I'm done with these cunts. Now fook off and let a professional handle this."

ROD ARGENT: No way was I gonna take that from a guy who'd been making a living by covering other musicians' songs. I mean, if you can't write your own sodding tunes, you shouldn't be ordering people around, right? Right.

So I told him, "I'm sorry, O great hunter, but I insist on being part of this battle."

Mick pointed his gun at me and said, "Stand down, Zombie."

I said, "I refuse."

He said, "Leave, immediately."

I said, "Never."

He said, "Piss off."

We went back and forth for a good long while.

GEORGE HARRISON: While those two idiots prattled on, I said to John, "Hey, how about you and I attack Jagger, and Paul and Ringo go after Argent?"

John said, "I have a better idea."

ROD ARGENT: Lennon tapped me on the shoulder, and next thing I know, we're at the Chess Records Studios.

MICK JAGGER: He wouldn't have been able to hypnotize me if I wasn't engaged with that Argent chap, I can tell you that much.

JOHN LENNON: There's little in this world I like more than fighting at a recording studio. Something about all that equipment gets those zombie juices bubbling.

But when I went to attack Mick in the studio, something felt wrong.

PAUL McCARTNEY: Right after we got to Chess, we dumped Mick and Rod into the recording room, then snapped them out of their spell. After all, we weren't ones to murder a bloke when he can't at least *try* to defend himself, y'know. When they got their bearings, I tried to rip off Argent's plonker, but the closer I got to his body, the weaker I became. On the other hand, whenever I walked toward all the guitars and basses against the back wall, I felt stronger than I'd ever felt. The moment I got a gander at the sunburst Fender Jazz Bass in the corner, some force made me pick it up and strap it on.

GEORGE HARRISON: It sounds ridiculous, but a 1952 Gibson Les Paul Goldtop just appeared in my hands.

JOHN LENNON: Next thing I know, I'm strumming a 1955 Gibson Les Paul TV. My hands automatically went to a blues in the key of A.

MICK JAGGER: I was a Willie Dixon fan, but I'd never heard his song "Built for Comfort" in my life. And yet there I was, standing in front of a microphone, singing it like I'd written it. The right key, the right lyrics, the right vibe. For that moment, any urge I had to murder the Beatles went right out the window.

ROD ARGENT: I didn't even like the blues that much, but I did some background harmonies behind Mick with a sense of soul that I never knew I had.

RINGO STARR: There wasn't a drum kit in the studio, so I sat on the floor and minded my own business.

PAUL McCARTNEY: We jammed until it was time to go back to the Amphitheater, about three hours. I don't recall how many songs we played, but before we set foot in the studio, we didn't know a single one of them.

We never heard or saw an engineer, but when we walked out of the studio, right on the floor near the front door were four reel-to-reel tapes, each labeled BEATLES/STONES/ZOMBIES BLUES JAM. Since

there were four Beatles, one Stone, and one Zombie, the Beatles got to keep them all. Majority rules.

When we made it back to the Amphitheater, I gave the tapes to Eppy, then never saw them again. Eppy told us that somebody nicked them from the dressing room. Bloody Chicagoans.

BRIAN EPSTEIN: Nobody nicked the tapes. Here's what happened.

I opened the boxes when I got back to my room after the show, and I swear to you, the tapes were alive. They were brown snakes with green dots, and their tongues were about six inches long, and they smelled like feces. It was grotty. Utterly, utterly grotty.

We were staying by Lake Michigan, so I left the hotel, ran across the street, and tromped through the sand, right up to the water. I flung the tapes as far as I could, and once the fourth one hit the water, a fireball rose from the lake and whizzed around about a meter in the air, like a giant soap bubble. It lit the entire area, so I could see thousands and thousands of dead fish float up to the surface. And then the entire lake turned red. And it bubbled and steamed. And it smelled like the snake, except a thousand times more potent.

At that point, I decided it was time to go back to the hotel and crawl under the covers. Or hide under the bed.

•

*O*ne *of the longest running jokes among music fans is, when Bob Dylan talks, people listen . . . but they can't understand a single word he says. It's been said that the man speaks like he has a mouthful of marbles or like he has cotton in his cheeks or like he has several ounces of hydroponics caught in between his teeth. Considering he's been a professional musician since 1961, and has thus successfully conversed* *with countless managers, promoters, agents, sidemen, engineers, road-ies, and groupies, I thought the whole you-can't-understand-Bob deal was an exaggeration.*

It wasn't.

In March 2007, I sat down with Dylan for a total of eight hours over three days, and, aside from "Hi there," "Send me a copy of your book when it's done," and "You'll pick up the check, right?" I couldn't make out a single complete sentence, rendering all of my interviews useless. Thus it was up to the venerable Eppy to tell the story of the Beatles' infamous first meeting with Dylan in New York on August 28, 1964.

BRIAN EPSTEIN: Bob liked the boys' records, and the boys liked Bob's, so when he and a writer named Al Aronowitz popped by our hotel, we were glad to invite them up.

They blathered about nothing memorable for a while, then Bob pulled out a joint. We were familiar with what Paul still likes to call "herbal jazz cigarettes," but the Beatles had never indulged, and frankly, considering how those pep pills affected them back in Germany, I wasn't entirely comfortable with the idea of them sucking down what some might construe as a foreign substance.

Ringo was the first Beatle to get high. He inhaled almost an entire joint all by his lonesome and was fine; all he did was giggle a lot. John, Paul, and George went next, and you could say they were fine, too. Their brains didn't melt out of their ears. Their eyes remained happily in their sockets. Their tongues didn't swell up like balloons. Their skin didn't turn any odd colors.

No, what happened was, they got gas. And they found the whole thing hilarious.

I remember John broke wind first, and he said, "Whoa, sorry about the air tulip, boys."

George followed suit and said, "Oopsie. Quite the trouser trumpet there. Apologies."

And then came Paul, who said, "Uh-oh, somebody let loose with a big, old rumbler, y'know, and I think his name is Little Paulie Macca."

And then the barrage started. One, right after the other, right after the other: some dribblies, a few rooters, a handful of rippers, a bunch of spoofies, a goodly number of piffles, a zump or two, a heap of flutters, a number of freeps, a gaggle of chuffs, and a collection of arse crunchers.

Now, I appreciate a good tooter as much as the next chap, but the weed caused a mess in the lads' respective gastrointestinal systems that took those pipe rotters to a whole other level. By the time they finished their second joint, the room was filled with noxious lavender-colored smoke.

After they were done smoking the marijuana, Bob stood up, breathed in a big lungful of the gassy purple haze—remember, heat rises—and said, "This is beautiful, man, just beautiful. I've never experienced such a beautiful moment. Beauty. That's what this is. Beauty. Beautiful." For a bloke who wrote such meaningful lyrics, Bob wasn't the most articulate gent in the world when he was surrounded by a bunch of undead quiffers. But I can't blame him, I suppose; I was feeling a bit woozy and silly myself.

I'm not sure how much longer we stayed. It might've been ten minutes, and it might've been ten hours. Lavender zombie poots have a way of making time a bit stretchy.

•

A*s a group, Ninjas, when they're not defending their turf or assassinating a politician, are an affable lot, and Ringo Starr was about as* *affable as they come. That being the case, most people appreciate and respect your typical Ninja, but there are pockets of folks throughout the world who despise these noble warriors. These anti-Ninjite malcontents tend to gravitate toward one another and eventually form hate groups. One of the most militant Ninja hate aggregations is based in Montreal; demonstrating a serious lack of creativity, they are known simply as the Fuck You Ninjas.*

Formed in 1959, the FYN was never the most skilled unit, but they got their strength through sheer numbers. In his unimaginatively titled 1980 manifesto All Ninjas Must Die: How to Kill a Ninja in Three Easy Lessons, *former FYN defense secretary Wilfred Hinckley White wrote, "Our plan has been, is, and always will be to surround, surround, surround our potential victim. If you put the Ninja in a box, cover all of his escape routes, and have one hundred men pointing one hundred guns at his heart, you're going to WIN! That was our plan for Richard 'Ringo' Starkey 'Starr': surround him and shoot him dead."*

Brian Epstein learned of the plan from a Canada-based Fifteenth-Level Ninja Lord named Roger Aaron. As Aaron, who'd infiltrated the FYN in 1962, explained to me in a December 2003 interview, the FYN versus Ringo waterloo went down during a concert at the Montreal Forum on September 8, 1964.

ROGER AARON: The FYN had only one plan for Ninja killing— encircle the target with as many armed men as they could recruit— and they used it over and over. It was unbelievably simplistic, but undeniably effective, and almost impossible for a lone Ninja to escape. It's possible that a single Ninja with, say, Sixty-sixth Level skills could put the kibosh on it, but I was only a Level Fifteen, so I had no chance . . . and neither would Ringo. My only hope of protecting him was to get the Beatles to cancel the show.

Brian Epstein didn't believe me, and I suppose I can understand

why. It was late '64, and the Beatles were just about the biggest thing in the world, so undoubtedly thousands of crackpots were coming out of the woodwork. Imagine if you answered the phone and a stranger said to you, "I'm a Ninja Lord who's been undercover for a few years with Canada's most dangerous Ninja killers. They're called Fuck You Ninjas, and they're planning to murder your drummer, and you have to leave the country immediately." What would you think? I know *exactly* what you'd think. You'd think, *This guy is a big bag of crazy.* So the show went on.

The night of the concert, the FYN didn't waste any time; they opened fire during the band's second number. (I still wish they'd waited, because I really wanted to hear the band do their thing.) As was the case with most of the Beatles' public battles, it was over in minutes, and if it hadn't been for the speed and exactitude of John, Paul, and George's counteroffensive, the death toll that night would've been in the thousands.

The second Wilfred White gave the go signal—no, not the second, the *milli*second—John was off the stage and in the audience, scooping up every firearm he could find. By my count, he himself disarmed seventy-three shooters in nine seconds, leaving the FYN with one hundred and twenty-seven armed attackers. Paul took care of another seventy-one, and George, sixty-three. Within thirty seconds, only twenty-something guns were trained on Ringo, and that's a manageable number for even a Fourth Level. For a Seventh Level like Ringo, escaping was a breeze.

Ringo was unharmed, and to his credit, he even managed to take out a few FYNs with a strategic toss of his crash cymbal. I'd venture to say that John, Paul, and George took between fifty and seventy-five bullets apiece, but none of them were of the diamond variety, so they also walked away intact, albeit pockmarked with steaming, noxious bullet wounds.

Sadly, fifty-three innocent mortals were killed in the attack, and another two hundred and seven were injured, but if it hadn't been for the Fab Four's quick thinking and quicker defense, we'd be looking at a stadium full of dead Beatles fans, and, worst of all, one very dead Ninja drummer.

JOHN LENNON: Nobody but *nobody* was going to kill a Beatle on my watch . . . unless it was me doing the killing. Like I always say, all for zombies, and zombies for all.

Besides, we were only millimeters away from hitting the Toppermost of the Poppermost, and I wasn't about to let anybody or anything stop us.

CHAPTER FOUR

1965

The Beatles' debut flick, A Hard Day's Night, *was a smash with fans and critics alike, so the canny Liverpudlians, not wanting to mess with a successful formula, brought director Dick Lester back into the fold for the film's follow-up,* Help! *They had a bigger budget this time around, which meant they were able to film not only in the UK but also in Austria and the Bahamas. Different and better locales meant different and better herbal jazz cigarettes; thus, according to Lester, it was lights, camera, duct tape, marijuana, action . . . and mayhem.*

RICHARD LESTER: They wanted to put a ski scene in the movie, and who was I to turn them down? Picture this: you've got three blitzed-out, blissed-out zombies on skis, wrapped completely in duct tape—completely, that is, except for the tiny holes over their mouths and noses that enabled them to breathe and, of course, to toke up—tottering around the side of a mountain. Man, I wish they had DVDs back then, because I would've put together one hell of a gag reel.

Eppy'd told me about how weed—and its aftereffects—had become a normal part of their lives, and my thinking was, *As long as they do their jobs, they can smoke and fart all they want.*

Which is exactly what they did.

They were sneaky about it; I didn't even know they'd gone to get high until, well, they'd gotten high. One minute, I see them calmly trying to figure out how to strap into the skis, and the next, I see them tearing off all their duct tape and engaging in an epic snowball fight. Now, that might not seem like that big of a deal—six-year-olds engage in epic snowball fights all the time, and they survive—but the snowballs got bigger and bigger, and the fighting became angrier and angrier, and it got ugly. It wasn't like they were mad at one another; I think it was more about the competition. They all wanted to be King Turd of Snow Mountain.

George was the first to take it up a notch, when he removed his leg and used it to whack a snowball at John. (Now, I'd never seen anybody use his leg as a cricket bat before, but this *was* the Beatles, so you have to expect the unexpected.) John followed suit by yanking off his right arm and hurling it at Harrison's noggin. He scored a direct hit, but the throw wasn't strong enough to knock off George's melon, which was fortunate, because had he been on target, we would've lost at least a day of shooting looking for a surgeon who could properly reattach the skull.

Paul, who, up until that moment, for reasons unknown, was throwing snowballs at himself, noticed the commotion. In two or three seconds, he'd put together an orb of snow as big as a boulder, and yelled, "Oi, if you cunts don't cut that out, you'll both be eating this for lunch, y'know!"

Using only his teeth, John removed his own left arm, spit the arm onto the ground, then kicked it toward Paul. Paul ducked, then kicked the massive snowball toward John. John avoided the snow-ball, and then, with blinding speed, retrieved and reattached both of his arms. Then he conked Paulie on his butt. And he hit him *hard,* so hard that Paul landed face-first in the snow, about seventy-five yards away. Even though the fight was messing up my shooting schedule, I was impressed. It takes a lot to bring down Paul McCartney.

George, who apparently had gotten his bearings back, took off one of his skis and whipped it at John, who dodged it neatly. Then George took off the other and chucked it at the prone Mr. McCart-ney. The sharp end of the ski lodged itself into Paul's back, theoreti-cally pinning him to the ground. But as anybody who's been attacked by any of the Fab Four knows, it's hard to keep a Beatle in-capacitated for long. So, without even removing the ski from his rib cage, Paul stood up; the ski remained lodged in his back, but only briefly, as he pulled it out without even a blink. Where his heart was supposed to be was a gaping hole, odd for a man who was known for writing such romance-filled ditties.

George tried to escape up the mountain, but Paul caught him easily. He grabbed George by the ankle, whirled him over his head like he was an Arsenal banner—a clever move he later told me he learned from John—then tossed poor Georgie up the mountain. Har-rison ended up what had to be six football fields' length away; the pile of snow that was kicked up when he landed looked like a mushroom cloud. Now I don't know if they got tired or bored or if the weed wore off, but right then, the melee stopped as quickly as it started.

They had a couple of more fights before we wrapped, the most notable being in the Bahamas, when George launched Paul into the ocean and he landed a solid half mile away. He made it back to shore but took a good long while. For the record, Liverpool zombies are slow, clumsy swimmers.

I got so wrapped up in watching these battles that it never dawned on me to roll camera, and I didn't get a single zombie-on-zombie clash on film. Frankly, ninety minutes of that sort of undead madness would've made for a better movie, that's for damn sure.

*

GEORGE HARRISON: After we finished filming *Help!*, we suffered from a bit of, I dunno, I guess you could call it malaise. All that Mania can get to a bloke.

PAUL McCARTNEY: We were exhausted, y'know, but I didn't think we should stop.

NEIL ASPINALL: The boys needed a break, but Brian wouldn't let that happen. They were knackered, and John was suffering the worst.

JOHN LENNON: I dunno if it was the grass or what, but I was hungry all the fookin' time, and human food wasn't cutting it. I could eat three steaks, four baked potatoes, six tins of beans, and eighteen boxes of Corn Flakes in one sitting, and I'd still be starved. The only way to placate my stomach was with the classic zombie meal of human brains with a side of bone marrow.

LYMAN COSGROVE: Lennon's 1965 murder spree was one for the record books. It rivaled the eating rampages of Earl J. Eaves in 1956—Mr. Eaves ate some thirty-two brains in seventeen days— and Martine Jefferson's 1961 onslaught, a three-day-long blood-bath that ended in twelve deaths and ten new Liverpool Processers. John held his own, downing twenty-eight brains in a two-week period. That was impressive, and one can't help admiring his single-mindedness.

What Eaves, Jefferson, and Lennon had in common was a notable weight gain. You see, Liverpool zombies rarely become ravenously hungry, and generally only need a handful of brains a year to survive. But when something triggers that eating mechanism, and they ingest brain after brain after brain, their gastrointestinal system goes off the rails. The fact that Lennon was inhaling an inordinate amount of cannabis didn't help matters.

JOHN LENNON: So I added one or two pounds. I don't think anybody noticed.

NEIL ASPINALL: John went through a tubby phase, no question.

RINGO STARR: His face got a bit fuller, his tummy got a bit wider, and his complexion got a big grayer. It wasn't attractive.

PAUL McCARTNEY: He certainly filled up his suits, John did, y'know.

GEORGE HARRISON: He was the fattest zombie I ever personally saw. And it slowed him down. He was still able to move well—he could chase down a mortal without too much trouble, so he was able to keep on eating—but if he'd needed to defend himself against, say, a Ninja, he wouldn't have stood a chance.

If there was a time for Ringo or me to take over the band, that would've been it.

RINGO STARR: One afternoon, Georgie invited me out to lunch, and he spent the entire meal telling me, "John's a fatso, Rings. He's slowed down, and you can take him out. Think about it: it's always

Lennon and McCartney this, Lennon and McCartney that. Isn't it time people start talking about Harrison and Starr? You can be the guy. *We* can be the *guys*! The best part is, if Johnny's gone, you can sing more than one song an album."

I told him I was perfectly content with the way things were, and if he wanted to start an uprising, he was on his own. He looked pissed off, and you don't want to be around George Harrison when he gets pissed off, so I became virtually invisible and scooted home. Aside from berating me for leaving him with the check, George never mentioned that lunch again.

JOHN LENNON: Eating brains isn't like eating food. There are hundreds of thousands of different human meals to choose from, but brains are all the same. The brain of a seventy-two-year-old Spanish gent tastes just like the brain of an eleven-year-old French girl. That being the case, in order to keep all these deaths quiet, I confined my meals to the Addenbrooke's Hospital geriatric ward.

If you were on your last legs, you were my breakfast. If you had one foot in the grave, you were lunch. If they were getting ready to pull the plug, you were dinner. I don't think you'd enjoy hearing about my in-between-meals snacks.

Brian thought I was being self-indulgent. It seemed like once an hour, he'd tell me, "You don't need all this food, John." I didn't think it was all that big of a deal. These people were close to the end anyhow; if they died a day or two earlier than scheduled, so fookin' what? They'd lived good lives, plus they'd get to tell everybody in the afterworld that they got eaten by a Beatle. I know for a fact that at one point in time, that earned you some serious cool points with the dead.

But yeah, no real weight gain for Johnny Lennon. Not much at all. Okay, I maybe gained a few pounds. Maybe three or four.

PAUL McCARTNEY: We put him on a hotel scale one night in Paris: sixteen stone. Two-hundred-plus pounds. That's a lot of excess brains, y'know. A lot of bloody excess brains.

BRIAN EPSTEIN: Image isn't everything, but it still matters, so I asked him to drop three stone. He pulled off his leg, wrapped it around my neck like it was a scarf, and said, "There's *five* stone right there, mate. Does that work for you?"

Up until that point, I never realized just how bad rotting zombie limbs smelled; I almost passed out from the stench. I shrugged and the leg fell to the ground. Then I nudged it away with my foot and said, "Johnny, lad, you'd best get it together immediately, because New York is waiting. That's a big gig, our biggest one yet, and you need your strength back, mentally and physically."

As I'm sure you know, John listened. Soon he was mentally and physically strong. Very, very strong.

✦

In June 1965, a mere week after graduating second in her class from Columbia University's Graduate School of Journalism, Jessica Brandice landed a job at The New York Times. *It's been said that* Times *publisher Arthur Sulzberger took a personal liking to Ms. Brandice—little surprise, considering how she simultaneously oozes intelligence and sexuality, even undead—which is why he ignored the unwritten reporter code and assigned her to the crime beat before she'd even written a single word for the venerable newspaper.*

Luckily for Sulzberger, it turned out that Jessica was far more than a brainiac and a pretty face; the girl was a terrific investigative reporter, as witnessed by her brilliant coverage of The Beatles' August 15 concert at Shea Stadium, coverage that ultimately led to the book The

Shea Stadium Riot: How the Beatles Almost Destroyed New York City, *arguably the finest examination of how, if a few things had shaken out differently, the British zombie invasion could have taken the United States off the map.*

Each August 15, Jessica honors the memory of the riots with a lecture at the New York Public Library. I sat down with her at length after her 2005 discussion; it was the fortieth anniversary of the Shea Stadium show, but Jessica remembers that horrifying evening like it was yesterday. Little wonder: once you get a look at the scars that run up and down her pretty gray face, you know that's a day she'll never forget, until the end of time.

(Note: Brian Epstein, Neil Aspinall, and three-fourths of the Beatles refused to discuss Shea either on or off the record. Lennon talked. Sort of.)

JOHN LENNON: The one thing I'll say about Shea is, you can blame it on my zombie nature.

JESSICA BRANDICE: It was one of the first rock concerts held at a major outdoor stadium, and the fact that a zombie band was performing had the city government on edge. As there was no precedent, putting together a security plan for Shea Stadium—not to mention New York City as a whole—was complete guesswork. Neither New York City mayor Robert F. Wagner, Jr., nor his staff had a clue how to deal with . . . well, the fact of the matter is, they didn't know *what* they'd have to deal with. It could have turned out to be a completely peaceful crowd. It could have turned out to be hundreds of thousands of screaming Beatlemaniacs and disturbed zombie fanatics ready and eager to trash Queens. It could have turned out to be something in between those two extremes. They had no clue.

My editor didn't assign me to cover the concert; the only reason I was there was because my boyfriend, Dave Errol, was the *Times* rock writer, and I was his plus one. I certainly wouldn't have attended of my own accord. I liked the Beatles as much as the next girl, but there's no way I would've gone to Shea, only to be surrounded by screaming teenage girls.

Now, the only time I'd seen the Beatles perform previously was their second appearance on *The Ed Sullivan Show,* the one where they blew up those poor cameramen. They'd looked perfectly poised on the television screen, right up to the moment when the screen went black. But that night at Shea, as they walked to the stage from the third-base dugout, I thought they looked twitchy.

They'd stuck me and Dave in the first-base dugout, which was about ten feet away from stage left. The dais was raised, and the dugout was below ground level, so the only Beatle we were able to see clearly was the Beatle who always stood stage left, John Lennon. I recently read an interview where Paul said that John "went crazy" during the concert, but it seemed to me he was acting a little crazy before they even played a note.

Dave said that the band was *too* energetic, and pointed out that Paul was counting off the songs too quickly, and they were racing through their two-and-a-half-minute tunes in about a minute forty-five. He also noted that it was weird they had an electric keyboard onstage for John, because as far as he knew, Lennon was, at best, an amateur pianist.

They had their amplifiers turned all the way up, and since we were so close to the stage, by the third number, our ears were ringing. So I took a tissue from my purse, ripped off two little pieces, wadded them up, and voila, makeshift earplugs. I did the same for Dave, and it was a damn good thing we did.

Seemingly only a few minutes later, the band went into the last

song of their set, "I'm Down." Lennon started playing the keyboard with his elbow . . . actually, he wasn't *playing* it but, rather, *bashing* it, sliding back and forth, and back and forth, creating a weird, dissonant mess of noise. When the song ended, Lennon hit the keyboard with his forehead, and then the stadium went silent. The screaming stopped. Fifty-five-thousand-plus people shut down, just like that.

And then Lennon grabbed a microphone, jumped on top of the keyboard, and whispered one word: "Poppermost."

And then the place went up for grabs.

In virtual unison, everybody in the crowd ripped their seats from the concrete and threw them onto the field. A good number of the hard, green wooden chairs hit the Beatles, but they seemed unaffected; for that matter, Harrison even threw a bunch of them back.

And then, the adults in the crowd froze in place, and the teenagers stormed the field. Watching the police detail try to stem the tide of boys and girls was laughable. The cops were standing a good ten feet apart, and the teens—who were all literally foaming at the mouth—plowed over, around, and through New York's Finest. To their credit, the police did their best, but they had no chance.

After the teens tore up and ate every blade of grass in Shea Stadium, the entire crowd—they were a mob at this point, really—stampeded to the exits; they moved quickly and violently, but almost politely, as if to make certain that none of their allies were injured. Aside from all the teens vomiting up half-digested grass, it looked to me like they were heading off to the train station.

At that point, the Shea Stadium concert went from being a music story to a crime story, so I told Dave to haul ass back to his apartment, because I had to follow this through to the end, and I couldn't

have him tagging along. He berated me for risking my life for a newspaper that paid me fifteen thou a year, and I told him to fuck off, this was a big deal, and money wasn't the issue. Then he asked me how the hell I expected either of us to get into Manhattan when the subways were going to be filled with hypnotized Beatlemaniacs who might be out for blood. I told him he had a point, but I had to follow the story. If he thought he could keep up with me, great; if not, I was going to have to go without him.

I'd been a sprinter at Columbia and was a considerably faster runner than Dave was, so I gave him a kiss, then zipped out of the stadium to the subway station. The next time I saw Dave, he was in the postsurgical recovery room at the Queens Medical Center. He was back to work eight weeks later, with a sixteen-inch zigzag scar running from his chest to his pelvis.

The mob took over the subway and that weird aura of politeness went out the window. From across the street, I could see they weren't just jumping the turnstiles—they were ripping them clean off and climbing over one another as if they were tigers on the hunt: grabbing, clawing, biting, spitting, roaring, not caring what or who they were hurting. There was no way I was getting on that train, so I hopped a cab.

My gut told me they'd ride from Shea to Grand Central Station, and I was right. According to reports, one-third of the crowd exited at Grand Central, while the other two-thirds transferred to other lines. Within an hour, the fifty-five thousand people who John Lennon had hypnotized were strategically dispersed throughout the city. I don't know if Lennon planned it that way, or if these poor people were acting on instinct.

If your readers want specifics on the riots—for instance, the Times Square bonfire, the complete destruction of the Bronx sewer system, or those brutal lynchings in Prospect Park—that's all in my book. What's *not* in my book is my own personal journey, and the only reason I'm able to discuss it with you now is because I've gone through a shitload of therapy.

I figured that Midtown was as good a place as any to get a good view of the action and stay out of danger, so I had the cabbie drop me at a hotel—I forget which one—on the corner of 43rd and Park, and I settled myself in the lobby, right by the picture window facing Park. The mob was moving methodically down the sidewalk, heading south, literally stomping over anybody who got in their way. Concertgoers were grabbing non-concertgoers and throwing them across the street, and throwing them *hard.* These people were crashing into the sides of buildings at thirty miles per hour. Eventually there were piles of shattered bodies and puddles of thick blood littering the Park Avenue sidewalks.

Once the mob was gone, I ran west, over to Eighth Avenue, figuring I could flag a cab and beat the crowd down to Greenwich Village. Nope. No way. By then, word had gotten around about the thousands of spaced-out freaks marching throughout the city, mindlessly attacking strangers, and the hacks weren't stopping to pick up anybody. So I opened my purse, fished out my wallet, a notepad, and a pen, threw the purse in the nearest garbage can, got on my high horse, and ran downtown. I made the two miles in just over fourteen minutes.

The mob was dispersed throughout the downtown area, but they seemed to be congregating in the West Village. I made my way over to this tiny park by Sixth Avenue and Bleecker and climbed up into a small tree. It was the perfect place to be: I had a clear view of the action, and I rightly guessed that the maniacs wouldn't be looking in trees for people to attack. There were plenty of folks on the street to torment.

The press referred to what I witnessed as the Greenwich Village

Massacre, but to me, *massacre* implies it was a single act that happened quickly, which wasn't at all the case. The downtown killings were random yet meticulous. I saw more people thrown into buildings. I saw a woman pluck off another woman's limbs, one right after the other. I saw a person of indeterminate gender rip a young man's heart from his chest. I saw two teenage girls pick up a Ford Galaxie and throw the fucking thing toward Houston Street; when the car landed, it exploded and started a fire that burned for almost forty-eight hours.

I don't know if their bloodlust was sated or if the spell wore off or what, but just after midnight, the mob dispersed and, save for the injured, the dying, and the dead, the streets were empty. As the ambulances rolled to the scene, I found a pay phone and made a collect call to the *Times* office. I feel sorry for whoever answered my call, because after I identified myself, I screamed nonsense for a good minute or two before I could even get a proper sentence out. Once I found my voice, I asked him if he could find out where the Beatles were staying. No, I didn't *ask* him—I *told* him. He put me on hold; then, five minutes later, he said two words: "Plaza Hotel." There still wasn't a cab to be found, and I wasn't comfortable getting onto a subway train just yet, so I walked up to the hotel, which was located on Fifth Avenue and Central Park South. Sixty-some-odd minutes and three miles later, I was standing in front of the Plaza.

There was a gaggle of print and TV reporters, as well as about fifty uniformed police officers, camped out on the street. The cops had cordoned off the entrance, and I'd prefer not to discuss how I made my way inside or how I learned John Lennon's room number.

The Beatles weren't in the penthouse, or even particularly high up; their rooms were on the sixth floor, as if they were any other guests. Lennon was in 606. I knocked on the door, and right away he called out, "Whoooo's therrrrrre?" He sounded practically giddy.

I said, "I'm a reporter from *The New York Times*. I can put my ID card up by the peephole if you'd like."

After he confirmed that I was who I said I was, he asked me, "Why should I let you in?"

I said in my sexiest voice, "I want to ask you some questions, and I'll make it worth your while."

He laughed, then said, "Love, if I wanted you to be my sex slave, you'd already *be* my sex slave." Then he opened the door and said, "I'll answer two questions. How does that sound?"

I said, "Okay. Why? Why did you do it?"

He said, "Couldn't help it. Zombie nature. Next question."

I said, "What exactly is 'zombie nature'?"

Lennon said, "You want to know about zombie nature?" He walked toward me, and the next thing I remember, I was at home, in my bed, showered, wearing my favorite nightie, undead as a doornail.

The final Shea Stadium concert toll: 1,051 dead, 3,198 injured, approximately two million dollars in property damage, and one *New York Times* reporter turned into a zombie.

GEORGE HARRISON: After the Shea business, the shows became, oh, let's call them *tense*. Not tense from our end, mind you. We knew there wouldn't be a repeat "zombie nature" performance from Mr. Lennon because Brian burnt that damn keyboard into ashes, and John promised to keep that bloody Poppermost shite under wraps when we were out in public. No, the tenseness came from the crowds, and I can't say I blame them. If the coleader of my favorite

band turned fifty thousand people into killing machines with a G-minor chord and a single nonsense word, I'd suppose I'd feel a bit dodgy about going to their concert myself.

Much of the remainder of the tour was a blur for me—it was Mania, Mania, and more Mania—but something nice happened in California. It wasn't as nice as it could've been, but it was nice enough. Okay, it wasn't nice at all. Let's just call it memorable.

∗

PAUL McCARTNEY: We were all enormous Elvis Presley fans, y'know, and very badly wanted to meet him. I don't recall if he invited us to his place, or if we invited ourselves, but the day before our concert at the Hollywood Bowl, there we were at his mansion: the four of us, Elvis's manager Colonel Tom Parker, a bunch of hanger-ons, and the King of Rock 'n' Roll himself.

We wanted to speak with Elvis without any, erm, prying ears, so I hypnotized Colonel Tom and the other blokes who were lolling about, then Ringo dragged them into the garage and pinned them to the wall with a couple hundred shuriken. I told Rings they wouldn't wake up until I woke them up, but he said he didn't want to take any chances.

Elvis was a little bit out of it when we got there, y'know—apparently he'd imbibed a handful of his favorite pharmaceuticals before we arrived—so George took him into his kitchen and slapped him around for a few minutes until he was more lucid.

When Elvis was more or less coherent and comfortable in his living room recliner, John started in on his recruitment speech.

JOHN LENNON: I kneeled down in front of Elvis—it was like he was royalty, and I was one of his subjects—and said, "Listen, King, your life is all about eating banana sandwiches and shoving down all the drugs you can find and playing music and making movies. Now, that sounds like a pretty fookin' good life to me, mate, and if I'm you, I'm wanting that life to go on forever. And let's face it: you're not getting any younger, and you're starting to get a little soft around the middle, and I dunno how many pills you take to get going in the morning, and I don't even know what to say about your wardrobe, but it's all going downhill. You're not looking as good as you did in the fifties, but the good news is that if you stay on this planet for all eternity, you can get your shite together like nobody's business."

He said, "What're you talking about?"

I said, "What am I talking about? Mate, I'm talking about making you a zombie who'll walk the Earth forever."

He said, "What kind of mess are you feeding me? Zombies don't exist."

I said, "Look at me, mate."

He said, "Yeah, I'm looking. So what?"

I said, "My face is gray. Like dead-guy gray."

He said, "So's Colonel Tom's."

I had to admit he had a point there. I said, "Okay, well, watch this." And then I took off both of my pinkies and played a little drum fill on his lap. "That's a zombie thing. Colonel Tom can't do that."

He shrugged, then said, "Yeah, but I seen a guy in Tupelo who could."

I said, "He was probably a zombie. Lot of undead in the American south, mate."

He said, "Zombies don't exist."

I said, "Yes they do," then I reattached my pinkies and removed my left leg.

He said, "No they don't."

I said, "Yes," then I reattached my leg and removed my right arm.

He said, "No."

I realized this could go on all day, so I put my arm back on and said, "Okay, King, let's pretend. Let's say that zombies did exist. Wouldn't you want to be one? Wouldn't you want to eat your fooked-up sandwiches and take lots and lots of drugs and sing songs and shoot mediocre-to-crappy films forever and ever and ever? Not to mention, you can fook all the birds you want and not worry about getting anybody pregnant or catching syphilis. Doesn't that sound top-notch?"

He nodded for a while, and I knew I had him. Right when I was about to dive into his neck and start the good ol' Liverpool Process, he said, "You know what, John? I don't want to be around forever. Me, I wanna die on the crapper, taking a righteous dump. That's how my daddy died, and that's how my daddy's daddy died. I'm not sure how my daddy's daddy's daddy died, but if I were a betting man, I'd wager that he also kicked the bucket while parked on the commode, laying some pipe."

Really, what can you say to that?

PAUL McCARTNEY: Ringo freed Colonel Tom and his gang, and then we went on our merry way. I was so depressed by the whole thing that I forced the incident out of my head. As a matter of fact, the next time I thought about it was some twelve years later, when Elvis died on the crapper, taking a righteous dump. Not exactly a kingly way to go out, y'know.

So here's how the phone call went:

"*Good day, you've reached Buckingham Palace. How may I direct your call?*"

"*Yeah, hey, my name's Alan, and I'm a journalist from Chicago, and I'm writing a book about the Beatles. Is the Queen available? I totally have to interview her.*"

"*Piss off, Yank.*" *Click.*

Okay, that's an exaggeration—your typical Brit is far too polite for that sort of behavior, and I'm somewhat more professional than that—but the Queen's people didn't exactly roll out the red carpet for me . . . that is, until they found out I knew a certain thing about a certain someone that that certain someone would probably rather be kept under wraps.

So. Out came the red carpet.

Blackmail usually isn't my style, but considering how insightful my brief November 2003 chat with the Queen turned out to be, it was worth sacrificing my principles for a minute or two.

QUEEN ELIZABETH II: I had mixed emotions about the Beatles. I was proud of what they had done for our country. They both inspired and instilled a lot of pride amongst our young people. But they also scared the tar out of almost everybody they ever met. I did not know if I should knight them or have an SIS sharpshooter end the madness with three diamond bullets. (I would spare Ringo Starr. Our country has far too few Ninjas; plus, he's too nice of a lad to seek revenge for the death of his cohorts.)

One of my advisors suggested that the public would appreciate me making the Beatles Members of the Order of the British Empire,

and I found that ideal. I would not need to have them knighted or killed. Lovely. Perfect.

PAUL McCARTNEY: John usually kicked up some sort of fuss at this kind of thing, y'know, but he was cool with the MBE. But something about it rubbed me the wrong way. It was like she didn't think we were good enough to be knighted. So I suggested that we accept the award; then, at the ceremony, knock her out with some zombie quiffs. That'd show her who should or shouldn't be knighted.

RINGO STARR: For maybe the first time, John was our voice of reason. He told Paul, "I love how you're thinking, mate, but messing with the Queen is too big for us. The FYZ would probably go international and kill Rings, and every bloke who can pick up a gun would buy up all the diamond bullets he could find, and we'd be in the ground within twenty-four hours, no matter how many hits we have on the charts. Let's go get our medals, smile for the cameras, and be done with it."

Paul said, "Can I at least eat the prime minister's brain?"

We all thought that was a fine idea, but Eppy talked us out of it.

QUEEN ELIZABETH II: I never heard any discussion about any attempt by the Beatles at mayhem during the ceremony. There might have been whispers about it amongst my staff, but as always, they did a superb job of keeping me insulated and worry free. Even if I had heard about it, I would have been skeptical. I knew the undead could sometimes be irrational, but at the end of the day, they were still polite English lads, and polite English lads do not break wind in the presence of the Queen.

But frankly, I almost wish they would have tried it. See, I

would've taken great pleasure in kicking their Liverpudlian arses up and down St. James Park, those fookin' arrogant zombie cunts.

*

The Queen may have been ignorant of the wind-breaking talk, but Mick Jagger was well aware of it. Yet as he'd lost Beatles battle after Beatles battle, it was clear to all that he couldn't go it alone anymore. Enter Mister Watts.

A man with no feelings one way or the other toward the undead, Rolling Stones drummer Charlie Watts became Mick's unwilling recruit in his eternal war against the Fab Four. Frustrated with his role in the various fracases, Charlie was more than willing to discuss with me the most memorable of his forays into zombie hunting after a Charlie Watts Orchestra rehearsal at Resident Studios in London in March 2007.

CHARLIE WATTS: Keith Richards and Brian Jones were heavy into the drug scene, and Bill Wyman was scared of his own shadow, never mind zombies, so when Mick heard that the Fab Four wanted to embarrass Her Royal Highness, I was the only one in the band who Mick could turn to for help . . . as usual.

The problem with him bringing me on board was that I personally thought John, Paul, and George were top geezers. (Ringo was also a fine bloke, but Mick didn't have personal issues with Ninjas, so Mr. Starkey was safe.) If the Beatles wanted to eat brains, let them eat brains, so long as they weren't mine or my family's or my bandmates'. So did I want to be a part of ending the Beatles' reign of terror? No. But was I obligated to help my bandmate? Yes. So on December 31, we hit the London streets in search of the three most famous zombies in the world.

Mick was always good at sniffing out the undead, so it took us a grand total of ninety minutes to track down the Beatles: they were all together, hanging out at Ronnie Scott's Jazz Club, digging on a New Year's Eve performance by an American guitar player named Wes Montgomery. After the bloke at the door let us in for free—that was one advantage of being a Rolling Stone; I never had to pay a cover charge—we took a couple of seats by the bar. I looked around the crowded club and asked Mick, "What are you gonna do, mate? Attack them in front of all these people?"

He said, "No, no, no, I don't want any civilians to get hurt."

I said, "What about me? Don't you want me to not get hurt?"

Mick said, "Don't be a baby." And that's all he said. None too reassuring.

When the set ended, much of the audience headed to the exit, and Ringo went off to the loo. Mick said, "Guard the door, Charlie. Don't let anybody in. Don't let anybody out. It's time to take out the trash."

I said, "Take out the trash? What the fook are you goin' on about, take out the trash?"

He said, "I'm taking out Lennon, McCartney, and Harrison. Sure, they're brilliant musicians. And sure, they've put British bands on the map, which'll help our band's cause. And sure, they're clever, and they're handsome, and they're out-and-out cool, but they're zombies, and thus, they're trash. Get it?"

I said, "Yes, Mick, I get it. You sound like a fookin' ponce, but I get it." He hated when I called him poncey, but I hated when he brought me into shite like this, so fair's fair. I said, "And what's this about me guarding the exit? How d'you expect me to stop people from going in and out of the busiest jazz club in all of fookin' Europe? I'm as skinny as a stick."

Mick said, "Dunno, mate. You're a smart man. Keep them distracted. Sign autographs or something."

I said, "Seriously, man, this is the last time."

He said, "Of course it is. Because it ends here."

He was always saying "It ends here." It never ended here.

So I guarded the door . . . or I pretended to. See, Mick was so wrapped up in starting the clash that I could've dropped my trousers and waved my plonker all about, and he wouldn't have noticed if I was guarding the door or taking a leak.

He quietly started doing his hip-wiggling and lip-pursing, which he claimed was a top weapon against zombies—but I wondered, if it was such a top weapon, why were the Beatles still around? John must've had a sixth sense about this sort of thing, because he was up and in defense mode within seconds. When he saw it was Mick, he started laughing, then tapped McCartney on the shoulder and said, "Oi, Paulie, look who's here!"

Paul turned around and laughed so hard that he spit out a mouthful of Scotch and Coke. He said, "Ooer, Mick's back. Give us a kiss, love." And then Paul blew him a smooch.

Mick said, "For you, McCartney, a kiss by any other name is the kiss of death."

George said, "Christ, Mick, you sound like a fookin' ponce."

I yelled out, "That's what I said!"

Ringo came out of the water closet and yelled back, "Right, good one, Charlie! How's it going, mate?"

I said, "Great, Rings. Heard Ludwig sent you a new snare drum. How's it working out?"

Ringo said, "Love it, just love it!"

Mick said, "The lot of you, shut up! On this ground, on the hallowed ground of this hallowed music venue, right now, right this

minute, I declare a battle to the death! Mortal versus zombie! Hunter versus hunted! Stones versus Beatles!"

Ringo did some Ninja thing and magically appeared behind Mick, then said, "You're sounding awfully dramatic, Mr. Jagger." Then he said in a most excellent Mick impression, "Your powers are useless against Ninja Lords, O great zombie hunter! Surrender or feel the sting of the shuriken!"

John, Paul, and George started giggling again. Paul said, "You tell 'em, Rings! Give 'em heck, an' that!"

George wadded up his napkin and threw it at Mick; it bopped him in the head, and I couldn't help laughing. Mick said to me, "Quit being a cunt, Charlie. If you're going to act like that, why don't you just piss off?"

I told him, "Cheers, mate." And I pissed off.

RINGO STARR: Jagger weighed next to nothing, so I picked him up, carried him outside, flagged down a cab, and threw him in. I said, "Happy New Year, Mick. And a piece of advice for you: you're not gonna get all three of them at once. Pick 'em off one at a time. You'll have a better chance."

He scratched his head and said, "That's actually damn good advice, Rings. I never thought of it, what with their 'All for zombies, and zombies for all' shite. But why're you telling me that?"

I said, "I like you, man."

He said, "Yeah, I like you, too. Hell, I even like them. But I can't let it go. I have to finish what I've started, or else I'll look like a prat."

I said, "Gotcha. But like I said, one at a time. If you do it like that, it'll be less embarrassing for everybody. You're never gonna beat them, but at least if you go one-on-one, you won't come off, ehm, looking like a prat."

Mick said, "Listen, Ringo, one at a time is no problem. All I need to do is give them a single kiss to the chest, and the Beatles will be broken up like no band has ever—"

I interrupted; "Yeah, yeah, yeah, I know that's all you need to do, but you're not gonna be able to do it. Nothing but *nothing* will ever break up the Beatles."

Mick rolled his eyes and said, "Now who's sounding dramatic?"

CHAPTER FIVE

1966

Circa 2008, what was the best way to track somebody down, be it an old girlfriend, an old high school classmate, or an old British reporter? That's right: Facebook. Thanks to this useful online social tool, I was able to track down Maureen Cleave, former pop culture scribe for the London Evening Standard.

On March 4, 1966, Cleave sat down with John Lennon for an interview that was, without a doubt, the most revealing of Lennon's Beatles years. In it, John was brutally honest with his opinions on literature, music, the pitfalls of fame, how he best liked to kill humans, and, most controversially, his faith, or lack thereof. (Odd that a few hyperbolic comments about God would create more of a ruckus than an internationally revered undead musician describing the manner in which he liked to murder, but that's religious types for you.)

Fearing a possible terrorist attack from the religious right or zombie haters in general, Maureen Cleave will never take a face-to-face meeting with a stranger, so I was lucky that in May 2008, she decided it would be okay to participate in an instant message chat session via good ol' Facebook.

Alan Goldsher: − x

Alan
What kind of mood was John in that day?

Maureen
fine. chatty. sometimes cranky. looked handsome.

Alan
When I interviewed him, he was always honest and
forthcoming.

Maureen
same here. painfully honest sometimes. when he described
how he procures and ingests brains, i got the chills.

Alan
Tell me about the religion business.

Maureen
i tracked down the original transcription for u. some of it
didn't make it into the original article. i'm cutting and pasting
THE important paragraph here.

Christianity will go. Maybe not today, maybe not tomorrow, but
come the middle of the twenty-second century—when I'm two
hundred sodding years old—Christianity will be dead. I don't
know what'll take its place. Possibly something led by zombies.
And I'll tell you why that might be the case: the Beatles are more
popular than Jesus. Shite, we're not just more popular than Jesus;
in some ways we're *better* than Jesus. Think about it: can Jesus
remove and reattach his arm? No. Did Jesus live forever on this
planet? No. Will we live forever on this planet? Yes. Except for
Ringo, of course, but I'm thinking of turning him soon.

Alan

Was there any point where you thought, Wow, this guy is messing with me?

Maureen

absolutely not. if u were there, if u were in britain in the midsixties, u would have understood why i felt the way i felt. the beatles WERE bigger, better, and stronger. and scarier. if u ran into john in a dark alley and he said, "believe in me or i'll kill you," you'd believe in him.

Alan

Could you have imagined the reaction by the religious types in the States?

Maureen

no no no no no no no!!!

Alan

Knowing what you know now, if you had to do it over again, would you have included John's religious rant in your article?

Maureen

NO NO NO NO NO NO NO!!! too many deaths. too much blood on my hands. too much, too much, too much.

*

In July 2006, I received an email from the address MyNameIsJohn-Smith@yahoo.com. The first line: "John Smith is not my name." Mr. Not John Smith went on to write,

> There is a ticket waiting for you at the American Airlines coun-
> ter at O'Hare Airport. It is a direct flight to Washington, DC. It
> leaves tomorrow at 8:00 a.m. At 1:00 Eastern Standard Time,
> you will meet me at a bench on the east side of the Washington
> Monument. The bench is painted with an advertisement for a
> local shyster named Zelman Berger. I will be wearing jeans and
> a red T-shirt with Che Guevara's face on the front. If you are not
> there, you will never hear from me again. If you are there, I will
> elaborate on some information regarding the Beatles and Elvis
> Presley that you may find very interesting. I look forward to
> meeting you. P.S.—Lunch is on me.

Being a bit of a conspiracy buff, that was an offer I simply couldn't refuse, so I updated my will, took out a five-million-dollar life-insurance policy, and hopped a plane to DC.

Smith was true to his word: Che T-shirt, jeans, a couple of turkey subs, and a fuckload of very interesting elaboration.

"JOHN SMITH": I was recruited by the CIA right out of Stanford in 1962. I was this skinny kid from the Arizona sticks who'd piss his pants if he ever saw a gun, so I couldn't figure out why they wanted me. Turns out, the Company needed some young recruits because none of those assholes knew shit about shit that happened after 1958. At twenty-four, I was the youngest agent by far, the only one with any concept of pop culture, and probably the only one who knew who the fuck Paul McCartney was.

I don't remember the exact date I got the memo, but it doesn't really matter, because the thing could've been sitting in somebody's in-box for a week or a month or a year. I don't remember the exact wording, either—so much shit came across my desk that one thing tended to blend into another—but the gist of it was, Andreas Cornelis van Kuijk, aka, Thomas Andrew Parker, aka, Colonel Tom, aka, Elvis Aron Presley's manager, had contacted one of our agents in regard to the Beatles. Long story short, van Kuijk wanted the Beatles banned from the United States.

As wacky as that sounds, van Kuijk's reasoning was almost sound. He claimed that: (a) the government should be concerned about a repeat performance of the Shea Stadium fiasco; (b) the United States wasn't equipped to defend itself against English zombies; and (c) as there had been whispers of sex slavery coming out of Europe, the Beatles' presence was a clear and present danger to girls and women between the ages of fifteen and thirty-five.

Now, if I was some asshole who'd been with the Company since Dub Dub Two, I probably would've put together an overly complicated plan to keep Lennon, McCartney, Harrison, and Starr out of our swell little country here. But I was a kid who knew that (a) Lennon took full responsibility for the Shea riots and swore up and down he wouldn't do it again (and I believed him); (b) Liverpool zombies were generally ultrapolite—some have said they're the pussies of the zombie world—and were eminently defensible; and (c) I'd never heard a single complaint about any alleged sex slaves from either a slave, a master, or a parent. It'd take a complete moron not to realize that Colonel Tom was scared the Beatles would wipe the Pelvis off the charts.

So I called van Kuijk and told him to fuck off. Then I got in touch with Brian Epstein. I figured that's the sort of thing his band might want to know about.

BRIAN EPSTEIN: The lads will always love Presley's music, but I think they lost interest in him as a person when he refused their invitation to join the undead movement, as it were. That being the case, they weren't particularly fazed or surprised when I gave them the

news about the King's attempt to banish us from his kingdom. But they weren't happy. I still don't know why they didn't decorate Graceland with his small intestines.

JOHN LENNON: If we'd have wanted to, we could've had him banned from the UK. After all, we were Members of the Order of the British Empire. And we have the medals to prove it.

We also could've zombified him against his will, but the paperwork on that would've been a disaster, so fook that.

No, we took the high road and let it lie, and let him live. We weren't *always* right bastards. Just sometimes.

●

There are myriad stories describing the Beatles' self-inflicted limb removals and subsequent reattachments, but few outside of the band's inner circle have actually experienced the joy, the fascination, and the horror of an up-close and personal view of John, Paul, or George calmly tearing off his foot, then even more calmly putting it back on. (I myself have seen several dozen versions of that act, and it never ceases to disgust . . . especially when George chows down on a French fry he'd just dipped into an open wound.) But that all changed in 1966, when the world was treated to photographic documentation of what many consider to be the Liverpool zombies' greatest trick.

The date: March 25. The location: a photography studio in the Chelsea section of London. The occasion: a photo session for an upcoming Beatles project to be determined. The photographer: veteran UK shutterbug Robert Whitaker. The outcome: equal helpings of controversy and disgust. The reasoning behind the Beatles' artistic concept for the session: nobody's quite sure, but in April 2003, Whitaker

offered the story behind one of the grossest moments in the band's un-
believably gross history.

ROBERT WHITAKER: I'd shot the Beatles dozens of times, and aside
from the time Paul picked me up over his head, then chucked me
over to John, who chucked me over to Ringo, who promptly
dropped me onto my hindquarters, the sessions had been unevent-
ful and oftentimes fun. The boys were always good for a laugh.

The day of the session in question, they arrived punctually, as
always, all wearing matching trench coats. At this point in their
careers, they had their fingers on the pulse of the fashion world,
so in terms of wardrobe, I let them make their own choices, figuring that they knew better than me what the clubbers were
wearing. If they told me trench coats were the rage, then trench
coats it was.

While my assistant prepared them some tea, John put his arm
over my shoulders and guided me into the corner. He said, "Listen,
Robert, we have an idea for how this should be staged. I don't know
if you'll like it, but trust me: everybody else in the world will."

Based on how many records they'd sold, I knew that John had a
far better idea of what "everybody else in the world" would like than
I did, so I said, "Of course I trust you. Do as you wish."

John said, "That's lovely, Robert, just lovely. Now, how about you
shove off for fifteen minutes while we get organized?" So I shoved
off for fifteen minutes. When I returned, I was greeted by a tableau
that could best be described as . . . arresting.

Save for Ringo, who was in his Ninja gear, the boys were all wearing their butcher jackets, but that wasn't the arresting part. John,
Paul, and George were perched on chairs one right next to the other,
and Ringo was lying at their feet, but *that* wasn't the arresting part.
What took me aback was what they'd done with their bodies.

All four of John's limbs were placed neatly on the floor in front of Ringo—the order went right leg, left arm, right arm, left leg. Paul had removed his left leg and was holding it up to his ear as if it were a telephone, and he'd snaked his tongue up the open part of the limb. George had taken off all ten of his fingers and tied them into a bundle with what appeared to be either his own small intestines, or a guitar string; as I walked into the room, he lovingly placed the bundle on his head. All four of the boys were covered with blips and blops of the eggplant-colored goo that courses through a Liverpool zombie's body.

As a human being, I was repulsed—in addition to the awfulness of the visual, the smell was beyond appalling—but as a photographer, I was thrilled. If these pictures came out properly, this session could be one for the ages. So I held a kerchief over my nose, did everything I could to keep my gorge down, grabbed my Kodak Brownie Auto 27, and, for the next forty-five minutes, took shot after shot after shot. As the afternoon progressed, the boys kept breaking off pieces of themselves, which they piled in front of Ringo. Eventually, John, Paul, and George were just torsos with heads, and Ringo was surrounded by a plethora of body parts. It was quite a sight to behold.

I suggested that they put themselves back together so we could snap a few shots with them fully intact, just in case somebody at the record label created a stink. They grudgingly agreed, but only if they could cover themselves in that purple zombie goo. I told them that would be lovely.

I stayed up all night developing the photos, and they came out smashingly. I still consider it the highlight of my career, so much so that I don't even mind that my studio, to this day, still smells slightly of wet zombie.

BRIAN EPSTEIN: I hated the photos, and Neil Aspinall hated the photos, and George Martin hated the photos, and everybody at the record label hated the photos, but it didn't matter what any of us thought; those boys had enough cache at that point that they could've taken a picture of Ringo juggling John, Paul, and George's detached genitalia while wearing a green-and-pink-checked tuxedo, and nobody would've questioned it.

When the record hit the streets in June, the public was less than thrilled.

The week after I interviewed Whitaker, I posed a question on my blog: What was your initial reaction upon seeing what came to be known as "the butcher cover"?

BEATLESNERD2121@YAHOO.COM: I have a pretty hearty stomach, but when I saw it at the record store, I puked all over the B section. I ended up paying for fifty-six records. Apparently the record store had a "you barf on it, you buy it" policy.

EVELUVZADAM@AOL.COM: I'm only fifteen, and I obviously didn't see a copy of the actual cover, but I saw a photo online. It was nasty, but I still thought it was pretty cool, so I set it as my screen saver. When my parents saw that, they took away my computer for a week.

123GUITARMEISTER321@GMAIL.COM: I was conflicted. On one hand, I respected them for sticking to their guns, but on the other, that shit gave me nightmares for weeks. It didn't change my feelings about their music, but I sure as shit wasn't inviting them to my bar mitzvah.

BRIAN EPSTEIN: The public spoke, and thank goodness the folks at EMI Records listened. They recalled all the butcher covers and replaced them with another shot from the Whitaker session. The replacement photo was atrocious in its own right—Paul was lying in a trunk, doing a weird vampire impression (God knows why), and the other three were drenched in that awful purple glop—but after its predecessor, it was comparatively tame. The whole to-do didn't hurt record sales, but I think it cost us a whole bunch of goodwill.

•

The loss of goodwill continued when word of Maureen Cleave's newspaper article—the piece in which John Lennon claimed the Beatles were on par with Jesus—made it across the pond. In the UK, the interview was taken with a grain of salt—the general feeling was, "Oh my, there goes Johnny again. He must be hungry. Somebody give the poor bloke some cortex to nibble."—but the American religious right took it a helluva lot more seriously.

Father Jeffrey Jenkins of the Cathedral of the Incarnation Catholic church in Nashville, Tennessee, was already a vocal opponent of the butcher cover, but when he heard of Lennon's pronouncement, he went over the edge. Jenkins became one of the most impassioned opponents of the Beatles and everything he believed they stood for. He was still bitter about the band when I spoke with him in May 2000.

FATHER JEFFREY JENKINS: I have no problem with zombies in general, so long as they know their place. There were three zombies in my congregation, and they were all quiet, respectful, and God-fearing, and we welcomed them with open arms. Heck, back in 1998, I even had a zombie over to my house for dinner. So zombies are okay with me.

My hatred for the Beatles has nothing to do with their state of being. Heck, considering their behavior, they could've been bogeymen or mole monsters or the starting offensive line for the mighty University of Tennessee Volunteers, and I still would've started the movement. I mean, if you put yourself on the same plane as Jesus Christ, which is exactly what that heathen John Lennon did, you deserve to be punished, am I right? When you flood the streets with filth like that horrible record cover, you deserve to suffer, and suffer badly. So I took it upon myself to see that the Beatles suffered accordingly.

I had trouble deciding on a name for our movement. My first choice was Parents, Sons, and Daughters Stomping Out Zombie Musicians from England, but I thought the media might have trouble with that one, and if we wanted to get our word out there, the media was an important ally. After days and days of rumination and prayer, I settled on God-Lovers Against the Beatles, or GLAB. That was easy enough for everybody to remember.

The goal of GLAB was simple enough: make every single person in the United States realize that the Beatles were evil and should be banished from our children's bedrooms, our retail establishments, and our God-fearing country. Our first step toward accomplishing our goal was to organize what we called Beatle Fires.

Beatle Fires were festive events in which our followers burnt all of the Beatles records and memorabilia they could get their hands on. They were a great success—heck, we probably ridded the world of almost eight thousand Beatles albums and singles in Nashville alone—but the zombie community made it known that they weren't happy with us. They didn't appreciate us going after their own, but I didn't appreciate them going after my God, so no matter how much fuss they kicked up, I wasn't backing down, no way, no how, no siree bub.

We were attacked during our seventh Beatle Fire. I couldn't tell you exactly what happened, because when that first zombie came over the hill, I hightailed it on out of there. I could've stayed and fought, certainly, but I decided it was important for the leader of GLAB to remain healthy and unharmed, in order to spread the word and carry out the mission, and I still believe that was the correct decision. GLAB suffered some bad losses that afternoon: twenty-six of us were killed, and more than twice that many were injured. However, none were turned into zombies, because the horrible, horrible undead men and women who staged the attack made it clear they didn't believe any member of GLAB was worth reanimating. I found that hilarious: a stinking zombie telling my followers that they weren't good enough to become stinking zombies. Give me a break.

After the attack, the Nashville division of GLAB drifted apart—it turned out that the majority of my parishioners were cowards—but the movement picked up steam across the country. Beatle Fires became commonplace, and it did my heart proud when I saw a photo of those gol-darned British zombies being burned in effigy down in Dallas. I also appreciated the group in Biloxi who torched that record shop. Unfortunately, by end of summer, the furor died, and, unfortunately, so did GLAB.

Was GLAB a success? That depends on your definition of success. Yeah, we lost more than two thousand people in various zombie attacks across the country, and we didn't stop the band from touring, recording, or entering the United States. On the other hand, we helped keep that butcher cover out of stores, and we burned hundreds of thousands of Beatles records, and I personally escaped any harm. So from where I'm sitting, yes, the GLAB movement was a huge success.

*

The Beatles were growing weary of touring, and began spending more and more time in the recording studio, which was a plus for a young up-and-comer at EMI by the name of Geoff Emerick. While Geoff never achieved Fifth Beatle status like his mentor George Martin, he became an integral part of the band's recording process, so much so that after he suggested that John record a vocal track through a Leslie speaker—an effect that captured his true zombieness for the first time on wax—Lennon and McCartney offered to find Stuart Sutcliffe and have Emerick turned into a vampire. (Apparently, Emerick had a minor nervous breakdown when the topic of zombifying him was broached, thus the vampire offer.) When Geoff nervously pointed out that Sutcliffe was dead, both Beatles clammed up, sprinted down the hallway, and the topic was never raised again.

As much as he enjoyed being in the studio with the Fab Four, nervous breakdowns notwithstanding, recording sessions weren't without their share of perils—especially, as he told me in November 2002, when the studio was invaded by a certain local zombie killer.

GEOFF EMERICK: I'd met Mick several times and found him to be a lovely bloke, so when John said to me one afternoon over lunch, "If that fooker Jagger ever shows up, tell us he's here, and then get the fook out. If he's around the same time we're around, make yourself scarce. You'll thank me," I thought he was having a laugh, and promptly forgot about it.

Late one night about two weeks later, George Martin and I were sitting in the recording room at Abbey Road, messing with some mix or another. We were exhausted, but it was a good exhausted, the kind where you're basking in the glow of a successful day's work.

We took a fag break, and after a couple minutes of comfortable silence, George said, "Jagger's back in town."

I said, "Cool, man. Haven't seen him in months."

George said, "You don't understand." And then he filled me in on
the eternal Beatles-versus-Stones conflict.

I didn't believe him, and said, "I thought that was all press hype."

George put out his fag in the ashtray. "Nope. All true. In a weird
way, Mick digs us, and in a weird way, we dig Mick, but he has
zombie issues, and when he gets in hunting mode, it's not pretty."

And then, as if it were planned, Mick burst into the studio, and
yelled, "Old Martin! Young Emerick! Lead me to Lennon! Lead me
to McCartney! Lead me to Harrison! If you don't, you shall feel the
sting of my sword!"

George said, "Hi, Mick. Good to see you. And you don't have a
sword."

Mick waggled his midsection back and forth, then said, "My hips
are my sword! They're hip swords!"

George shook his head and said, "Your hip swords aren't very
hip, Mick. They don't work on mortals. They barely even work on
zombies, for that matter."

Mick dropped the dramatic delivery and said, "They work on everybody but the fookin' Beatles. Speaking of which, are those sad
cunts around?"

George said, "They shoved off hours ago, Mick. Geoff and I are
working on a mixdown. You're welcome to stay and listen. You
might actually like it."

Mick walked over to George, crouched down, and said, "Oh, I'll
stay, George Martin. Do you want to know why?"

George kind of rolled his eyes at me, then said, "Sure, Mick. Why
are you gonna stay?"

Mick whispered, "Because I have a thirst for Beatles blood . . ."

I said, "The Beatles don't really have blood, Mick. Well, Ringo does, I suppose."

Mick told me to quiet down, then repeated to George, "I have a thirst for Beatles blood. But since the Beatles aren't here, I shall taste the blood of George Martin!"

George rolled his eyes again and said, "For crying out loud, Mick, it's two in the morning . . ."

When Mick picked up a chair and hurled it through the glass window, George's eye rolling came to an abrupt halt. Mick yelled, "Prepare for battle, Martin!"

George popped up and yelled, "I'm from Highgate! Highgaters don't fight! I'm from Highgate! I'm from Highgate!"

Mick said, "Yeah, well, I'm from Kent, and in Kent, we fight and fight and fight some more!" Right before he was about to do some serious damage to George, the studio, and probably the tapes of that afternoon's session, I picked up the metal garbage can that was under the mixing board, dumped its contents onto the ground, and clocked Mick on the noggin.

While Mick was unconscious, George and I tied him up with several meters of reel-to-reel tape, after which I asked George, "So what now?"

George was still shaken up and didn't say anything for a while. Eventually, he strode across the room, picked up the phone, and quickly dialed a number. After a few seconds, he said, "Hello, it's George . . . Mick went off . . . Yeah, Emerick knocked him out . . . Yeah, he's secured . . . Great . . . So can I bring him around? . . . Wonderful . . . See you in a few." Then George picked Mick up—which couldn't have been that difficult, as Mick weighed next to nothing—then bade me a good night and took his leave of Abbey Road.

The next day at the studio, Paul came in late, wearing a shit-eating grin. He called out, "Lads, come here! Now! I have a new necklace, y'know!"

Ringo said, "Sod your necklace. Plug in your Höfner, and let's get to work."

Paul said, "Not until you look at my jewelry."

Harrison shook his head and asked, "Seriously, Paulie, you're really not gonna play until we look at your new toy?"

Paul said, "Erm, seriously."

So after we all trooped over to Macca, he puffed out his chest, pointed at the necklace, and said, "Check it out, boys. Check it right on out."

I said, "Paul, that's a tooth."

Paul said, "That's correct."

George Harrison said, "It looks like there's something shiny in the middle."

Paul said, "Correct again."

I asked, "What it is?"

Paul said, "It's a diamond."

I said, "A diamond, eh? Does a diamond embedded in a tooth symbolize something?"

Paul said, "Yeah. It symbolizes that we won't be hearing from Michael Philip Jagger for a while."

*

A*rguably the world's leading expert on psychedelic drugs, Dr. Timothy Leary was the first person I spoke with for this book, and to be honest, I'm still not 100 percent certain why a legendary figure like Leary would invite a novice journalist into his hospital room, as he rested on what would soon become his deathbed. I'd yet to publish anything of note, I had no direct connection to any of the Beatles, and I didn't even do drugs. So why me?*

It turns out that for decades, everybody in Doc Leary's inner circle

*pooh-poohed the legitimacy and importance of zombies to modern cul-
ture, and, as best I can figure, he wanted to rap about the undead with
somebody before he went off to the great LSD lab in the sky. And in the
spring of 1996, mere days before his passing, that somebody was me.*

DR. TIMOTHY LEARY: I worked with plenty of other otherworldly
beings. For instance, I gave mushrooms to a Satyr—the poor guy
couldn't get vertical for the next three days—and peyote to a werewolf, who scratched his pubic area raw, a terrible sight. But I'll
always have one professional regret: that I never had the opportunity to test a single drug on a single zombie in a laboratory.

I couldn't procure one undead individual volunteer for one
measly controlled experiment, and my assistants were of no help
whatsoever, because none of them gave a damn. It was a great big
hole in my research, and I pray that someday, somebody will pick
up the baton and run with it. The world needs to know specifically
if or how zombies are genetically affected by psychedelics. Someday,
the fate of mankind may depend on it.

Before the Beatles got dosed, I had my theories. We know that
drugs of any sort—be they herbal or over-the-counter—alter a zombie's coloring, and I always hoped to see a zombie take acid and
watch his pallor transition from the traditional gray to rainbow. I
envisioned some melting of the skin and some oozing of the brain.
Spontaneous combustion of the internal organs was a distinct possibility, as were mossy fungus growths in and around the ears.

But the real question, the *important* question was, would my
trusty old lysergic acid diethylamide make these beings happy?
Would it open their minds and give them a better perspective on
life and undeath? Or would it give them the munchies and compel
them to eat more brains, thus exponentially raising the world's zom-
bie-induced death toll?

My hope—no, my *dream*—was that one tab would bring the undead back to a blissful, eternal life, and I was willing to spend the time and money to figure out how I could make that happen. Zombies are beautiful creatures, and they deserve a shot at happiness. This is why I was so curious to see what would happen when the Beatles started in with the stuff.

Turns out I was wrong up and down the board. Very wrong.

GEORGE HARRISON: The story goes, we were slipped the dreaded lysergic for the first time by a local dentist at a party, but that's a crock. The truth is, we were far more proactive about it. And the person who was the most proactive was, of all people, Brian Epstein.

PAUL McCARTNEY: From the first day he signed us, Eppy was very protective of our image, especially in light of the fact that we had what he called "an annoying tendency" to, erm, eat our fans. His thinking was, if things played well for us in the press, and if we stayed on the cutting edge, the public would overlook such minor things as a brainless corpse here, or a decapitated body in a dark alley there. That made perfect sense to us, y'know, so whenever he said, "Dance, lads," we'd say, "What step?" If he gave us a suggestion, we'd generally take it without complaint—even a suggestion like we start experimenting with hard drugs.

RINGO STARR: I'm not sure how Eppy heard that LSD was the flavor of the month, but when he called a band meeting and told us he wanted us to take acid in order to stay ahead of the curve, we went along quite willingly. The only problem was that Eppy wasn't the kind of guy who knew where to buy illegal drugs, and we all agreed that it would be a bad idea for a Beatle or a Beatle associate to

wander the London streets looking for a dealer. So he decided to get into the manufacturing end of things.

BRIAN EPSTEIN: I'd always had a keen interest in science and was happy to take a crack at making my own lysergic. The tale of how I rounded up the proper equipment and ingredients is a long and boring one involving a lot of phone calls and numerous drives to Ireland and back with Mal Evans. Suffice it to say, I procured everything I needed without anybody from our camp getting arrested.

It was a hit-or-miss process. My first week of work, I started four large fires and countless small ones that led to several first-degree burns and the unfortunate destruction of my record collection. I eventually found my sea legs and managed to put together what I believed was a respectable batch. Neil Aspinall volunteered to be the test subject, and God bless him for it, because if I'd have given the first three lots directly to the lads, who knows what would've happened?

NEIL ASPINALL: I don't remember most of what happened from the summer of '65 to the spring of '67. John's always told me I didn't miss much, but I think he's just saying that to make me feel better.

PAUL McCARTNEY: After throwing down the first dose of Brian's brew, Neil walked around the house bent at a ninety-degree angle. When he straightened up five days later, Eppy gave him a tab from the second batch, which had poor Neil speaking in animal noises for two or three weeks. Finally, the fifth batch in, Eppy felt comfortable enough to give Ringo a hit.

RINGO STARR: I turned on, tuned in, dropped out, and it was smashing. When I came down from my first trip, I called 忍の者乱破 and tried to get him on board—if there was a guy who needed to open his mind, it was 忍の者乱破—but he wasn't having it. He gave me some rubbish about how Ninja Lords need not use synthetic means to attain a higher consciousness, and our Earthly work should fulfill us and keep us properly connected to the cosmos, and blah, blah, blah. I told him to piss off, then hung up the phone and took another hit. Eppy was a bloody genius.

BRIAN EPSTEIN: After Ringo survived sixty-three lysergic trips in eight days, I was ready to give it to the rest of the lads . . . but not all three at once. I could afford to have a single Beatle go on "vacation," but I couldn't have the entire lot out of commission. Naturally, John volunteered to go first.

PAUL McCARTNEY: We all went over to John's flat—me, Ringo, George, Neil, and Eppy—and removed all breakables from his living room, then threw pillows and blankets all over the place. Johnny was chomping at the bit, so we gave him the tab, and everybody shoved off except for yours truly, who got elected to sit around and make sure he didn't hurt himself or anybody else.

It kicked in immediately and, long story short, he died.

JOHN LENNON: The minute I get to the afterlife, I run into Jesus Christ, and the first thing he says to me is, "You were right in that interview, mate. You Beatles *are* better than me. After I read that fookin' thing, I tried getting that guitar sound from the beginning of 'A Hard Day's Night,' and I couldn't get close. Then I got a bunch of angels together to harmonize the chorus of 'Nowhere Man,' and it sounded like shite. And I'm fookin' embarrassed to tell you what happened when I tried to copy Paul's bass line on 'Ticket to Ride.'

So cheers, Johnny—it'll be a pleasure to have you up here with us. You wanna go and grab a pint?"

Christ seemed like a top geezer, and I think I'd have been fine hanging out with him for all eternity. But Mr. Showbiz wasn't having any of it.

PAUL McCARTNEY: We had albums to record, y'know. We had gigs to play. We had birds to fook. We had a thick-lipped, skinny-arsed Rolling Stone to torment. Death for John Lennon was not an option.

LYMAN COSGROVE: Reanimating the rare dead Liverpool Processer who wasn't killed by a diamond bullet is a dicey proposition. There's no definitive way to make it happen. Different techniques work on different zombies. With some zombies, nothing works at all.

PAUL McCARTNEY: I went on autopilot. My animal brain took over, and my zombie body followed its instructions. If I'd been in better control of my faculties, I probably wouldn't have smashed John in the face with his Framus acoustic guitar, nor would I have torn off his left hand and his right foot, then reattached them in reverse. If I had been thinking, I probably would've done the Liverpool Process . . . which would've been exactly the wrong thing to do. Turns out that would've been lights-out for John. Forever.

What happened next was purely instinctive, y'know. I tore off John's head, yanked out his brain, ran it over to the bathtub, and gave it a quick soapy soak, maybe three minutes in all. The brain was quite slippery when I pulled it out of the tub, so slippery, in fact, that I almost dropped the bloody thing onto the bathroom floor. After I dried it off, I ran it back to the living room and slid it into its proper resting area in what I hoped was the, erm, proper position. Then I went into John's linen closet, and thank Christ he had a sewing kit. Seconds after I stitched his head back onto his neck, John Lennon was back, sober, and crankier than ever.

JOHN LENNON: The afterlife was looking all right. No pressure. No commitments. No Brian Epstein dragging us all over the world. No Paul McCartney telling me to get back to work. Just Christ and me, drinking ale and hanging out with dead artists. Right when I'm getting comfortable—and right when my man Jesus is about to introduce me to Charles Baudelaire—I feel this tug, and I'm back in my living room staring at Paulie's puppy-dog eyes.

Paul kissed me on the cheek and said, "I thought we lost you, mate."

I said, "Nope. You didn't. I'm back. Lucky me. Say, is there any more of that fookin' lysergic left?"

JESUS CHRIST: I was fookin' sad to let Johnny go back to Earth, and I would've loved to find a way to keep him around, but Dad gets pissed when I break a rule, and when Dad gets pissed, it's bloody hell for everybody.

GEORGE HARRISON: After the John disaster, I couldn't *wait* to try Eppy's next batch.

BRIAN EPSTEIN: I tweaked the recipe, so George's experience was far better than John's, in that he didn't die. But he had his own problems, the most notable being a nasty case of leprosy that lasted several weeks.

GEORGE HARRISON: The high was nice, but it wasn't worth losing any limbs over. On the plus side, if it wasn't for Brian's LSD, I never would've come up with the skintar.

NEIL ASPINALL: A few days before we were to leave on a tour of the Far East—and while he was in the midst of his leprosy problem— George rang me up and told me to get to his flat *immediately* because he had something to share. When I showed up at his place an hour later, I rang the bell, and he yelled, "Come in! Door's open! I'm not leaving the house!"

One look at him, and I understood why he didn't want to be seen in public. Aside from the fact that one or two of his fingers plopped onto the floor every few minutes, his skin was, well, his skin was *gone.* Okay, it wasn't *totally* gone, just the first two layers, and the one layer that was left was translucent; I could see practically every bone, organ, and muscle in his body. It was very Midpointery. I told him, "Looking good, Georgie. Leslie Langley's been asking about you. Why don't you give her a jingle? You're as handsome as I've ever seen you."

He said, "Very funny. Listen, I have something very serious to share. You're the first person who's ever seen this, and you can't be judgmental about it, and, most important, you can't freak out."

I said, "George, after what I've seen over the past four years, nothing can possibly freak me out."

He said, "If you say so."

And then he reached behind his sofa and pulled out something that freaked me out.

He said, "So what do you think?"

I asked him, "Is that what I think it is?"

He said, "Dunno. What do you think it is?"

I said, "I think it's a guitar fashioned out of the skin that slid off your body. Now if you'll excuse me, I'm going to shove off to the loo and say good-bye to my lunch."

GEORGE HARRISON: For the previous several months, I'd been hearing different musical noises in my head, sounds that my trusty old Epiphone wasn't capable of making. So when the first two layers of my skin slid off during my LSD trip, I got out my tools and went to work.

The first thing I did was bake my fallen skin in the oven at a low temperature for about forty-five minutes, so it'd stiffen up without rotting, and hopefully get a bit darker in color. I watched it carefully, because if I overcooked it, it'd get crispy and lose its pliancy and resonance. Once the skin was heated to my satisfaction, I brought out an X-Acto knife, set one layer of the epidermis aside, and cut the other layer into what I believed would be the perfect shape for an instrument. I then cooked up some porridge—overcooked, actually, so it'd be nice and thick—and slathered it all over the skin; then I put the whole mess back into the oven for ten or so minutes. Meanwhile, I rolled up the other skin layer into a nice, tight tube, then went to the oven and removed what was about to become the instrument's body, then glued the two pieces together with some more porridge, then put it back in the oven for a few more minutes, then after it cooled down, I covered it with shellac. When it dried, I put eight strings on it—if six is good, eight is better—and voila, a skintar.

One strum, and I fell in love with the sound—full, singing, and meaty—but I knew right off the bat that keeping it in tune would be an issue.

NEIL ASPINALL: When I came out of the bathroom, George said, "You're the roadie, so here's a question for you: Can I bring the skintar on tour with us?"

It was grotty, utterly grotty, but, even more problematical, it didn't sound particularly good, so I told him, "Best you leave it at home, Georgie. I have a hunch the Japanese won't take too kindly to that sort of thing. They're already cheesed-off with Ringo, and we don't need any more trouble."

George nodded, and said, "Oh. Right. That Ninja shit. Good point."

*

RINGO STARR: Eppy had scheduled the Tokyo shows months before, and since we'd never been to Japan, the country was going mad. Aside from the Japanese wanting to hear us live, Japan has a very small zombie population, and since most of the population had never seen any undead, the curiosity level was through the ceiling.

This isn't to say they were looking forward to seeing us. See, Japan had a huge warrior population, and, as I soon found out, Japanese warriors weren't big fans of British Ninja Lords.

Like me.

PAUL McCARTNEY: That press conference in Tokyo was a nightmare. Those journos are lucky John didn't attack them, y'know.

JOHN LENNON: Hey, if you're fookin' with Ringo, that means you're fookin' with me.

RINGO STARR: The writers thought I was a phony. They made it clear that the belief around the country was, the only reason I'd been given Seventh Level status was because I was a rock star, and I was besmirching the good Ninja Lord name. I tried to explain that I reached the Seventh Level before joining the Beatles, but they either weren't listening or didn't believe me. I wanted to cry, but Lords above Fourth Level aren't allowed to cry in public.

JOHN LENNON: Ringo clammed up, but it wouldn't have mattered if the poor guy was reading the Magna Carta, because all those bastards would've shouted him down anyhow. I leaned over to Ringo and said, "You've gotta do something physical."

He mumbled, "The only thing I want to do is get out of here."

I told him, "Listen, the only thing these cunts'll understand is a demonstration of your Ninja talents. Be a warrior. Show them the skills, mate. And if you have to make one of 'em bleed, so be it. I give you full permission, because nobody but *nobody* can shit on the Beatles without incurring our wrath."

RINGO STARR: John had a point. If I showed them Seventh Level skills, there was a better chance they'd accept me. Problem was, I wasn't comfortable frivolously using my Ninja techniques, especially near the actual birthplace of the Ninja movement. Defending yourself during a physical attack is accepted—encouraged, even—but going on the offensive during a verbal barrage isn't.

But once the bloke from the *Sekai Nippo* newspaper threw a spitball at me, all bets were off.

PAUL McCARTNEY: I knew Ringo could move fast, but I didn't know *how* fast. If I could've actually seen what he did, I'm certain it would've been a sight to behold, y'know, but I only saw the results. A dozen or so reporters were screaming accusations at our poor drummer, then I blinked, and the bloke from *Sekai Nippo* is hanging from the ceiling fan by his tie, and two other reporters are pinned on the wall with Ninja stars, and the rest of the lot are face-down on the ground, their wrists tied behind their backs. That little stunt probably cost us thousands and thousands of dollars in lost record sales, but I couldn't blame Ringo one bit.

It shouldn't have ever happened, really. These guys were Japanese, for goodness sake. They were raised at the home of the Ninja, and they should've known better than to piss off an honest-to-goodness Ninja Lord.

RINGO STARR: The story was all over the news, and the fans weren't happy. The next day, we started our run of three nights at the Budokan Hall, and the crowd booed before each song, during each song, and after each song. When they weren't booing, they were yelling for my scalp. But the Japanese are generally a peaceful lot, and they never went after me; it was just a bunch of noise.

Still, I couldn't wait to get out of that country and over to the Philippines. I knew it would be far, far better.

GEORGE HARRISON: The Philippines were far, far worse.

JOHN LENNON: We were always going, going, going, and we barely had the opportunity to check out our own local newspapers, so how was I supposed to find the time to read what was happening in the fookin' Philippines?

PAUL McCARTNEY: The Filipinos had it out for us from the get-go. Had we known what had happened there the year before with the zombie population, we probably would've skipped it altogether.

●

A*n award-winning reporter for* The Philippine Star, *Rizal Guintu is the kind of guy who would run into a burning building if he thought there was a story to be written. Unflappable and unafraid, his coverage of the 1965 undead uprising in Manila is believed by those in the know to be the most accurate depiction of the havoc that can be wreaked by a Filipino zombie, a belief that I wouldn't dispute after interviewing him in July 2000.*

RIZAL GUINTU: As a group, we Filipino are, size-wise, a small people, but the majority of our undead have the strength and quickness of the biggest North American zombie you can find. And they are aggressive, these zombies, very, very aggressive.

The year before the Beatles' visit, Ferdinand Marcos had taken control of the country, and one of his first acts was to change the laws regarding zombies. For the previous five or six decades, the government and the zombies had reached a comfortable accord: the undead were segregated in an area on the outskirts of Antipolo, and in exchange for their promise not to interact with the general population, they were given the brains of the nearly dying for sustenance. It was not a perfect system, but it kept the inevitable undead-versus-human conflicts to a bare minimum.

Then Marcos changed the laws for no reason other than that he desired to put his own imprint on the country. It was *his* administration, and he was going to do things *his* way, whether or not it made sense. The primary tenet of the new law was that zombies were allowed to walk among the human population, but Marcos took away their access to sustenance—in other words, when it came to brains, they were on their own. This led to mass murders, which led to hundreds of incarcerated zombies, which led to thousands of angry zombies, which led to a storming of the Malacañan Palace.

Marcos and his family escaped the attack unharmed, but fifty-four members of the Presidential Guard were killed, and the army—who most believed up to that point was impenetrable—lost ninety-nine men. Not a single zombie was hurt.

In order to quell any further war action, Marcos reinstituted the previous undead laws, and sent the zombies back to Antipolo. There was an uneasy truce, and there was still the sense that the situation could explode with the slightest provocation.

The blood of the dead military men and the tears of their families had barely dried when the Beatles landed at Ninoy Aquino International Airport on July 3, so few were surprised when the Liverpool zombies were not greeted with open arms.

BRIAN EPSTEIN: Police surrounded us from the second we landed at the airport. We thought they were there to protect us. What we didn't know was that we actually needed to be protected *from* them. Fortunately, these dunderheads had no idea how to harm a zombie, which explains why they did such a horrendous job quashing the uprising in the first place.

They tried poisoning our food, which was completely ineffective. My stomach was in knots, so I couldn't eat a thing, and Ringo was appalled by Far Eastern cuisine, so he lived on the baked beans he'd brought from home. John, Paul, and George, however, happily chowed down on kare-kare, binakol, and pancit . . . all of which was laced with copious amounts of strychnine. It gave the lads horrible gas, and their skin turned neon blue, but no harm was done.

The next assassination attempt came the night before the concert, when the police threw John out of his twenty-fifth-floor hotel room while he was still asleep. He woke up briefly when he hit the pavement, then went right back to dreamland. Eventually the police came and told him to get back to his room, as his snoring was scaring the local children.

But that wasn't the end. The morning of the concert, they kidnapped Paul, who went along with it for about an hour. When he got bored with the exercise, he hypnotized his captors and made them bring him back to the hotel. Under the power of his puppy-dog eyes, they quickly became enamored with Macca, so much so that they offered him the services of several of the city's finest prostitutes, which he gracefully declined.

Then we were invited to lunch with the president and the first lady. We were going to take a pass, but they trained several guns on me and explained that attendance was mandatory, and if we refused, I was a dead man. John said, "You know what, boys? Let's do this. It'll be a giggle."

JOHN LENNON: You could tell by the way Marcos governed the undead that he was a cunt. I'm not one to get out there and protest for zombie rights, but the way my Filipino brethren were treated was appalling, and if I had the opportunity to do something about it, I'd take it.

Paul, George, and I weren't exactly eager to eat any more strychnine—we'd just gotten our gas under control—so we zombie types took a pass on the meal. Ringo and Eppy didn't want to die a horrible death, so they also gracefully declined. Marcos and his cunty wife, Imelda, pretended to be insulted that we'd declined the tainted food. They were horrible actors, those two. Marcos then started in with a bunch of We're-honored-to-have-you-in-our-fine-country-and-you-should-be-honored-to-eat-the-food-we-have-so-kindly-provided-for-you claptrap, and Paulie just burst out in giggles. Marcos then lost his composure and yelled, "What are you laughing at? I welcomed you into my country and invited you into my home, and you disrespect me at my own dining table? This is an outrage!"

I pointed at my plate and said, "You tried to fookin' poison us."

Imelda made a painfully fake insulted face and said, "How dare you accuse us of such treachery. That is the ultimate insult. We would never commit such a heinous act."

Paul said, "Is that right?" He pushed his plate toward her, and continued, "Then what say you take a little nibble of this?"

RINGO STARR: Imelda turned white and said, "Thank you for the offer, Mr. McCartney, but I'm quite full." She gestured toward her plate, which was practically untouched.

Paul said, "You don't need to take a full bite, love. Just a nibble, y'know."

Imelda said, "I couldn't."

Paul said, "You can."

Imelda said, "I shouldn't."

Paul said, "You should."

Imelda said, "I won't."

Paul said, "That's too bad." Then he looked over at the president and said, "How about you, Ferdie? Can I interest you in a taste of death?"

Ferdinand looked at Imelda, and Imelda looked at Ferdinand; then, at the exact same time, they stood up and ran toward the nearest exit.

The security guys stared at one another for a minute, then the only one who spoke proper English said, "You are free to go, Beatles."

Brian said, "Thanks, mate. We'll show ourselves out."

BRIAN EPSTEIN: Showing ourselves out of the palace wasn't a problem, but showing ourselves out of the country was a whole other issue.

What happened was, they unleashed the undead.

JOHN LENNON: Christ, those midget Filipino zombies are strong.

RINGO STARR: When those itty-bitty undead types were waiting for us at the airport, I made myself invisible. I sensed what they were about, and I wanted no part of it.

NEIL ASPINALL: There were at least five hundred of them on the tarmac. They created a human pyramid—or, I suppose an inhuman pyramid—and blocked the plane. The pilot refused to move.

PAUL McCARTNEY: All I can say is, thank God Filipino zombies are very, *very* susceptible to hypnosis.

BRIAN EPSTEIN: It was over in thirty seconds. John, Paul, and George sang some odd phrase in harmony—some rubbish like "Jay garoo divided um"—and those zombies broke up their pyramid, then removed their heads and flung them straight up into the air. As far as we knew, those heads never came down.

GEORGE HARRISON: For me, that was the final straw. The Mania had overtaken our lives, and touring became a nonstop drag. If it wasn't some Filipino fascist dictator trying to poison us, it was some American bird trying to steal our plonkers. Me, I was ready to pack it in altogether.

JOHN LENNON: Nothing felt fun anymore. Touring was a nightmare. Playing the same tunes night after night was boring, boring, boring. Yeah, we still loved one another, but sometimes the sight of George's gray face or Paul's puppy-dog eyes got my stomach churning. It seemed like we were moving farther away from the Poppermost, and that "all for zombies, and zombies for all" business was getting tired. I needed a break . . . maybe a permanent one.

RINGO STARR: I wanted two things: to reach the Eighth Level, and for everybody in the band to be happy. Whatever the majority wanted was cool with me. If they voted to keep moving forward as if everything was hunky-dory, fine. If they voted to call it a day, fine.

If they voted to launch an offensive on Buckingham Palace, fine. If at least two of the blokes were happy, then I was happy.

PAUL McCARTNEY: The Beatles were not going to break up. The Beatles were never going to break up. Not if I had anything to say about it.

CHAPTER SIX

1967

GEORGE MARTIN: The sessions that ultimately produced the *Sgt. Pepper* album were dizzying. The studio always seemed to be filled with special guests, some invited, some not: a full-blown orchestra, zombie groupies, visiting *shinobi* dignitaries from Borneo, and a few confused vampires. It was a revolving door, a parade of diverse faces and colorful clothing, and at one point on New Year's Day, I swear I saw Stu Sutcliffe. When I mentioned that to the boys the next night, John laughed it off, called me a nutter, and then strongly suggested I never mention Stuart Sutcliffe again. When John Lennon strongly suggests you don't do something, you don't do it.

John and Paul were especially intrigued with the string section; having all those violins and cellos at their disposal seemed to tickle their fancy. I'm not sure whether they were taken by the sound of the orchestra, or whether they got off on controlling a dozen-plus musicians with a mere baton, but whatever it was, they were entranced. Naturally, that led to trouble.

NEIL ASPINALL: We'd just finished up with the bit at the end of "A Day in the Life" where all the strings start out quietly sawing away, then get louder and louder and louder, until it all ends in a burst of orgasmic pleasure. John was so blown away by the whole thing that he actually had an orgasm that blew through the front of his trousers. There was dustmen everywhere, and a poor harp player named Sheila Bromberg caught the brunt of it. Dustmen is white, and Sheila's dress was black, and it wasn't pretty.

After Johnny changed his pants, he stood up on a chair in front of the orchestra and said, "My lovely string section, you've given us a gift. You've given us joy. You've given us something that will endure until the end of time. And now, Paul McCartney and I would like to return the favor."

Paul said, "We would?"

PAUL McCARTNEY: I'd seen that look in Johnny's eyes many, many times, y'know, and I knew *exactly* what *favor* meant.

JOHN LENNON: I thought it was a brilliant idea then, and I think it was a brilliant idea now, and if I had it to do over, I'd do the same fookin' thing.

NEIL ASPINALL: I dunno if John and Paul were getting old or tired, or if all the various drug "experiments" had affected their reflexes, but their attacks weren't as quick as they used to be. That didn't mean their victims had a significantly better chance of escaping. All it meant was that it was easier for a bystander to see exactly what they were doing. Which, if you aren't a fan of having nightmares for two consecutive weeks, wasn't a good thing.

GEOFF EMERICK: After John gave his little speech to the orchestra, he turned to Paulie and said, "What do you think, mate? Are you with me or not."

Paul said, "Not. You're on your own."

John said, "No, I'm not on my own. You're with me. I was being rhetorical. It wasn't a question."

Paul said, "Yes it was. You said, 'Are you with me or not?' You started your sentence with the word *are.* By definition, any sentence with the word *are* at the beginning of it is a question."

John said, "That's not necessarily true. I didn't upturn my voice, and if there's no upturn, there's no question. Like if I say, 'Paulie's a git?' and I upturn my voice, it's a question. But if I say, 'Paulie's a git,' *without* upturning my voice, it's a declarative statement. Get it? 'Paulie's a git.' Statement. Period."

Paul said, "Are you saying I'm a git?"

John said, "No. I'm explaining that if I say, 'Paulie's a git,' without upturning my voice, it's a statement. Ipso facto, 'Paulie's a git' is not a question."

Paul said, "You *are* saying I'm a git."

John said, "No, I'm saying it's *not a question* that Paulie's a git. Now, are you gonna help me murder the orchestra, or what?"

Paul said, "Now *that's* a question."

NEIL ASPINALL: Three years earlier, John would've been able to do the whole lot all by himself, but now he needed Paul, and he probably knew that. However, that didn't stop him from diving in solo.

GEORGE MARTIN: John went after the violinists first. He didn't transform them individually but, rather, three at once: chomp, chomp, chomp; suck, suck, suck; tongue, tongue, tongue; spit, spit, spit;

glue, glue, glue. It was a veritable zombie assembly line. The problem was, he bit off more than he could chew, so to speak, and he wasn't plugging up the neck holes quickly enough, and there was blood *everywhere*.

PAUL McCARTNEY: I dunno what it was about those violinists, but they were *gushing*. It was like their veins were jet-propelled. Within seconds, the floor was covered, just *covered*.

GEOFF EMERICK: The pools were getting bigger and bigger, and our microphone cables were getting closer to being in harm's way, so instinct took over, and I ran out of the control room and into the studio, where I promptly slipped and fell face-first into a blood puddle. I bloodied my nose . . . or, at least, I think I did. Everybody was leaking red, so the blood covering my face might've come from the cello section.

GEORGE MARTIN: Paul ran to the corner of the studio and grabbed his bass, then placed it on top of an amplifier; then he said, "Sod it," and jumped into the fray. I know Paul didn't want to be part of zombifying this truly talented batch of orchestral musicians, but I suspect he went to help because he thought John wouldn't be able to seal the wounds himself, and the tidal wave of blood would destroy every piece of equipment in the place.

PAUL McCARTNEY: We were now ankle-deep in the red stuff, and it was only gonna get worse. Once I knew my Höfner was out of harm's way, I came to John's rescue. No way he could've handled it himself. He'd lost a step. Hell, we'd *all* lost a step.

JOHN LENNON: I was faster than ever, and I absolutely could've handled it myself.

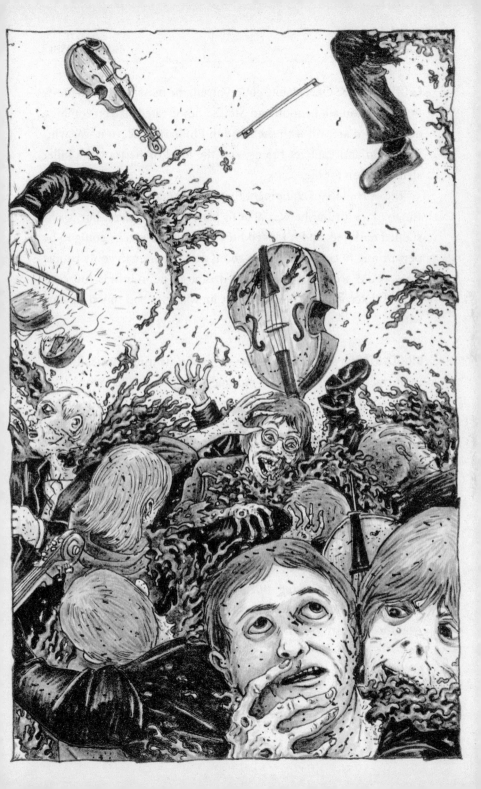

GEOFF EMERICK: Once Paulie got involved, the massacre ended pretty quickly. All in all, Lennon and McCartney created sixteen zombies, all of whom are still with the London Philharmonic, so it was win-win. John and Paul got brains, and the local orchestra got a killer string section for life.

The only piece of equipment that was permanently damaged was Ringo's kick drum; he was able to play it, no problem, but it was stained dark red, and it looked hideous. But we weren't going to be performing in concert anytime soon; thus, we were the only people who would see his bloodstained drum, so nobody was too concerned. Except, y'know, Ringo, but he was in a bad mood to start with.

RINGO STARR: John and Paul were experimenting musically and multitracking and killing off our guest musicians, and George was off messing about with his skintar, so they were all in their element, which left me with a lot of free time. So what did I do with myself? Write some of my own tunes? Nah. Work on drumming technique? Nope.

I called 忍の者乱破 and scheduled a meeting. I was gonna make Eighth Level if it killed me.

忍の者乱破: Richard Starkey was disciplined. Richard Starkey had a good heart. Richard Starkey was a spiritual being who was in touch with his inner *everything*. But Richard Starkey was, is, and always will be a Seventh Level Ninja Lord. Nothing more, nothing less. And there is nothing wrong with that.

RINGO STARR: I trekked over to 忍の者乱破's dojo on Molyneux Road back in Liverpool and was greeted with a reception worthy of a Fifty-fifth Level: streamers, balloons, and hundreds of shuriken stuck in the wall in a pattern that spelled out BEATLES 4-EVER! I almost wept. 忍の者乱破 wasn't one for public displays of respect, so that was special.

忍の者乱破 guided me to a seat in the middle of the room, clapped his hands twice, and, out of nowhere, in an impressive display of cool Ninja skills, two dozen of his students materialized. They put on a private show that would've had the Shaolin monks on their feet: astounding choreography, mind-blowing feats of strength, and disappearing and reappearing. It went on for two hours, and as far as I was concerned, that wasn't long enough.

Once the twenty-four Ninjas packed it in, 忍の者乱破 stood me up and guided me to the door. He said, "Young Starkey, you are a credit to Ninja Lords throughout the planet. Speak to the masses. Show them your skills. Make the public aware that Ninjas are a singular breed that deserves the respect of the world. I love you. I know you love me. Now spread love, because love is all you need." Then he kissed me on the cheeks, and next thing I knew, I was out on the sidewalk. After I heard the front door click shut behind me, I hopped into the car and drove back to Abbey Road. What else could I do?

忍の者乱破: Quality drummer, passable Ninja. I did not want to put him through another Eight Level test. It would have been shaming for everybody.

RINGO STARR: I showed up at the studio around dinnertime, and there're George Martin and Geoff Emerick crawling around the lawn on their hands and knees, clearly in search of something. When I asked what was going on, Mr. Martin gave me a disgusted look and said, "Go up on the roof and find out for yourself."

GEORGE HARRISON: We were in the midst of a playback, and suddenly, John said, "It appears the walls are growing tentacles. Gotta go," then he ran all the way up the stairs. Having seen our fair share of tentacles, Paul and I figured out pretty quickly that somebody'd dosed John. We never found out who, we never found out how; best we could figure is that one of the groupies who were parading in and out of the studio snuck a tab in his Corn Flakes.

I found John on the roof, sitting on the edge, farting up purple clouds and screaming, "Come back! Come back! Come back!"

I called out, "Oi, Johnny, what is it you want to come back?"

John said, "My fookin' fingers!"

GEOFF EMERICK: Harrison yelled down to us from the top of the stairs, "Emerick and Martin, please go find John's left pinkie and right thumb. They should be somewhere on the lawn out front. McCartney, please join me on the roof."

John's fingers had fallen onto the street side of the studio, and our primary concern was that they'd rolled into the street and gotten splatted by an oncoming bus. Fortunately, there wasn't much traffic, and we didn't see any flattened digits on the street, so unless one of the fingers somehow jumped into somebody's tailpipe, they were around there *somewhere*.

So, George Martin and I—while wearing ties and nice trousers, mind you—got on our hands and knees and poked through the bushes. Nothing. Then we went through the front lawn. Nothing. I asked George if he wanted to run to the roof and make sure John wasn't messing with us. He told me that, as I was the junior member of the team, it was my job to handle the talent, so I should get my arse up there.

As I headed upstairs, I worried about how the talent would handle me.

PAUL McCARTNEY: John was inconsolable about the potential loss of his fingers. He said, "How'm I gonna play guitar? How'm I gonna play keyboard? How'm I gonna fix my hair so I don't look like a prat?"

Harrison and I tried to calm him down, but when a zombie's on acid, there's no talking to him, y'know. He went on and on, and his moaning was getting more zombie-like and starting to attract attention. Right then, Geoff shows up, and says, "Good news, boys: we found the fingers!"

GEOFF EMERICK: We hadn't found the fingers.

PAUL McCARTNEY: John sprang up—almost falling off the roof in the process—jumped at Geoff, and tried to give him a kiss on the neck. Not an undead kiss. Just a *kiss* kiss.

GEOFF EMERICK: I ducked, and he sailed right over me and crashed headfirst into the door. No way I was letting John Lennon get anywhere my neck.

PAUL McCARTNEY: John popped right on up, shook out the cobwebs, gave us a big old smile, and said, "Right, then. I'm heading downstairs. And the next time you see good ol' John Winston Lennon, he'll have ten fookin' fingers, just like the rest of you cunts." He paused, then said, "We should do a concert up here someday. It'd be a larf."

GEORGE MARTIN: Geoff yelled at me from the roof, "Get a move on, mate! Johnny's on his way down! He thinks we found his digits!"

I'd come up empty-handed, if you will: no pinkie, no thumb, bugger-all. Thinking fast, I went over to the nearest tree, ripped off a branch, and broke off two finger-size pieces. It was dark. John was high. At the very least, it would buy me some time.

When I gave John the sticks, he wept with joy. While he embraced me, I patted him on the back and told him, "Don't reattach the fingers just yet, John. You're a bit addled, and you don't want to do something that serious until you're in a good headspace. Go have a lie-down on the cot in the control room. I'll be back in a few."

It took me two more hours to find his fingers. Turned out they'd landed in a robin's nest. The mother bird took a nice chomp out of the pinkie, but otherwise, they were in fine shape. Paul reattached them while John was asleep on the sofa, and he was never the wiser, and Mr. Lennon's hands lived happily ever after.

GEORGE HARRISON: Brian had initially wanted the press and the general public to know we were experimenting with the dreaded lysergic, but the results of said experiments were such failures that we decided to keep it amongst ourselves. Or at least, John, Ringo, and I did.

PAUL McCARTNEY: The writer asked me a question, y'know. I answered it. I told the truth. Who knew it would lead to what it led to?

BRIAN EPSTEIN: After Paul told that newspaper reporter that the boys had tried acid, a lot of our American fans went a little bananas. The English press wasn't particularly concerned—it seemed like everybody in London was tripping that summer, so who cared if a few rock stars were messing about with the stuff?—but in the States, it was another story. Especially for tens of thousands of teenage girls.

•

The lone zombie psychiatrist in the entire state of Wisconsin, Dr. Jennifer Everett, wasn't the first young woman to join one of the so-called Beatles suicide acid cults that popped up across the United States, nor was she the last. But she is one of the few who escaped both alive-ish and with her mind more or less intact.

Jennifer's cult leader—a zombie who tried to pass as a man and went by the snappy moniker of Reverend Starkey Best von Pollywog— did a superb job of brainwashing his followers, so Dr. Everett's memories of her two weeks as a member of the Merry Undead are iffy at best. But in January 2000, she told me enough to paint a picture that was, at the very least, disconcerting.

DR. JENNIFER EVERETT: Considering how crappy the modern music scene is, people who weren't around when the Beatles were in their prime will never understand how a little rock group from England could wrap me so tightly around their little finger. And since that cult had an irrevocable impact on my life, and I wouldn't have joined the cult had it not been for the Beatles, I think about that constantly. Was it their songs that roped me in? Their voices? Their look? The era? No clue. Still haven't been able to figure it out. All I know is that there hasn't been a single band either before or since who could get me physically, emotionally, and sexually aroused by simply *being*.

I would've followed the Beatles anywhere, but by '67, they weren't touring, so the only way I'd be able to be with them would be to move to England, but little girls from the Wisconsin heartland didn't move to England, especially when their parents vehemently despised both rock 'n' roll and zombies. So when I heard about Reverend Pollywog, well, the Merry Undead seemed to be the next best thing.

At the time, the Merry Undead was very shrouded in mystery, but if you took away the rainbow-colored school bus, the dashikis, and the copious amounts of acid, it was just a cover for a random nut job trying to fuck as many young girls as he possibly could. The reality was more nasty than mysterious.

Reverend Pollywog was a marketing genius. He somehow got all the hippie girls in the streets to talk him up—"Oh, the Merry Undead are soooooo beautiful, and they've got the best drugs, and they hang out with all the coolest zombies"—so when the bus rolled through Milwaukee that summer, Pollywog didn't have to do any recruiting. He had his pick of the Beatle-loving litter. He thought I was cute. I was in.

I have vivid memories of getting on the bus, but after Pollywog shoved his tongue down my throat, it gets hazy. I remember the other twenty-three girls and I were constantly naked. I remember eating lots and lots of Corn Flakes—and to this day, when I walk down the cereal aisle at the grocery store and get a glimpse of that white Kellogg's box, I get the heebie-jeebies. I remember a lot of tambourines. Oddly enough, I don't remember listening to much music.

In the end, only two of us were actually turned into zombies—me and this seventeen-year-old from St. Louis named Annie—but I'm pretty certain that wasn't the game plan. I think Pollywog wanted us all undead, but for some reason, the other girls never got reanimated. We never got an explanation, because when we woke up in a back alley in Taos, New Mexico, the Reverend was long gone. We pieced it together as best we could and decided that Pollywog had gotten a lousy batch of acid that had killed everybody so quickly, he had time to zombify only the two of us. I was happy to not be six feet under, but on the minus side, zombies weren't welcome in my part of Wisconsin, so I haven't seen my family since.

*

John Robert Parker Ravenscroft—aka, John Peel—was one of the UK's most in the know disc jockeys, always presenting the hottest and hippest tunes on his radio show, always seen at the hottest and hippest musical gatherings throughout London. On June 25, 1967, Peel wasn't yet an employee of the British Broadcasting Corporation, but he managed to sneak into the BBC studios, where the Beatles were scheduled to perform a tune to be shown via satellite to a worldwide audience. (The Beeb, who'd commissioned the number, nixed the first draft of the song, which Lennon had entitled "All You Need Is to Die a Painful Death." It still hasn't been established whether or not John was yanking some Beeb chain.) When I spoke with Peel in June 2004, only four months before his death, he explained that he wasn't the only music-biz luminary in the studio audience that viewed the event The Sun dubbed "the literal and figurative definition of a bloody mess."

JOHN PEEL: The joint was crawling with stars: Eric Clapton, Keith Moon, Marianne Faithfull, Graham Nash, the works. I was so uncool that I wanted to run around and get autographs, but I was cool enough to not actually do it.

Some of the lot were perched in their seats, while some were on the floor, when the director gave the go-ahead. But before John could even get through the first verse, who bursts through the door and jumps right into the fray, lips a'kissin' and hips a'wigglin'? That's right, kids, everybody's favorite zombie hunter.

Mick Jagger strode right up to John, raised his arms to the sky, and said, "O zombie Lennon! It ends here. In full view of a worldwide audience, you shall taste death."

John said, "You're right, Mick. It ends here." And then he ripped off his headphones. And then the madness began.

If I hadn't seen the videotape in slow-mo, I wouldn't have believed it went down the way it did. It was one of those things so utterly inhuman and *wrong* that my mind couldn't even process it. What happened was, John ripped Paul's bass from his hands and pulled off the neck—it was a shiny new Rickenbacker, which is probably why Paul got so pissed—then gnawed the end with his teeth until it was as sharp as a knife. He then lifted it above his head and brought it down through Mick's right shoulder. Mick's arm detached and flew across the studio and fell right at Eric Clapton's feet, staining his nice hippie-dippy outfit bright red, and let me tell you, Slowhand wasn't pleased. John grabbed Mick by the back of his neck, then wrapped his entire mouth around Jagger's gaping arm wound; his cheeks puffed in and out for a bit, then Mick collapsed on his arse. From where I was sitting, Jagger looked deader than the Big Bopper.

John yelled at Eric, "Oi, Clappy, toss that arm over."

Clapton yelled back, "Are you a fookin' nutter, mate? I'm not touching this thing!" He then kicked Mick's arm—which flew smack into the side of Marianne Faithfull's noggin—then stood up, and sprinted out the door.

Marianne shook her head and said, "What a pussy," then, as John requested, she tossed Mick's arm across the room. I should note it was a perfect throw. That Marianne was a keeper.

John caught it neatly with one hand, then said to McCartney, "A little help, Paulie?"

Paul, who was staring at the remnants of his bass and practically weeping, said, "Not today, John."

John gave Paul a disgusted look, then asked George, "How about you? Are you on board?"

George sighed, and said, "I suppose so," then he walked over to Mick's fallen body, made a fist, stuck his hand into the open stump, and lifted Jagger over his head. He didn't seem too happy about it, truthfully, but he managed to walk Mick over to John.

And then came another moment that my mind couldn't quite process: John took Mick's body from George, licked both Mick's arm and stump, then jammed the whole mess back together. Almost immediately, Mick's eyes popped open and, with the biggest smile on his face, he said, "Holy fook! Undead is life! Why didn't you tell me, John? Why didn't you say something?"

John wiped the blood from his lips and said, "Would you have listened?"

Mick said, "Probably not, probably not." He looked around the room, then asked, "So, erm, where does a guy procure some brains around here? That's what you zombies do, right? Procure brains?"

John said, "It's not *you* zombies, Mick. It's *us* zombies. *Us* zombies. You are we, and we are us, and we are all together."

They gave each other a long hug, and if John's mouth hadn't been covered with drying blood and dead skin, and if Mick hadn't been turning gray before my very eyes, it would've been a terribly touching moment.

＊

GEORGE HARRISON: After the BBC fiasco, I needed to get out of the country for a while. The Mania of touring was no longer a problem, but the Mania of living in London with John, Paul, and Ringo was becoming more maniacal than ever, so I shoved off to San Francisco. Why San Fran? Well, it was apparently the place to be if you wanted to experience the Summer of Love. Also, I'd heard that San Francisco was the acid epicenter of the United States. I didn't particularly enjoy my experiences with the dreaded lysergic, but it's possible that Eppy didn't do a good job of mixing the stuff and I was missing out on the real thing. So, as the song says, California, here I come.

I was surprised at how many zombies were wandering around the city—why zombies would migrate to San Francisco, I have no clue—and I was also surprised at how badly they cared for themselves. As a lot, the undead are nasty to begin with—our scent is horrific, and you can't even imagine what it's like to live with these insurmountable skin problems—but we're very meticulous about our personal hygiene, because if we don't properly groom ourselves, we'd be shunned even more than we already are, and that's saying something.

Those Bay Area zombies, however, were disgusting. They lived on the streets, and the moist San Francisco climate exacerbated their odor and skin issues. Their clothes were tattered and torn, the kind of clichéd gear you'd see in one of those Hammer Productions movies that John and Paul were always going on about. Worst of all, most of them were missing a limb and/or some digits and didn't seem concerned about replacing them.

Now, I dunno if this all meant that the acid was really bloody good or really bloody bad, so I didn't want to take any chances. On the other hand, I couldn't leave San Francisco without trying *some* drug, so my second day in town I smoked some terrific weed, farted a few impressive rainbow clouds, then called it a day.

I had an open-ended airline ticket, so I could go back to London whenever I wanted, but if I'd returned after only three days, I'd have looked like a prat. So I went to Oakland in search of the Hell's Angels.

●

Every morning when I wake up, I thank whatever force is in charge of the universe that when the late Hunter S. Thompson was trashed, his *gun-aiming skills went right into the crapper. You see, when I set foot on his land in Woody Creek, Colorado, in September 2004, Thompson took four potshots at me before I was anywhere near the house.*

But it was important I speak with the Gonzo guru, so while he was reloading his Remington, I waved an issue of ESPN The Magazine *in the air as if it were a white flag, and said, "I contribute to this! You contribute to this! We're practically related!" Always a contradictory sort, Hunter told me to fuck off, then invited me in.*

Thompson's 1966 book Hell's Angels: The Strange and Terrible Saga of the Outlaw Motorcycle Gang *was a groundbreaking piece of you-are-there journalism that almost got him killed by the hair-trigger bikers, and it was believed that after the book was published, Thompson became persona non grata among the Angels. Not true. Hunter had made nice-nice with a number of high-ranking gang members, and up until he ran for sheriff of Colorado's Pitkin County in 1970, he had his finger on the pulse of all that was Angel.*

Thompson wasn't in Oakland when George Harrison and Angels godhead Sonny Barger had their little summit meeting, but Thompson's sources were impeccable, and as he was one of the great journalists of his era—even when he was whacked out of his gourd on some substance or another—one can take his depiction of the Harrison/Barger get-together as fact.

HUNTER S. THOMPSON: Yeah, yeah, I know George Harrison has the strength of ten mules, but he was a fucking idiot to go meet Barger without any backup. Sure, he could've taken that fucker Sonny one-on-one, but Sonny was hardly ever alone, and I think even a hard-strapped zombie would have trouble against fifteen or twenty of those Angel motherfuckers.

There weren't too many Angels who gave a rat's ass about the Beatles, so when Harrison showed up at their clubhouse, unan-

nounced and un-goddamn-invited, it could've been a clusterfuck. The Angels could've opened fire on Harrison or gone after him with tire irons before he even said hello. But before they started pounding on him, one of those assholes recognized him and put the kibosh on the beat-down. Beating up a Beatle would've been horrible PR, and no matter what they say, those bastards care about how they're viewed by the public.

Barger was always a bit of a star-fucker, so he was all into meeting Harrison. My inside man didn't get close enough to their conversation to find out what they specifically discussed, but from what I know about Sonny, and from what I've read about Harrison, my guess is that it was some disjointed fucking discourse.

After they were done chatting, Barger, Harrison, and my inside man went in search of some good shit. See, apparently Harrison told Sonny that the LSD in San Francisco sucked, and Sonny insisted they could track down some good shit in Oak-town, and that was indeed the case. Except that shit was *too* good, and the only reason Harrison made it back to merry old fucking England with his faculties more or less intact was because my inside man didn't take a tab, and protected them from reality during their trip. Had they all gotten high, there's a good chance all three of those motherfuckers would've ended up at the bottom of the San Francisco Bay.

Those wasted morons wandered around the city for over forty-eight hours, but it would've been a lot less if Harrison's nose hadn't have fallen off in fucking East Oakland. I still can't believe they found that thing. If it happened today, no way he would've gotten it back. East Oakland's a shithole, and those people need bread *badly*. Imagine how much George Harrison's schnozz would go for on eBay.

They brought Harrison back to the clubhouse, and, since Barger was Barger and the Angels were the Angels, they got into a fight, and it turned out that three dozen Hell's Angels couldn't take down a lone Beatle zombie. My inside man was a smart dude, so he got the fuck out of there when the melee got bad. He found out the next day that five Angels were killed, and every single one of those motherfuckers in the place got hurt . . . except for Harrison. The moral of the story is, don't get into the shit with the undead unless you've got a fucking werewolf in your crew—and everybody knows that werewolves don't exist.

GEORGE HARRISON: Almost permanently losing my nose was a wake-up call, so after Oakland, I was done with acid, but I needed something to fill the ever-increasing void in my soul. Music wasn't getting me excited, nor was murder, so I went on a search that'll last me the rest of my undeath. My first discovery: the Maharishi.

RINGO STARR: George hipped us to this bloke called Maharishi Mahesh Yogi, who apparently had the ability to get us in touch with our inner something-or-other through meditation . . . and my inner something-or-other was in serious need of touching.

I didn't think 忍の者乱破 or the High Ninja Council would approve of me studying with Maharishi—those Ninjas are very proprietary about spirituality—but they'd denied me an opportunity to reach Level Eight, so, you know, sod 'em.

PAUL McCARTNEY: If Ringo and George were doing it, *I* was doing it.

JOHN LENNON: If Ringo, George, and Paul were doing it, *I* was doing it.

GEORGE HARRISON: One of the great things about being a Liverpool zombie is that we can remove our brains and give them a good cleanse. Some cold water, a drop or two of dish soap, and a quick pat dry with a towel, and voila, your synapses are firing better than ever. But it is a tricky process, and you don't want to do it all that often, because why take chances? What if your brain slips out of your hand and falls onto the floor? Who's to say your Alsatian won't wander over and take a nibble?

That all being the case, the fact that we were able to find a way of cleaning our brains without actually physically cleaning our brains was nothing short of a revelation.

We went up to Wales for a few days, and Maharishi taught us about Transcendental Meditation and gave us each a mantra, and it *worked*. Within hours, I was more relaxed than I'd been since elementary school. The fact that some pink gunk began leaking from my nose when I reached a higher consciousness didn't even bother me.

JOHN LENNON: After only two hours with Maha, the sky looked bluer, the grass looked greener, the sun and stars shone brighter, and the brains tasted better.

And I didn't like it one fookin' bit.

PAUL McCARTNEY: I was in my hotel room, sitting on my bed, reciting my mantra, contemplating the universe, and, erm, mentally running some sales figures, when John pulled my door off its hinges. Without so much as a hello, he said, "The Maharishi must die."

JOHN LENNON: If I was relaxed, how was I supposed to maintain my artistic edge? If I was in a positive headspace, how could I defend myself and my band against attacks? If I was at one with the universe, chowing down on a living brain would be practically impossible, zombie nature or no zombie nature. I couldn't take a chance that I'd get led to a happy place, so I couldn't take a chance that the Maharishi continue to walk the Earth.

PAUL McCARTNEY: I told John, "If you're concerned about him walking the Earth, you don't need to kill him; all you need to do is cut off his legs, y'know."

He said, "Paulie, you're a genius. But just to play it safe, I'm gonna cut off his arms, too."

JOHN LENNON: I went to his hotel room and told him, "Maha, your teachings are genius. Never in my life have I felt so at peace. The wisdom you exude is an inspiration. But you're ruining my groove, so you have to suffer, and suffer badly."

The entire process took about ten minutes, and he never felt a thing, and he couldn't have been more gracious. He even thanked me when it was done. Let me go on record as saying that Maharishi Mahesh Yogi was the kindest, most gentle person I'd ever had the honor of fully dismembering.

Without limbs, Maha's authoritative presence wasn't nearly as compelling—one of his minions had to haul him around in a wicker container, and it's hard to take a guru too seriously when he has to travel in a picnic basket—so I was able to unrelax. Without arms and legs, Maha was much more fun to be around, and we probably would've stayed a few more days if Eppy hadn't topped himself.

And losing Eppy, man, that broke my unbeating heart.

BRIAN EPSTEIN: Like I told you, I died, and I wanted to stay dead, and now, thanks to John Lennon, I'm undead. Take that as you will.

*B*ack in early 1966, Lennon was recruited by the band's favorite director, Richard Lester, to take on a co-starring role in the satirical military flick, How I Won the War. *For the second time in his otherwise
Beatle-worshipping career,* Liverpool Herald *arts critic Irvine Paris
pulled out his Howitzer and took some potshots at Beatle John's performance in a review that was released three days before the film's of-
ficial November 8th London premiere.*

HOW I HAD A SNORE
Smart Beatle Misfires in Stupid War Film
By Irvine Paris

November 5, 1967

Director Richard Lester's *How I Won the War* is the first
collaboration between Lester and John Lennon since the
Beatles' 1965 almost classic *Help!*, and the twosome should
have packed it in after that impressive romp. In this new se-
rio-comedy, Lennon—who is inexplicably wearing a pair of
round glasses that no self-respecting undead man should
be seen alive in—plays the role of one Musketeer Gripweed,
a zombie on a mission to take over first his own unit, then
the entire British Army, then the whole world. In other
words, Lennon played an exaggerated version of himself.
Unfortunately, he did not play it well.

The movie has myriad problems, but the worst offence is
that there is no plot to speak of. Time and again, conversa-
tional scenes alternate with fight scenes, until the credits
roll. A typical transition has Lennon chatting amiably

(albeit stupidly) with the film's leading man Michael Crawford about the lack of zombies in the military, then, two minutes later, Lennon is tossing Crawford across a field, twenty meters in the air. Admittedly, when Lennon flings Crawford—and when he similarly tortures fellow costars Lee Montague and Roy Kinnear—it looks painfully true to life, especially the disconcerting moment when Montague's shoulder seems to pop out of its socket. But quality stunts and realistic special effects doth not a quality film make.

Attempting to break that theoretical fourth wall, Lester often has Lennon speaking directly to the audience. The technique is legitimate, certainly, but when Lennon tells the camera that, "Zombies eat brains while riding trains in the rain, and they never leave stains, merely much pain," and, "Bombs kill people, but nothing kills me. You'll be dead, and alive I'll be," one can imagine poor Luigi Pirandello spinning in his grave and thanking his lucky stars he will never be reanimated to see this drivel in a theater.

Lester uses Lennon's/Gripweed's undeadness as a clumsy metaphor for the pointlessness of war—a fair conceit, granted—but both gentlemen depict the numerous zombie attacks in such a ham-fisted manner that one wishes for a *deus ex machina* moment (for instance, a hail of well-aimed diamond bullets shot from behind enemy lines) to put an end to this dreary picture.

NEIL ASPINALL: That *Herald* review threw John for a loop. He stayed with me at my flat for the two days leading up to the premiere, and all he did was moan, "They're gonna kill me. They're gonna kill me. They're gonna kill me." I wasn't sure whether he meant the critics,

the general public, or some cheesed-off undead bastards. I dunno if *he* knew who he meant, either.

GEORGE HARRISON: John forbade any of us from attending the premiere. After what that bloke in the *Herald* said, I was fine with that. If John got too upset, he'd go on a rampage, and if he went on a rampage, I'd get sucked into it, and frankly, I wasn't in the mood.

RINGO STARR: Irvine Paris was a pretty sharp guy, and if he said something was shit, it was probably shit. Now I don't know if Richard Lester made any changes to the film between the day the *Herald* article hit the street and the night of the premiere, but the reviews that were published the next day were a helluva lot more generous.

PAUL McCARTNEY: When the *Herald* ran that goofy retraction, my first thought was, *Irvine Paris must have found himself the best blotter in Liverpool, because the cut of the film I saw last week was awful.* My second thought was, *Lester must have reedited the movie in record time.* My third thought was, *Wait a sec, I thought Johnny said he'd never hypnotize anybody into liking him.*

HOW I WON THE WAR *IS HELL, NO MORE!*
Genius, Thy Names Are Lennon and Lester
By Irvine Paris

November 9, 1967

One of the most wonderful things about my job is that my editors give me the opportunity to right any of my wrongs, and right here, right now, I would like to right the wrongest wrong of my career. After I finish typing this article, I will climb to the top of Scafell Pike and scream to the heavens above, *"HOW I WON THE WAR IS BLOODY BRILLIANT!!!"* The characterizations are wrenchingly realistic, the dialogue is snappy, and the cinematography is beyond lovely. It makes for a magical filmgoing experience, and I can honestly say that a better movie has not been released this decade . . . or possibly ever.

I still do not know where my mind was on November 5. For that less-than-flattering, off-base article, I offer heartfelt, sincere apologies to Richard Lester, United Artists, and especially the genius that is John Winston Lennon.

JOHN LENNON: I would never, ever, *ever* use my zombie powers to influence a writer's opinion of me. And for any of you reading this fookin' book who ever questioned those good reviews of *Life with the Lions*, you can fook right the hell off.

✳

S*howbiz hyphenate Steven Spielberg is best known for such family fare as* E.T. *and* Raiders of the Lost Ark, *and yet he claims the 1967 UK television film* Magical Mystery Tour *to be an indelible influence on his own art. Today's film experts probably find Spielberg's stance odd, because immediately after its release, this patently nonfamily movie became a punching bag for critics throughout England.*

It took me five-plus years and a whole lot of palm grease to get an audience with Spielberg, but when I sat down with him in September

2009, he explained why he had such affection for this universally re-viled piece of celluloid.

STEVEN SPIELBERG: What happened was, the best *Magical Mystery Tour* stuff never made it onto the screen. If I could get Lennon, Mc-Cartney, Harrison, and Starr to sit down and put together a full-length director's cut, you'd understand why I find this film so brilliant. But when I purchased the hours and hours of unused foot-age from Paul back in 1976—right after I got my first *Jaws* royalty check—I signed an agreement barring me from releasing any of the material. However, the agreement didn't say anything about dis-cussing the movie, so here goes:

The original movie's structure—which was based around an un-scripted bus ride—was flimsy at best, and the extra footage, while interesting and well-shot, wouldn't have made the plot any clearer, but there was a whole lot of action that would've lifted *MMT* close to classic status. The most memorable material involved a surprise visit from Rod Argent. Rod, who was apparently still upset about the Beatles allegedly ruining the Zombies' careers, bum-rushed the set on day three, and to my eternal happiness, Lennon, McCartney, et al. kept the cameras rolling.

Word is that Argent had been in training for that very moment since the Beatles beat him up in Chicago back in '64, and he must've been training well, because he looked like a defensive lineman: muscles on top of muscles; head attached directly to his shoulders; walking like his quadriceps were overdeveloped to the nth degree; sweating like a pig; ready for a fight.

You could tell by the way he looked around the set that he hadn't come with a specific game plan. He went after Starr first, probably because Starr was the first Beatle he laid eyes on. The only reason he was able to do any damage is that he snuck up on Ringo; had Ringo seen him coming, the battle probably would've been over before it started. But Argent got in a couple of good shots with a rock to the back of Ringo's neck—nothing major, just enough to draw a few drops of blood. By the time Ringo turned around to respond, Argent was gone; Rod somehow out-Ninja'd the Ninja.

Seconds later, Argent reappeared behind Harrison, and, before George even knew what was happening, Argent ripped George's right arm off, then threw it on top of the bus. Even though it lasted only a few seconds, that single moment was more graphic than the whole twenty-minute section of *Saving Private Ryan* when the troops storm the beach at Normandy.

At this point, Lennon and McCartney became aware of what was going on, so they took off after Argent. Argent was fast, though, and for a few hundred meters, he outpaced the zombies. But he ran out of gas, and that's where the fun began.

Lennon grabbed Argent by his long hair and tossed him toward the sky. The sun was shining brightly, and the camera wasn't equipped to handle that sort of explosion of brightness, so it was impossible to see how high Argent went, but since he splatted onto the ground a full forty-five seconds later, you can assume that Lennon got some good lift.

By now, Harrison had retrieved his right arm from the top of the bus, and you could tell he was pissed off. Using his left hand, he balled up the right fist, then hurled the arm at Argent like it was a javelin. If I may be permitted to make a horrible pun, it pounded Rod right in the rod. All the fight went out of Mr. Argent. But not Mr. McCartney.

Paul picked up Argent like he was a sack of feathers, then threw him back up in the air, probably even higher than Lennon had. Harrison zipped on over and caught Argent before he splatted again, then he contorted the poor man into a pretzel.

And then George said to Paul, "This guy is a bloody cunt, but I kind of dig his band. Maybe we should show some mercy."

Paul said, "Yeah, that cover of 'Goin' Out of My Head' they did is solid, y'know. Should we, y'know, do the do?"

Ringo said, "It *would* be a nice thing. Positive karma, and all that."

John said, "I vote yes. What one of you geezers wants to go for it?"

George said, "It was my idea, I suppose, so I'll take the reins. Ringo, can you please finish off Rod so I can have access to his brain?"

Ringo said, "It'll be my pleasure." And then he punched Argent in the heart, and that was it.

George seemed to take great pleasure in transforming Argent—it came off on film as a celebration, albeit in a weird zombie kind of way—but there's no way they could've put that particular moment in the final cut, as it was to be shown on BBC, rather than in theaters. It made an impression on me, though; that scene informed a number of the rougher set pieces in *Poltergeist* and, believe it or not, *Schindler's List*.

It's probably best I don't discuss the remainder of the footage, which could be best summarized in two words: snuff film.

•

PAUL McCARTNEY: All four of us were in a horrible state after *Magical Mystery Tour* went belly-up. Ringo and George found their own ways to amuse themselves, which was lovely for them, but John and I needed something to occupy our minds, because had we become idle, bad things could've happened, y'know. Very bad things. Unspeakable things. So, erm, I shan't speak of them.

There were days at the end of 1967 when John and I couldn't be in the same room—we'd been together almost every day for ten years, and his scent was nauseating me more and more each week, and I'm sure my stink was getting to him too. George was off experimenting with more weirdo guitars; he'd developed something called a Hair-ison, which was a mandolin strung with strings fashioned from the pubic hair of his female victims. Nobody knew where the fook Ringo was, and it was a mess. With Eppy gone, the Beatles were like a barely functioning airplane flying over the Bermuda Triangle. One harsh gust of wind, and we would be done.

CHAPTER SEVEN

1968

GEORGE HARRISON: I planned a trip to India to get a few Transcendental Meditation lessons with Maharishi. I invited the guys—I thought they'd benefit from it, plus it might keep us from becoming more splintered—but John didn't want to go, because he was still on that "I'm afraid of losing my edge" kick. I insisted it would be impossible for any zombie to lose his edge, especially one as grouchy as he was. He yanked off my arm and beat me with it for about five minutes, then the lightbulb clicked on, and he said, "Oh. Hunh. You may have a point there, mate."

I said, "I *know* I have a point. Besides, after what you did to Maharishi in Wales, he'll probably tweak your lesson plan however you want it tweaked. I mean, the only extremities of his you didn't tear off were his head and his plonker, and I think he's gonna want those, so if you say 'Jump,' he'll say, 'How high?'"

John mumbled, "Something tells me that legless git won't want to discuss jumping."

JOHN LENNON: Maha wasn't the kind of cat who'd get an artificial limb—he'd rather display his wounds so everybody'd know he was at one with himself, or whatever—so when we pulled into his compound in Rishikesh, they had to wheel him over in this sharp little wagonlike thing, covered with diamonds and jewels, and being pushed by three of the most gorgeous women I'd ever seen. I elbowed George and said, "That's enough to make you wanna rip off your own limbs and chuck 'em in the garbage, eh?"

He rolled his eyes at me, then told Maha, "Thank you for welcoming us to your home. As a small token of my appreciation, I'd like to play you a song I've written especially for the occasion." And then he pulled out that fookin' skintar, and those gorgeous birds ran off to the hills, screaming like banshees.

Maha, who suddenly looked a little green himself, smiled and said, "That's okay, my son. A tune is not necessary, as the songs of nature fill my soul. Besides, your positive vibes are powerful, very powerful, and that is enough for me." Then, in a dead-on Liverpool accent, said, "Now put that smelly fookin' piece of music-making machinery back into its case before I toss me curry."

Don't let anybody tell you that old Maha didn't have a sense of humor.

RINGO STARR: Paul and I got to Rishikesh a few days after John and George, and by the time we showed up, the two of them were already bored to tears. When we got to the compound, they were off under some tree, way away from the action, playing strip poker. They'd obviously been playing for a while, because they were both not only naked but also legless.

John looked up at Paul and said, "Macca, it's so fookin' dull here that I'm even glad to see you."

Paul said, "Cheers, mate. But if you're so bored, why don't you do something productive?"

John said, "Like what?"

Paul said, "Oh, gosh, erm, I dunno, maybe write some songs or something."

George said, "Not a bad suggestion. But I have a better idea."

JOHN LENNON: The irony is that I was always the guy who came up with those sorts of schemes. I never thought George had it in him.

RINGO STARR: George was the most spiritual zombie I'd ever met, but when he laid his plan out for us, I realized there was a limit to a zombie's spirituality.

PAUL McCARTNEY: On one hand, I thought George's idea was a horrible one that'd lead to bad press and bad juju, an' that. But on the other hand, I was really, really hungry, y'know.

GEORGE HARRISON: That American actress Mia Farrow was at the compound with us, as was her sister Prudence. Mia was a good egg and participated in all the activities and ate all of Maharishi's shite food with us. Hell, she even joined us for a round of strip poker. Prudence, on the other hand, was always up in her room with the door locked, doing who knows what. So my idea was, let's eat Prudence. But not just her brain: *everything*. Skin, bones, organs, muscles, eyeballs, the entire shebang.

Ringo said, "The brains I can understand, by why the whole thing?"

I said, "Because we can. Plus she's a pill, and nobody'd miss her anyhow."

JOHN LENNON: Right at that moment, right when he suggested we make a meal out of dear Prudence, I couldn't have been prouder of George Harold Harrison. My little boy had finally become a man.

PAUL McCARTNEY: We decided to sneak into Prudence's room in the dark of night, but truthfully, everybody at the compound was so wrapped up in their own heads that we could've wandered in there at high noon carrying signs that said PRUDENCE FARROW IS ABOUT TO BECOME OUR LUNCH, and nobody would've blinked an eye.

GEORGE HARRISON: I hypnotized her first, so she never felt a thing. Just because she was an antisocial bore didn't mean she deserved to die a painful death.

JOHN LENNON: It wasn't a big to-do. We butchered her, then called it a day. We were quite tidy about it, and we didn't leave a single drop of blood or gristle in her room; after all, eating a fellow TM student isn't the way a good TM houseguest should act, so the least we could do was be neat about it.

Our picnic was very civil. I got the drumsticks, George got the thighs and the wings, Paulie got the breasts.

PAUL McCARTNEY: What can I tell you? I'm a tit man, y'know. Plus I've always been partial to white meat.

RINGO STARR: It took everybody a full two days to realize that Prudence was even missing, and another two days for any of the Maharishi's people to question us about it. Actually, they didn't question *us* about it—they questioned *me*. And I ratted the lads out.

JOHN LENNON: Yeah, Ringo went all Guy Fawkes on us, and they chucked the lot of us, but that was fine with me, because I was ready to get the fook out of there. That peace shit was getting on me last nerves.

The next day, we get to the Nagpur Airport, and guess which wally shows up out of nowhere?

ROD ARGENT: I was still on the fence about my newfound zombie life. The powers were nice and all, but did they make up for my horrible scent, or the fact that my family and girlfriend shunned me? Yes and no. Eternity on Earth seemed like it would have its advantages, but it would've been nice to get a hug from my loved ones, you know? I think all mortals who become undead later in life have to deal with this sort of internal conflict.

The main thing that cheesed me off was that I wasn't given any choice in the matter. It would've been nice had Ringo or Paul said, "Oi, Roddy, I know you've been trying to mess us up for the last five or six years, but as proven by your dreadful showing while we were shooting *Magical Mystery Tour,* no matter how much you train, no matter how many muscles you develop, and no matter how fast you might get, you don't have a shot. So what say we zombify you and turn it into a fairer fight? You still won't be able to take us because we outnumber you—plus we have a Ninja in the fold—but maybe, just maybe, if you score a point or two off of us, like maybe if you briefly remove John's arm or throw George off a cliff, you'll feel better about the whole thing."

I probably would've told them no, then thrown in the towel and concentrated on my music. I mean, there're only so many times you can get your face bashed in before you realize it's time to call it quits. But they didn't ask. They just did it. Thus, the battle continued.

The press covered the Beatles' every move, so they were easy enough to track down in India. I thought that going after them in an unfamiliar airport would be something of an equalizer. Like launching an attack at, say, Abbey Road Studios would've been suicide . . . not that I could've actually died, but you get the point. Also, I wanted as many journos to capture it as possible; a few good newspaper articles would've boosted the Zombies' record sales, and we needed all the help we could get.

They were flying a private plane, naturally, and they probably thought that taking their own aircraft would keep them safe. Little did they know that ol' Roddy Argent was waiting for them on the tarmac.

PAUL McCARTNEY: Argent looked pissed, and he had zombie powers now, and I was still feeling logy from having eaten Prudence Farrow's sweet bristols, y'know, and I didn't want any part of him, so after Rod issued his challenge, I flipped him the bird and got on the plane.

RINGO STARR: I missed London like you wouldn't believe, and I wanted to get home as fast as possible. Besides, I'd eaten nothing but Heinz baked beans for the last two weeks—no way I was touching that Indian shite—and I wasn't in any shape to fight Rod. So I flipped him the bird and got on the plane.

GEORGE HARRISON: I was hauling seven instruments: my skintar; my Hair-ison; my double-reeded plonker-phone; my toe-monica; my hi-head-hat; my nose flute; and my jaw harp. These were all delicate pieces, and I had zero urge to get involved with some pointless Mania with Rod Argent, so I gently put down everything I was holding, flipped him the double bird, and got on the plane.

JOHN LENNON: Rod looked heartbroken when we didn't accept his invitation to battle, so I walked over to him and said, "Listen, mate, we dig why you've always been upset with us. If four giant beetles started a band and sold a bunch of records based on a tenuous connection with us, I might get upset, too. But just because we're zombies doesn't mean you can't be a Zombie. Besides, you're a zombie now anyhow, so you might as well roll with it. We all wish you the best of luck, and you should probably know that if we ever see your face again, we're going to rip it off and throw it into the Atlantic Ocean." Then I reached into my pocket and pulled out a few thousand rupees, handed them over, and said, "Go buy yourself a first-class ticket home, mate. You've worked hard trying to kill us, and you deserve something special."

And then I flipped him the bird and got on the plane.

ROD ARGENT: All the fight went out of me. I went back to the terminal, bought my first-class seat, and never saw the Beatles again.

*

PAUL McCARTNEY: We'd been discussing starting up our own record label for a while, but we got serious when we got back from India. John wanted to call it Maggot Music, but that was summarily voted down. By me.

JOHN LENNON: To us, the music industry didn't work. A band would get a record deal; then, unless they immediately hit the charts, they'd become persona non grata. There was no nurturing. No vision. No love. And no monsters.

PAUL McCARTNEY: Outside of the Grateful Dead, we were the only successful rock band that had a zombie, y'know. There were plenty of jazz monsters around—Miles Davis is a vampire, of course; and Thelonious Monk is an unclassifiable deity, kind of like our old friend Roy Orbison, I suppose—and the classical world was littered with swamp things, but in rock 'n' roll, *nothing*. So we decided that our new baby, Apple Records, would have a roster consisting entirely of otherworldly beings. (George came up with Apple, because it reminded him of the satisfying crunch of a fresh skull. Good one, Georgie.) Thing is, it's not easy to find monster musicians in Europe, as England isn't loaded with clubs that offer open-mic nights for so-called creatures, so we had to put the word out all by ourselves. And that meant hitting the streets. And the sewers.

JOHN LENNON: Neil and I designed these leaflets alerting the monster world that we were accepting demos from non-mortals of all shapes and sizes. We hung the posters all over London, and got only one single demo from one single band, and we didn't consider signing them, because, well, let's just say that "Something Fishy's Going On" by the Raspberry Blueberry Booger Boogie Beat Extraction featuring Willie the Hydra wasn't exactly a toe-tapper. We found out quickly that the chance of finding a solid, well-oiled all-monster band was unlikely, as your typical moleman doesn't have the means to buy a decent guitar or rent a decent rehearsal studio.

So we ripped down the old notices and replaced them with new posters announcing a one-day-only audition. Be you monster, human, man, woman, or child, if you were good, you'd get signed. But if you were bad, you'd get killed.

PAUL McCARTNEY: John talked a good game but didn't follow through. We didn't kill anybody at the audition, although John took a couple of token swipes at an American bloke named James Taylor, who hightailed it right on back to Heathrow, y'know. Once we abandoned the monster idea, we gave the label a rest. That left us with a lot of time on our hands, y'know, so John and I put our heads together and came up with what seemed like a damn good idea.

By the late-sixties, zombies were accepted in most parts of society, but that didn't mean we were catered to—like, good luck finding an undead restaurant. So John and I decided we should give something back to our zombie brethren.

One way that zombies are like regular people is that they have three basic necessities: food, clothing, and shelter. As long as there are living beings with working brains walking the Earth, the food portion of the program is covered. Shelter is generally easy enough to find: if there aren't any available flats and all the zombie hotels are full, there are always the sewers. Clothing, however, is another matter altogether. Unless you have a tailor who knows what he's doing, your tattered rags will always look like tattered rags . . . and smell like them, too. So we decided that in conjunction with our new label, we'd open up a store that sold gear specifically tailored for the undead.

JOHN LENNON: Up until we launched our little clothing establishment at the end of '67, the words *zombie* and *fashion* were rarely heard in the same sentence.

PAUL McCARTNEY: We named it Apple Boutique, and as far as I was concerned, it was the cat's pajamas. We offered a vast array of clothes for the stylish zombie, everything from tattered rainbow slacks to tattered silk shirts to tattered feathered hats to tattered blue jeans to tattered checkered sport coats to tattered ladies' unmentionables. And everything but *every*thing was lined with a laboratory-developed anti-stink shield. If you were a zombie, you could come by the Boutique and leave looking good and smelling good. Okay, you wouldn't smell *good,* but you'd at least smell *better,* y'know. I mean, there's only so much twenty-three Nobel Prize–winning scientists can do.

JOHN LENNON: Our first week in business was brilliant. Every zombie who was anybody came by and dropped fifty, one hundred, even two hundred quid on the slickest rags they'd ever owned. But after that, despite the multicolored mutilation mural on the side of the building that was supposed to hypnotize everybody into dropping their paycheck at the Boutique, the shop died. Practically each day for six months, Paul and I stood in front of the building and all but begged people to come in. Didn't work. They hated our clothes, they hated the *Mystery Tour* movie, and it felt like they hated us.

The two biggest problems were that zombies didn't have any money, so they couldn't buy anything; and living beings couldn't wear zombie gear without breaking out in oozing acne, so they *wouldn't* buy anything.

PAUL McCARTNEY: We didn't think any of this stuff through. We weren't good filmmakers. We weren't good businessmen. We weren't good clothing gurus. The only two things the Beatles could do successfully were make music and transform living beings into hideous-looking, odiferous creatures that most humans couldn't stomach. I think we were all looking for some change. But some of us questioned the changes because, erm, they were questionable.

●

JOHN LENNON: I met Yoko Ono back in '66, at the Indica Gallery. She was presenting this exhibit called *Undead Death March . . .*

April . . . May . . . June, and in retrospect, I think that was meant specifically to get my attention.

I didn't go in with any expectations. Yoko was an artist, and I like art. If her art was exciting, great, I'd hang out for hours. If it was dull, I could go over to Paul's place and throw his Aston Martin into his living room.

Turned out it was exciting.

There were about five dozen tiny photographs of her in various states of undress all throughout the gallery. For example, in some, her face was covered with a hood, while in others, she had a rope of machine gun bullets wrapped around her waist. The only commonality was that in each shot, she was holding a sword. And that sword looked awfully familiar, like something Ringo might mess about with.

I wandered over and introduced myself. She pointed at her mouth and shook her head. I said, "So what's this, then? You're not talking?"

She said, "Nope." Then she got a stricken look on her face, pulled a Ninja star from her pocket, and poked a tiny hole in her forearm; there were already about fifteen or twenty wounds there. After she wiped up the dot of blood, she again pointed at her mouth and shook her head.

I said, "The sword that's in the photos. Can you tell me about it?"

Yoko said, "Well, John, it comes from . . ." Again, she covered her mouth, and again, she stabbed herself in the arm. There was a bit more blood this time, and I was impressed. Any bird who could tolerate that kind of pain—especially if it was self-inflicted—was okay with me.

She then grabbed a pad of paper and wrote that the weapon was her Ninja sword, and she was an Ninth Level Ninja Lord, but she was concerned that the Great High Ninja Poobahs would disown her for utilizing it for art's sake, because Ninjas are never supposed to utilize their weapons for anything other than defense. Thirty-seven pages later, she finally stopped writing, and I was entranced. She had stamina, she enjoyed being photographed in the buff, she knew her way around a piece of equipment that could neatly sever somebody's head, and she was a Ninja, just like Ringo. I thought, *That's the kind of girl the other blokes'll love to have hanging around with us at the recording studio.*

It was a good two years before Yoko and I finally did the do, and it was worth the wait, because that girl knew how to plunk a plonker. Our first night together was endless, and after twelve hours worth of messing about with her, I ran down to my basement studio, snatched up my reel-to-reel tape player and a microphone, took it back up to the bedroom, fired it up, and then Yoko and I curled up in bed and laid down what I still consider to be the greatest achievement of my career.

RINGO STARR: The night after John did the do with Yoko—and "did the do" were his words, not mine, thank you very much—he came over to my flat and played me the tape. It was twenty-nine minutes and twenty-seven seconds of John letting loose with a zombie moan, and Yoko harmonizing it with a Ninja yell. No verse. No chorus. No lyrics. Just noise.

John said, "So? D'you like it?"

I said, "Well, it's not exactly 'Day Tripper,' now, is it?"

He said, "I *know*! Isn't that *great*? Let's be honest here, Rings: nobody'll be listening to 'Day fookin' Tripper' even five years from now, but they'll be playing this baby on the radio into the next millennium."

I'd known John at that point for almost six years, and the smile he laid on me was the biggest I'd ever seen plastered on that gray mug of his, so I knew that if I was honest and told him I thought it sounded like the Undead Tabernacle Choir tripping out on Eppy's first batch of acid, it'd break his heart. So I deflected the question with a question, and asked, "What're you gonna do with it?"

He said, "I've got it all figured out. Remember the Robert Whitaker photos those fookers at EMI wouldn't let us use for that album cover?" I nodded, and he continued, "Well, Yoko and I are gonna do something like that—you know, rip off our arms and plonker, and the like—except the big surprise is we'll be naked."

I said, "Wait a minute, rip off *our* arms? Yoko's a zombie?"

He said, "Oh. No. She's not. Didn't think of that."

I said, "Yeah, last time I checked, you remove limbs from a real person, and we're talking either death or zombification. You want to zombify her this quickly? Maybe you should get to know each other a little better."

John ran his hand through his hair, which was practically down to his arse by then, and said, "Cheers, Rings, I see your point. Maybe I'll just have her put her arms behind her back or something."

I said, "John, no matter what she does with her arms, there isn't a single record label in the world who'd touch it."

He gave me that smile again, and said, "Oh, yes there is."

PAUL McCARTNEY: I told John, "A half hour of groaning wrapped with a photo of your shriveled zombie dick resting on top of Yoko's head? There is no way Apple Records will release this. No way, no how, no sir, no, no, no."

JOHN LENNON: Here's an interesting fact that not too many people are aware of: Ninjas who're Ninth Level and above have a way of making zombies feel physical trauma. No idea how they do it, but they do it. And that's something James Paul McCartney became painfully aware of one summer night, after he was paid an unexpected visit by a certain Asian performance artist.

PAUL McCARTNEY: Oh, Yoko hurt me that night, all right. But she never hurt me again.

JOHN LENNON: Oh, she hurt him constantly. *Constantly.*

RINGO STARR: Over the strenuous objections of three-fourths of the Beatles, Apple Records ended up releasing *Two Virgins.* Actually, it wasn't Apple, per se. It was a subsidiary of Apple that John dubbed Crapple. No comment.

Surprise, surprise, the press reception for *Two Virgins* was dreadful. *Mersey Zombie Weekly,* who'd always been one of our biggest boosters, called it, "The aural incarnation of an eight-stone ball of Limburger cheese that'd been rolled through the sewers under the Anfield Cemetery, then eaten, digested, and excreted by a human, then balled up again and eaten, digested, and excreted by a zombie, then cooked in a vat along with a puree made from the seven-week-old maggot-infested carcass of a boar that, for his entire life, had been fed nothing but solidified rabbit farts and brussels sprouts coated with last month's head cheese."

Personally, I thought they were being kind.

PAUL McCARTNEY: They took a beating in the papers, but they weren't fazed a bit, and by the time we had to hit the studio, John and Yoko were attached at the hip.

GEORGE MARTIN: I couldn't figure out exactly what he saw in her. She wasn't the most dynamic girl I'd ever met, and in terms of conversation, she didn't bring much to the table. Admittedly, her ability to crawl on the ceiling was impressive, and she could sure take a punch, but as far as I was concerned, Yoko Ono did not belong anywhere near a recording studio . . . or, at least, one that housed the Beatles.

While she was quiet enough, John was always distracted by her presence. Now, I'm not the kind of person who angers easily, but after six weeks of him spacing out in the middle of a tune, I finally had to speak my mind. One afternoon, after yet another blown take, I pulled him aside and said, "Listen, John, we have a record to finish. Yoko's getting in the way, and you know it. She has to be gone—at least part of the time."

The whites of John's eyes flashed red, and for a second, I thought he was going to do me like they did Mick Jagger and Rod Argent. But then he gave me a sappy smile and said, "I love her, Georgie. She stays."

I said, "But she's destroying the—"

His eyes flashed red again, and he yelled, "I said, *I love her*. I said, *she stays.*" And then he grabbed Yoko by the wrist and stomped off to the Abbey Road basement to sulk.

Paul and I discussed the matter for hours and hours, and we eventually decided the best way to get John to cut the cord—or at least loosen it—wasn't with anger or violence but, rather, sweetness and reason. So one evening, while the lads and I were sitting in the break room eating a late supper, and Yoko was off in the loo, Paul said to John, "Listen, mate, we all know she's your girl, and we all respect that, but even you have to admit she's changing up the vibe here, y'know. When we make records, it's always been just the four of us, and the four of us love one another, and, erm,

having that special sort of love seems to have worked for us, right?"

John said, "Of course. But it never hurts to add a different kind of love to the mix."

Paul cleared his throat and said, "But, erm, if I can be frank, we don't love Yoko . . ."

And then, with a single flick of his index finger, John sent Paul flying through the break-room wall and across the studio, where he landed on and subsequently destroyed yet another guitar amp. John yelled, "You don't get it, mate! You don't *really* understand love!"

Very calmly and coolly, Paul stood up, dusted himself off, and said, "Of course I don't *really* understand love. Neither of us *really* understands love, because neither of us has a beating heart." Then his fuse finally blew and he yelled, "But one thing I *do* bloody understand is how to make a bloody Beatles record, and the only people who should be in the bloody studio when we're making a bloody Beatles record are the bloody Beatles!"

John ran through the hole in the wall, picked up Paul's favorite Rickenbacker bass, and drop-kicked it through the ceiling. Then he tracked down Yoko and they stomped off to the Abbey Road basement to sulk . . . again.

After a few minutes of silence, George said, "Fellows, if we're ever gonna get this record in the can, it seems a new plan is in order." He turned to Ringo and said, "Yoko's a Ninja. You know the Ninja brain. Any thoughts on how to get her out of here?"

Without saying a word, Ringo walked through the hole in the wall, went to the opposite side of the studio, and sat down at his drum kit. He did a neat little snare fill, then he threw his drumsticks into the air; they stuck point-first into the ceiling. He took a long pull of his ale and said very quietly, "The answer is wonderful in its simplicity. I think you gents know where I'm going with this."

Paul said, "I know *exactly* where you're going with this, mate, but how do you propose we make it happen? Trust me on this: the bird can hit, and hit hard."

Ringo polished off his drink and said, "As our Mr. Harrison pointed out, I know the Ninja brain. I know what she's going to do before she does it."

Paul said, "Doesn't that mean *she* knows what *you're* going to do before *you* do it?"

George said, "And she's a level higher than you, right, Rings?"

Ringo said, "Two levels higher, actually."

George said, "*Two* levels? You don't stand a chance."

Ringo said, "Cheers, thanks for the support, mate. We've gotta try something, because what's happening right here and right now ain't working. It's only a matter of time before Johnny starts in with more of that *Two Virgins* shite. Do you want that? Because I sure don't." And then, after a pause, he repeated, "The answer is wonderful in its simplicity."

The three of them took a vote, and it was decided that Paul would go down to the basement and invite Yoko into the recording room for a confab . . . alone, sans John. Turned out that wasn't a problem, because she *wanted* to have a little chin-wag with the boys.

Yoko was in the same outfit she'd been wearing since the recording sessions started: studded leather underwear, studded bra, a black hood, and a pair of swords crisscrossed between her shoulder blades. She unsheathed one of her swords, rubbed her index finger along the blade, and said, "I think I know what you gentlemen wish to discuss. I want to discuss it, myself. I respect that you all love John. But please respect that I love John, too. I love him in ways you can't imagine."

George said, "I don't *want* to imagine."

Yoko yelled, "*Silence, guitar monkey,*" then pulled a Ninja star from who knows where and flung it at him.

The star found its target: George's forehead. He calmly plucked it out and said, "Right, then. I'm going to the loo." He looked at Ringo and said, "Would you like to take over now?"

Ringo said, "Gladly," then he hurled a timpani mallet across the room.

If Yoko had moved a thousandth of a second slower, the mallet would've struck her in the eye, and she would've been blinded, and the battle would've been over before it started. Considering what happened to Abbey Road that evening, that probably would've been best for everyone.

Ringo then fell on her with a sense of fury and fire that I sometimes wished he applied to the drum kit. Yoko reached for her sword, but Ringo stepped on her wrist; she let out a *Two Virgins*–sounding scream that broke three of the VU meters in the recording room and caused poor Geoff Emerick's ears to spurt blood.

The main problem for Ringo was that Yoko had two levels on him, and he'd be able to keep control of the battle for only so long. She threw him off—quite easily, it seemed—rolled out of his reach, then leapt up onto the ceiling like some sort of supernatural cheetah. While she was hanging upside down, she said, "Not a single scratch, fellow Ninja. But I'm not surprised that's the best you can do, Starkey. John told me your powers are questionable at best."

I don't think I'd ever seen Ringo look so hurt. He asked Yoko, "Did John really say that?" I thought he might burst into tears.

Yoko said, "Yes, Ninja Lord. John really said that."

Once he gathered his composure, Ringo ripped off his striped button-down shirt and flung it over his shoulder. Now, I'd never seen Ringo topless, and was shocked at his muscles, because they

weren't just muscles; they were muscles on top of muscles on top of more muscles. He gave Yoko his best steely glare—which wasn't very steely, because Ringo really is a sweetheart—then said, "Yours are the only powers that are questionable, fellow Ninja," dashed to his drum kit, tore his ride cymbal from its stand, and whipped it at Yoko. She skittered quickly across the ceiling, but not quite quickly enough; the cymbal buzzed through her right biceps, and several dollops of blood dripped onto Paul's amplifier.

Paul stared at his favorite amp as it shorted out, and whispered, "Yoko Ono must die, y'know." And then he clenched his fists, raised his arms to the sky, fell onto his knees, and yelled, *"Yoko Ono must diiiiiiiiie!"* He let loose with a moan that caused chills to run down my spine, then picked up his blood-soaked amp and launched it at Yoko. Since she was nursing her arm wound, she never saw it coming. Yoko fell from the ceiling onto the floor in a heap, landing headfirst. She must've had one hell of a hard head, because she didn't even blink. She stood up and spit out some unintelligible noise; it might've been something in Japanese, or it might've been some nonsense syllables, but whatever it was, it summoned John from the basement, and John was not happy.

John glanced at the blood gushing from Yoko's arm and the lump that was growing on her forehead, walked over to Paul, and whispered, "You did this."

Paul said, "Actually, it was Ringo."

John said, "Ringo would never commit such a heinous act. I know it was you, because I know you better than you know yourself. For over ten years now, together, we have moved the heavens and the Earth. Together, we have made beautiful music. Together, we have created armies of the damned. And now this. And now,

James Paul McCartney, you must feel the hurt that I feel. You must taste the pain that I taste. My suffering is infinite, and you shall suffer equally."

Ringo turned to George, who'd just returned from the WC, and said, "Here we go again."

George said, "Indeed." He checked his watch and said, "What say we go to the pub for a quick one." And then they shuffled off, leaving John and Paul alone in the studio to destroy each other, Abbey Road Studios, and quite possibly the world.

After George and Ringo left, Paul said, "John, can't we discuss this before we dive in? We're on a contractual deadline with this record, plus a fight'll cost us a fortune in studio time. Besides, I'm afraid I might actually hurt you."

John ripped off his own arm and began beating himself on the head. "Look at me, Paulie! What're you going to do to me that I can't do to myself?"

Paul took a step backward and said, "Erm, that's a new one, mate." Then he took off his sport coat, took a deep breath, and said, "Right, then, let's get this over with."

And thus yet another battle began.

GEOFF EMERICK: By then, I'd been working with the Beatles for the better part of two years, and the novelty had worn off. At first, it was a thrill to listen to George work out an intricate guitar part, or to hear John and Paul overdub perfect six-part harmonies, or to watch the two of them try to beat the stuffing out of each other without causing too much damage to their own instruments. But now, it was all a matter of course: *Oh, look, what a surprise, John's destroyed another of Paul's amps,* or, *My, my, my, John's been decapitated, haven't seen that one before.* There's only so much busted gear, or so many stray limbs, one can see before one gets bored.

Sure, the Yoko fight was the worst one yet—the only piece of equipment that didn't get totally annihilated was George's skintar, which seemed to be indestructible—but when you put it in the simplest terms, it was just another Lennon/McCartney hissy fit. I was so fed up that, as I watched Paul reattach his feet, and John carry the bleeding Ms. Ono out the door to theoretical safety, I said to George Martin, "D'you think you could get me a job with the Kinks?"

George shrugged, and said, "D'you think *you* could get *me* a job with the Kinks?"

RINGO STARR: I don't recall exactly how many injuries Yoko sustained—I know she had a nasty laceration on her skull and at least six broken bones—but like most Ninjas, she was a quick healer, and within a couple of days, things were as they were before, with Yoko hanging out in the studio, and John losing focus, then Paul throwing microphones at John's forehead. Ah, the joys of being a Beatle.

In all seriousness, the joy was gone. I couldn't sleep that entire week after the fight, because all I could hear was Yoko's voice, over and over again: *John told me your powers are questionable, John told me your powers are questionable, John told me your powers are questionable.* I know I wasn't 忍の者乱破, or even Yoko herself, for that matter, but I was still pretty good. It was eating at me, and I was miserable.

So one day, at about five in the morning, without having slept a wink, I decided that if John didn't believe in me, maybe he should find himself another drummer.

GEORGE HARRISON: It was about six in the morning, and there's Ringo, in his pajamas, banging on my front door and yelling, "Georgie! Georgie, open up!" I ran downstairs, brought Ringo into the kitchen, and prepared him some tea. When I asked him what was going on, he said, "John hates me because he thinks I'm a shitty Ninja, and Paul hates me because I didn't finish off Yoko the other day, and you hate me because you think I can be replaced by a set of tablas. So I quit."

I told him, "I don't hate you, Rings. But it's funny you mention that. Because I'm quitting, too."

RINGO STARR: I thought, *Great, here we go again, another Beatle stealing poor little Richie Starkey's thunder.*

GEORGE HARRISON: Ringo said, "What're you talking about?"

I said, "Yeah, John hates me because, deep down, he's pissed that my skintar sounds better than any of his damn Epiphones, and Paul hates me because I shoved off during the battle with Yoko, and you hate me because everybody else hates me, and you have a tendency to succumb to peer pressure."

Ringo said, "I don't hate you."

I told him, "I don't hate you, either. So how about we go over to John's and tell him what he can do with his Poppermost?"

JOHN LENNON: It was about seven in the morning, and there're George and Ringo, in their pajamas, banging on my front door and yelling, "Johnny! Johnny, open up!"

I ran downstairs, brought the two of them into the kitchen, and prepared them some tea. When I asked what was going on, they started shouting at me at the same time: "You want to murder us because of this, and Paul wants to murder us because of that, and blah, blah, blah, and we quit."

I said, "Funny you mention that. Because I'm quitting, too."

RINGO STARR: I could see the headlines. It'd say in big, bold capital letters HEAD ZOMBIE LEAVES BEATLES, EARTH STOPS SPINNING ON ITS AXIS. Then, underneath, in small type, *That Drummer Ninja Bloke Whose Name We Forgot Also Did Something.*

GEORGE HARRISON: I asked John, "So you're miserable, and I'm miserable, and Rings here is miserable. What next?"

John said, "How about the three of us start our own band?"

Ringo said, "Brilliant! Let's go tell Paul."

PAUL McCARTNEY: It was about eight in the morning, and there're John, George, and Ringo, in their pajamas, banging on my front door and yelling, "Paulie! Paulie, open up!"

I ran downstairs, brought the three of them into the kitchen, and prepared them some tea. When I asked what was going on, they started shouting at me at the same time: "You want to murder us because of this, and we want to murder you because of that, and blah, blah, blah, and we quit."

I said, "Funny you guys are telling me this. Because *I'm* quitting, too, y'know."

Ringo said, "You're quitting? *You're* quitting? Fook that. I'm joining up again."

George said, "Well if *you're* joining back up, then *I'm* joining back up."

John said, "The Beatles can't be just you two sad sacks. I'm back in."

I said, "You know what, lads? Count me in, too."

John's face lit up. He said, "We're back, and back *forever,* mates! If each one of us quitting the group didn't break us up, we're *never* breaking up. We're a band, a true *band,* and will be that for all eternity. Nothing can come between us—*nothing.* And I will kill, maim, or destroy any living being or supernatural entity that tries to separate us from one another. Four equals one. All for zombies, and zombies for all, and all zombies for Ninja Lords, and Poppermost, here we come!" He paused and said, "Now I'm sick of the sight of you cunts. Stay out of my fookin' face until 1969."

CHAPTER EIGHT

1969

GEORGE HARRISON: We didn't see one another for a good three months. Ringo flew off to either the North or South Pole—I don't recall which—to engage in some Ninja foolishness. Paul went on an eating tour of Europe, which meant two-hundred-some-odd people unknowingly sacrificed their brains and lives for the good of rock 'n' roll. John and Yoko created a hybrid cannabis seed that enabled a zombie to get high without it changing the color of his skin or causing him to excessively break wind. Mr. Lennon grew a lot of it, and Mr. Lennon smoked a lot of it; he had constant munchies and ended up glomming down a couple of hundred human brains himself. Me, I built a few more instruments, got deeper into my meditation, and took a tour of the Wormwood Scrubs prison, where I chowed down on the cortexes of some of the blokes who were serving life sentences. Just because John and Paul got their tasty brain treats from innocent people didn't mean I had to follow suit.

We were all having a lovely time apart from one another, and it turned out that this was one of those instances where absence did *not* make our unbeating hearts grow fonder. When we got together to shoot the film *Let It Be* at the coffin-like Twickenham Film Studios, things went downhill immediately.

RINGO STARR: The other three blokes had eaten more gray matter in three months than they'd eaten in their entire adult lives combined, and I'd been studying with an Eighty-Eighth Level Ninja Lord at this tiny island in the Weddell Sea, and the skills I learned, well, as they say in the movies, if I told you about them, I'd have to kill you. Point being, all four of us were stronger than ever, which made sitting in a dank studio doubly frustrating. And John brought Yoko along, which didn't help matters.

JOHN LENNON: We weren't in Twickenham for ten minutes, when Paul launched an unprovoked attack on my girl.

PAUL McCARTNEY: I swear on Robert Johnson's eternally damned soul that I didn't mean to hurt Yoko. All I did was kiss her on the cheek. But—and I know this is going to sound clichéd, but it's the absolute truth—I didn't know my own strength.

GEORGE HARRISON: The second Paul's lips touched Yoko's face, she went flying across the room; she landed on a cameraman, who promptly died . . . and whose brain I promptly ate. Can't let fresh gray matter go to waste, I always say.

The only reason John didn't rip off Paul's head on the spot was that he tripped over a microphone cord. When he fell, he landed face-first in a pile of dust.

And then he sneezed.

RINGO STARR: John's sneeze wasn't particularly loud, but it had the strength of a hurricane, and it blew a hole in the concrete floor. Let me reiterate: *John sneezed through concrete.* He stared down the hole for a bit, then sat up, wiped his nose on his sleeve, and sneezed again, killing the rest of the camera crew.

GEORGE HARRISON: When Paul went to help Yoko up, he accidently winged her up to the ceiling. In typical Yoko fashion, she hung up there like a bat and said she wasn't coming down, *ever.* Paul mumbled, "We should only be so lucky." I shudder to think what would've happened had John heard him.

RINGO STARR: We were at Twickenham for just over two weeks, and here's the scorecard: George quit, and then returned to the band six times; seventeen cameramen, three production assistants, and two grips were killed; Yoko suffered another twelve broken bones; and John and Paul whaled on each other for a combined total of twenty-six hours. When John knocked down the entire west wall of the studio with his left index finger, we knew it was time for a change of venue.

In an ingenious move, we decided to shoot the remainder of the movie at Abbey Road. In an *un*ingenious move, John asked Magic Alex to redo the studio.

*

P*eople go to Paraguay for two reasons: to eat sugarcane or to disappear. A loosely governed country with plenty of remote places to make oneself scarce, Paraguay has been a favorite getaway for Nazis, white-collar criminals on the lam, and escaped prisoners for almost a century.*

*Yanni Alexis Mardas—known to Beatleologists as Magic Alex—
isn't running from either the law or any of Simon Wiesenthal's minions, but there are four gentlemen who he isn't exactly anxious to
break bread with. Those four gentlemen are the Beatles, and—as Alex
admitted to me in June 2009, while we were huddled under an oversize umbrella in a field far outside the city of Fuerte Olimpo—John,
Paul, George, and Ringo have a legitimate reason for wanting Alex's
scalp.*

MAGIC ALEX: It was 1965, and I was twenty-one, and it seemed like
every man I knew was enjoying the era of free love . . . but not me.
Ladies weren't interested in a kid from Greece who spoke lousy
English and had really thick eyebrows. This is why I decided to
end the Beatles. If I finished off the biggest band in the world, I'd
become famous, and if I became famous, I could get a pretty girl
to love me.

I was a scrawny young man, and I knew a physical approach
wouldn't work for me—after all, look what they did to a strong,
learned zombie hunter like Mick Jagger. So if I was gonna put the
Fab Four to eternal death, I'd have to go a different route. And that
route was electronics. But all I knew how to do was change a lightbulb, plug and unplug a cord, and turn something on and off, so
step one was to learn something about electronics. It took me a few
weeks to figure out how to take apart and put back together a telly.
So that was a start.

Step two: meet some or all of the Beatles and earn their trust,
which was easier than it sounded. See, John Lennon liked watching
the telly, so I paid an old Grecian Ninja pal of mine to break into
John's house while the band was on tour, and destroy his TV. The
next day, I put a leaflet in John's mailbox advertising my services as

a repairman. He called me, I fixed his television, gave him some good acid, and we were fast friends.

Step three: build a machine that would act as an aural diamond bullet. Naturally, that proved to be more difficult. It took three years to build and cost me two toes, as well as the lives of six other zombie hunters, but it was worth it. I created a set of speakers that, when properly placed, created a frequency that would kill any zombie within a two-meter radius. I hoped.

Step four: convince the band to let me install my system at Abbey Road. I'd earned John's trust, so it was a go. No problem.

Step five: convince George Martin to let me install my system at Abbey Road. *Big* problem.

GEORGE MARTIN: Magic Alex was the most ridiculous person I'd met in my life. Electronically speaking, he was good at three things: changing lightbulbs, plugging and unplugging cords, and turning things on and off. Apparently he could fix a television, but I never saw him do anything that would lead me to believe he even knew what a tube was.

But John believed in him, so he was not only happy but eager to have ridiculous Alex set up his ridiculous speakers in what was about to become a ridiculous playback room.

MAGIC ALEX: Boy, oh boy, did those speakers sound wonderful.

GEORGE MARTIN: The playback sounded like it was coming from seventy-two transistor radios, a third of which were working at half power. But I couldn't say a bad word about it, because in 1969, what the Beatles wanted, the Beatles got.

RINGO STARR: I was there right when Alex was putting the finishing touches on his system. When he fired up half of the speakers, it sounded like shit. But it didn't just sound bad, it sounded . . . *wrong.*

MAGIC ALEX: My biggest tactical error was not setting up zombie test runs. Finding a zombie to listen to some tunes from Magic Alex's magic speakers wouldn't have been a problem, because in London, the undead are always hard up for work, and I could've gotten one to come by my studio by offering him ten pence.

RINGO STARR: Once Alex got all seventy-two speakers going, it sounded a little bit better, but only a little bit. Even so, something still wasn't right.

MAGIC ALEX: I don't care what anybody says, but Ringo Starr is as good a Ninja as you'll ever find. I never saw him coming. All I felt was a whoosh, and then I was naked. And then the studio temperature dropped. A lot.

RINGO STARR: I slammed the door shut and said, "Right, Alex, you'll get your clothes back when you tell me what this is all about."

He started shivering and whined, "I'm c-c-c-c-c-cold."

I said, "And I'm c-c-c-c-c-curious. Tell me about your little system here. It's all treble and midrange. Why can't I hear the bass? Who puts together a sound system that doesn't have any bottom?"

He said, "The b-b-b-b-bottom's there. You just can't hear it."

MAGIC ALEX: The human ear can't hear fifty-eight thousand hertz, but the body can *feel* it. I don't think the zombie ear can hear it, either, but my working theory was that fifty-eight thousand hertz, combined with the proper amount of treble and middle, would create an identical frequency to that of a diamond bullet being fired from a Howitzer. One E-flat-minor chord, three dead zombie Beatles.

RINGO STARR: Alex gave me some gobbledygook about low frequencies being good for the soul. It took only one shuriken to the chest to get the truth out of the little Greek freak.

MAGIC ALEX: After Ringo coerced a confession out of me by cutting off my left nipple, he said, "I'm gonna let you live, but only because I don't want George Martin to have to scrub the bloodstains from his mixing board again. I am, however, gonna tell the other lads exactly what went down here, so I recommend you leave the continent as soon as possible. I'll give you a one-hour head start, then I'm gonna make three quick phone calls."

I went to Greece, then the United States, then Canada, then Mexico, then back to Europe, and now here I am, in beautiful Paraguay. And you know what? I don't care if you print how and where I'm living. It's been thirty years, and I can't imagine the guys are still mad at me.

JOHN LENNON: Wait, you know where Alex is? Give me that little fooker's address . . .

◆

PAUL McCARTNEY: After George Martin put the studio back together, we finished shooting the movie, and since the film didn't really have a climax, y'know, we decided to stage a concert on the Abbey Road roof. And everybody knows how that went.

GEORGE HARRISON: From the get-go, that show was a mess. I don't know what the exact temperature was outside, but it was the kind of chill that could cut through even cold-blooded blokes like us. The cold also wreaked havoc on my instruments; the double-reeded plonker-phone was barely staying together, and my skintar got chapped like you wouldn't believe. Making matters worse, we were several stories up in the air and couldn't catch a positive vibe from the crowd; but even if we'd been at ground level, it wouldn't have made much difference, as most of the crowd was comprised of cops, and London's finest don't have much in the way of positive vibes to offer.

By the time we launched into our third tune, I was in a foul mood, simply foul, so when John accidentally knocked my patch cord out of my amp, well, my reflexes took over.

NEIL ASPINALL: Can zombies fly? Not by themselves, but when pushed by another zombie, they can cover quite a distance in the air. Which is exactly what happened when George shoved John off the Abbey Road roof.

JOHN LENNON: I was just standing there, caught up in the moment, playing what I thought was a nice little solo, trying to do my best Eric Clapton impression, minding my own fookin' business, wrapped up in the tune, when all of a sudden, I'm wrapped up in a juniper bush three blocks away, with the neck of my Epiphone jammed into my chest, right where my heart resides. It was the dictionary definition of impalement, and if I'd been a vampire who prayed at the altar of Les Paul rather than Jesus Christ, I'd have been done for.

I yanked my guitar out of my chest—neither my axe nor my

body were badly damaged, thank goodness—and ran like the wind back to Abbey Road.

PAUL McCARTNEY: From the moment John landed in the bushes to the moment he returned to the roof, we're looking at, erm, fifteen seconds, maybe twenty. To give you some context, George kicked him off during the tune's bridge, and he was back by the end of the third verse.

After we finished the song, John leaned into the mic and said, "Thank you very much, ladies and gentlemen. And now, for your listening pleasure, I present to you Mr. George Harrison." Then he unplugged George's guitar and shoved him down onto the pavement.

GEORGE HARRISON: I landed on a fat policeman, so I didn't sustain any significant damage. The policeman, however, didn't look too smashing, but I didn't have time to help him out; after all, I had a concert to get back to. A wonderful, horrible, lovely, terrible concert.

RINGO STARR: When George came back onto the roof, he pushed Paul out of the way to get to John. I don't think he intended any harm, but it appeared that Paul didn't give a damn about George's intentions, especially when Paul landed arse-first on one of the bobbies.

After that, it was every zombie for himself.

GEORGE MARTIN: I had turned the mixing board over to Geoff Emerick so I could grab some lunch in my office up on the third floor. I was seated at my desk, one bite into my BLT, when I saw

George fall past my window. Before I could even get up to look at where he'd landed, there went John. And then, in due order, Paul. And then, astoundingly enough, George again, and then, naturally, John. It was boom, boom, boom, boom, boom, one right after the other.

I sat back down, afraid to look at what was happening down on the ground, so I pulled rank, called Geoff, and told him to go outside and give me a report.

GEOFF EMERICK: By the time I made it onto the sidewalk, the boys had stopped shoving and started making music, so I only saw the aftermath. The single useful observation I can offer is that those Beatle blokes had some terrific aim: five separate falls, five separate cops landed upon. It was a breathtaking display, truly breathtaking, and from that moment on, as far as I was concerned, those bastards could do no wrong. If they wanted to take over the world, they had my vote, because nobody else would be able to do it better.

✱

JOHN LENNON: Tossing George and Paul from the roof, then watching them fall on those pigs, jazzed me up. It felt like I was back at the Indra Club or the Star-Club or the Cavern Club, speeding on greenies, playing music all night long, and doing damage upon whoever or whatever tried to block me from getting to the Poppermost. I thought, *This is a good way to feel. This is how all zombies should feel. No, this is how all humans should feel.* So after Yoko and I tied the knot, the two of us started a protest. Our motto: give war a chance.

PAUL McCARTNEY: I sympathized with John's sentiment—what fun is life without a little bit of spilt blood?—but the press was

killing him, and I thought it best to let him fly solo. For that matter, I started to distance myself from him and the band altogether.

RINGO STARR: I wasn't surprised to see John encouraging the masses to beat the crap out of one another, but seeing it from Yoko was another story. She was a Ninja Lord, and Ninja Lords don't condone pugnacious, aggressive behavior—in other words, we don't start shit, we finish it. And there's Yoko, standing right beside the most pugnacious, aggressive man in rock history, rooting him on. 忍の者乱破 rang me up, and he was pissed, and it takes a lot to piss off 忍の者乱破.

He was so angry, in fact, that he strongly suggested I call up Rory Storm and organize a Hurricanes reunion. He felt we needed to demonstrate that Ninjas who were part of the rock 'n' roll world weren't all violence-mongering performance artists.

I told him I'd consider it. But I didn't. Maybe I should've.

GEORGE HARRISON: I ignored John's whole bloody protest. Talk about Mania.

JOHN LENNON: Yoko and I weren't going to take to the streets and start tearing things up. That would've led to riots, and riots are too messy for anybody's own good. No, Yoko and I were looking for real wars, with real battle plans and real strategy. Any random wanker could throw another random wanker off a roof—Paul McCartney and George Harrison are two excellent examples—but it took a special kind of person to participate in a well-organized military action.

I wasn't looking to start World War III, and something like Vietnam was too sloppy for my taste. I suppose if you put a gun loaded with diamond bullets to my head and asked me to choose what kind of conflict I wanted, I'd have said, "How about a re-match of the Revolutionary War? I bet we'd kick those Yanks' arses this time."

In the end, it was Yoko who came up with what I initially thought was a brilliant idea: build a giant bed in front of the Sexmuseum in Amsterdam, surround it with bombs, barbed wire, guns, and the like, and lie about in it for seven straight days. My wife was a fookin' genius.

NEIL ASPINALL: John knew that Paul, George, and Ringo wouldn't fly out to Denmark and give him a hand with his ridiculous bed idea, so he called me. He knew that when it came to him, my hand was always available for the giving, even if I knew his idea was the stupidest thing in music history.

After day two, the public began avoiding the Sexmuseum like John and Yoko had the plague. But wouldn't you? First off, there was the smell. On a good day, John's zombie stink was tough to handle, but after forty-eight hours without a shower, you could get a whiff of eau de Lennon from half a kilometer away. Second off, there weren't too many folks, undead or alive, who were sympathetic to his cause. If you're a zombie, and you've got that so-called zombie nature working for you, sure, violence is lovely, but far from essential. And for people like me—you know, people who enjoy living—giving war a chance was just silly.

JOHN LENNON: We packed it in on the fourth day. Like they say in the United fookin' States, you can't win 'em all.

*

The *music world's most notorious, ball-busting-est accountant, Allen Klein, was retained by the Beatles in 1969 to tidy up their fi-*

nancial affairs, affairs that had grown progressively messier after Brian Epstein's untimely death. Thing is, not all four Beatles agreed with the hire, the lone dissenter being Paul McCartney, yet another bullet point in the ever-growing list of reasons why it was all but impossible for John, Paul, George, and Ringo to be in the same room together.

I met with Klein in February 2009, and even though he was nearing the end of his long, colorful life, Klein was a force to be reckoned with, and it's easy to see how and why he scared the shit out of high-profile clients, because—as every sentence he delivered was yelled at the decibel level of a small jet—he scared the shit out of me, without even getting up from his deathbed.

ALLEN KLEIN: Listen, brother, managing musicians is a pain in the ass. They're all *kvetch, kvetch, kvetch,* and *"Where's my money, where's my money, where's my money,"* and *"Find me a private plane in an hour,"* and *"Help me get rid of this dead hooker,"* et cetera, et cetera, et fucking cetera. And that's just regular human musicians. Add three honked-off zombies, a confused Ninja, and a royally screwed-up financial portfolio into the equation, and you're looking at a pain in the ass like you wouldn't believe.

I have no clue what happened between John, Paul, George, and Ringo that made them hate one another so much. Might've been that they had creative differences. Might've been that they were growing up and growing apart. Who knows? All I know is that our numbers meetings turned into hours and hours of recriminations and finger-pointing . . . and, for that matter, finger removal.

The fit hit the shan, as some say, in the winter of '69. I was sitting through another Beatles bitchfest in the big conference room up at Apple Records' offices, and as usual, John and Paul were in each other's faces, throwing the periodic punch, and George was sitting on the floor in the corner, in a trance, trying to get in touch with his inner I-don't-know-what-the-fuck, and Ringo was slumped down into a chair, looking like he was gonna cry. It was a sad, sad scene, and if I wasn't getting paid a huge fucking pile of money, I'd have told them all to break up and fuck off, then I'd have flown back to Jersey and washed my hands of them. But I *was* getting paid a huge fucking pile of money, and I thought it might be nice to do something to earn it, so after Paul threw John into a file cabinet, I grabbed a stapler and chucked it out the window. Nothing. Then I grabbed the phone and chucked that out the window. Nothing. Then I grabbed the tranced-out Mr. Harrison and chucked *him* out the window.

That got their attention.

When George came back up, I told them all to sit the fuck down and shut the fuck up, because it was time for Professor Klein to give them a lesson in how to be a rock star. I said, "Listen to me, you undead limey schmucks, you have dozens more records to make, and they'll all go platinum fifty times over, and right there, you have money. If you get off your undead asses, you can start touring again, and you'll sell even more records and have even more bread. If you stop throwing one another off buildings, you might see a newspaper article in which you're not referred to as 'thrill-seeking has-beens.' Five words, boys: Get. It. The. Fuck. Together."

After McCartney cracked Lennon in the head with a clipboard, he said, "You might be right, Allen. John turned me into a zombie so we could make music together forever, and you know what? That was only twelve years ago. That's twelve years down, and eternity to go. Now, I don't know any zombie musicians who're as good as John Lennon and George Harrison, and aside from the brilliant Ringo Starr, I don't know any Ninja musicians who aren't shite."

John looked around the room, nodded, and said, "I hear you, Paul. I hear you loud and clear." Then he overturned the conference room table. With his pinkie. At that point, I got the fuck out of there. I had a hunch it was all over but the formalities, and I sure as shit didn't want to be there when the formalities started.

Two weeks later, I get a midnight phone call from Lennon: "Oi, Kleiny, wake up, mate, we're packing it in. Call Paulie and tell him that if I ever see his ugly mug again, I'm shoving a diamond bullet so far down his throat, he'll shit five carats."

I said, "That sounds great, John. I'll send you my bill."

And then I hung up. And that was the end of the Fab Four.

*

MICK JAGGER: I owe the Beatles, I really do. Who knows where I'd be now without receiving Lennon's and McCartney's zombie kiss. Dead in a Soho gutter? Maybe. Singing in a Rolling Stones tribute band in Galway? Possibly. Raising money to make a documentary on undead hunting? Perhaps.

But going on the *Bigger Bang* world tour in 2006? Absolutely not.

GEORGE MARTIN: When some people lose a significant other, they'll keep bits and pieces of that person around as a reminder of their love. Sometimes it's a shirt that retained a certain scent, or a sweet message on an answerphone. I like that idea. I like that a lot.

They put me through hell, but I truly, truly love John, Paul, George, and Ringo, so I held on to dozens of physical Beatles memories, such as the mixing board that Paul melted with his mind during the *Revolver* session, and the Gibson J-160E that George ate, then regurgitated, while we were cutting *Beatles For Sale*. For that matter, I still haven't cleaned the stain on the carpet from the blood that Ringo spilled near the end of that devastating fight with Yoko during *The White Album* session. And you know what? I never will.

BRIAN EPSTEIN: I loved every minute of what George always calls the Mania: the endlessly creative recording sessions; the excitement of touring; seeing the world from a first-class seat; watching John and Paul mess about with the press. Even the Shea riot was somehow magical.

I'm just glad I was dead for most of the bad bits.

PAUL McCARTNEY: We had a good run, but enough was enough, y'know. I mean, how many times can you fight the same argy-bargy with the same fighters? Getting mashed or mangled or beheaded or disemboweled day in and day out didn't physically hurt me—*nothing* physically hurt me—but I was bored. Wouldn't you be? Imagine waking up knowing you'll have to beat John Lennon with a two-by-four in the morning, then shove a chainsaw up his arse in the afternoon, then rip off both his ears after supper. And then imagine you'll have to do it again tomorrow, and the next day, and the day after that. And then imagine you'll have to do it for all eternity. Just thinking about it is getting me exhausted.

Nobody deserves that. It's no way to live. It's no way to die. And, erm, it's especially no way to be undead.

GEORGE HARRISON: It was the Greek dramatist Menander who first said, "Time heals all wounds," but clearly he wasn't a zombie, because our wounds are everlasting. The scars and stitches and bloodstains aren't going anywhere. Our zombieness is a uniform we can't ever remove . . . or, for that matter, properly wash.

But I don't think we undead get enough credit for our sensitivity. Everybody assumes that just because we would kill a man as easily as we would shake his hand, we have no feelings. Every time John called me a rotting corpse who can't find his way through a C-sharp-minor scale without a flashlight, it stung. Every time Paul told me I'd be a better guitar player if I put my left fingers on my right hand, and my right fingers on my left, I felt it. And whenever Ringo chastised me, well, that was especially painful, because Ringo never chastised *anybody*.

To me, we pulled the plug on the band at exactly the right time. Think about it: how many shots to the heart can one zombie take? I can tell you unequivocally that that number is finite . . . even if that heart is inanimate.

RINGO STARR: I could've gone on playing with them. Hell, if any of the others had given even the slightest hint of interest in continuing, I'd have done anything to make it happen, *anything*. But zombies are a stubborn lot, and once they make a decision, it's all but impossible for anybody to unmake it.

Shutting it down wasn't all bad. My drums weren't going anywhere, so I'd always be able to play. I had dozens and dozens of Ninja Lord levels to conquer. And besides, murdering humans for either food or a few sadistic laughs wasn't exactly my bag—I didn't even like *witnessing* that sort of behavior—and if I could curl up in bed knowing that I wouldn't have to watch John snake his tongue up the bloody hole in some poor fan's neck the next morning, well, that wasn't a bad thing.

JOHN LENNON: We were a rock band. Nothing more. Nothing less. I don't even know why we're talking about it. The records are there, and the corpses are there, and that's all you need, because at the end of the day, that's what the Beatles were about: music and death.

EPILOGUE

1970–Present

What with the five major riots, the eighteen arrests, the dozens of, ahem, odd musical choices, and the countless number of assassination attempts, recapping Lennon's, McCartney's, Harrison's, and Starr's post-Beatles life would require an entire book unto itself. After spending so much time in close confines with zombies, my health-insurance rates have skyrocketed, so I'll leave that journey to another intrepid journalist.

While checkered and oftentimes disparaged, John's, Paul's, George's, and Ringo's post-Beatles careers have had some definite highlights, my personal favorite being John Lennon's spectacular destruction of Phil Spector. After the legendary producer remixed— and, in Lennon's mind, ruined—their album *Let It Be,* John tracked him down in his underground compound in Bolivia and hypnotized the hell out of him, turning the already unhinged Spector into a raging, wig-wearing nutbag. To me, that was far more elegant and appropriate than a mere murder. Death is over in a heartbeat, but insanity lasts a lifetime.

Conversely, there were also plenty of lowlights. Lennon and Mc-Cartney's two-year post-breakup press battle in *Mersey Zombie Weekly* was an embarrassment for everybody involved. Harrison's stab at starting his own religion—which he clumsily dubbed Undead Transcendental Inner Outer Everythingness—was a very expensive, very public fiasco. Starr's awkward traveling Ninja demonstrations would've been impossible to watch even if they lasted only fifteen minutes. But six hours? You're the man, Rings, but come on.

The lowlights eventually far outweighed the highlights, and by the turn of the millennium, the band was all but forgotten. Sure, you'd periodically stumble across a Beatles tribute on some college radio station, and every once in a while you'd hear about a Beatles convention in a random town like Bismarck, North Dakota, or Portland, Maine, but at the beginning of the aughts, the Fab Four was yesterday's news.

What was most heartbreaking about the situation was that the boys' financial situation had gone to hell, and—save for McCartney, who was a canny investor—the Liverpudlians were all but broke. Doubly heartbreaking was that because hip-hop, sampled beats, prefab bands, and tarted-up pop tarts, were the music industry norm, nary a record label or concert promoter was interested in financing a Beatles reunion.

That is, until 2003, when Max Brooks's book *The Zombie Survival Guide: Complete Protection from the Living Dead* climbed onto the bestseller charts, and all of a sudden, zombies were kind of cool again. The following year, the remake of the zombie classic *Dawn of the Dead* and the undead farce *Shaun of the Dead* were box office smashes. Three years later, Brooks followed up *Survival Guide* with another bestseller, *World War Z: An Oral History of the Zombie War,* then three years after that, Seth Grahame-Smith's *Pride and Preju-*

dice and Zombies: The Classic Regency Romance—Now with Ultraviolent Zombie Mayhem helped turn the undead into a legitimate cultural phenomenon. As the decade came to a close, zombie flicks were clogging up the movie theaters, and zombie clothing stores were clogging up the malls. Next thing you know, it was safe for a zombie to walk the streets without fear of persecution, be it a high-functioning behemoth or a low-functioning groaner.

Next thing you know, the Beatles are again a viable entity.

◆

The only Beatle who stayed in touch with me after I finished my interviews for this book was Ringo Starr, so it was a bit of a shock when the name JOHN LENNON popped up on my cell's caller ID. I put my phone on speaker, clicked RECORD on my digital voice recorder, hit the phone's SEND button, and said, "Hey, John. Long time, no hear."

"Good afternoon, scribe, good afternoon. And of course it's long time, no hear. Why the fook would I bother calling you if I didn't have anything specific to talk to you about?"

I wasn't offended. That was just John being John. "Understood," I said. "Which means you have something specific to talk to me about."

"I do," John said. "I most definitely do." He paused, then said, "Here's a question for you, mate: If you Google the phrase, 'The band is reuniting,' how many hits do you get?"

"What are you talking about, John?" I said. "That makes no . . . wait a sec. Are you saying what I think you're saying?"

John ignored me. "Four hundred and twenty-nine thousand, that's how many. Now, how many hits do you get if you Google 'the Beatles'?"

"No clue," I said.

"Three hundred and eighteen thou. Point being, a search of 'the Beatles' needs to exceed a search of 'The band is reuniting.' So, y'know, the Beatles are reuniting. And you need to cover our first show."

"Are you kidding?" I said. "I wouldn't miss it for the world. Where's it happening? Wembley Stadium? The Rose Bowl? Folsom Field?"

"Nope," John said. "Double Door."

"You're kidding," I said. Double Door is a Chicago dive club a few miles away from my apartment. It has a capacity of about four hundred, and is a haven for either up-and-coming or come-and-gone indie rock bands who have cult (read: limited) audiences. "Why in God's name would the Beatles play Double Door?"

"It's a practice run. Next Wednesday. Six o'clock. We're not even advertising it."

"No advertising on a Wednesday evening?" I said. "Sir, you are gonna be playing for an empty house."

"As long as there's one person there, we're cool. So you'll be there, right."

There was no question mark at the end of that sentence. John wasn't asking. John was telling.

◆

Size-wise, the Double Door dressing room adds up to approximately the total square footage of four airplane lavatories. The walls are covered with hand-drawn flyers, graffiti, and stickers, and the floor is gummy with months-old booze—not exactly the kind of place you'd expect to see John, Paul, George, and Ringo prepare for their big return.

The guys were genial enough to me, but quite distant, which I attributed to flat-out nervousness; after all, they hadn't played a live concert for a paying audience since 1966, and you'd have to be inhuman and heartless not to have a case of the jitters.

Paul asked me to take a peek into the club and get a head count. Including the bartender and the bouncer, there were a grand total of eleven bodies. "Great," Paul mumbled. "That won't even cover our gas money up to Milwaukee."

We silently ate a few pieces of crappy pizza and drank a few bottles of beer, then it was time. I wished them luck, and John, Paul, and George trooped off to the stage. But Ringo, who was decked out in his finest Kabuki finery, held back.

He fixed me with a long look and asked, "What do you think of all this, Alan? You think it'll be good?"

"Who knows?" I said. "It could stink, but it could be a blast. One thing I do know is that, no matter what, it'll be interesting."

Ringo gave me a little smile and said, "Interesting. Right." Then he reached into his pocket and pulled out a pair of earplugs. "Here," he said. "Wear these."

I joked, "Why? Have you guys gone metal? Are you turning it up to eleven?"

He shook his head. "Just trust me. I'm wearing a pair myself. Now put 'em in, or I'll go Ninja on your arse." The plugs were a bit hollow, and didn't block out much noise, but Ringo was a trustworthy gentleman, so I went with it.

After I gave him one of those hipster handshake/hugs, I told him, "I'll see you after the set, man. Break a leg."

He gave me a weird smile, shrugged, and said, "I'll probably break something."

Like in many small rock clubs, the Double Door sound system leaves something to be desired, so after Paul counted off one-two-three-four, and they launched into "All My Loving," it sounded like shit. George's guitar fed back, and Paul's bass sound was a mushy mess, and the only piece of the drum kit that could be heard with any semblance of clarity was the hi-hat. I assumed the onstage sound wasn't much better, but oddly enough, the boys didn't seem fazed; quite the contrary, they seemed to be having a blast, especially John, whose smile lit up his face and whose skin tone was as close to vibrant as a zombie's will ever get.

Once the tiny audience realized they were watching the honest-to-goodness Beatles, they fired up their cell phones and started spreading the news, and within twenty minutes, the club was packed. Forty-five minutes and ten well-performed classics later, John said, "We'd like to thank you all for coming tonight. Before we call it an evening, there's one thing I'd like to say." And then he uttered a brief five-word sentence. I still don't know what language it was in. Possibly Latin. Possibly Sanskrit. Possibly an ancient dialect that only zombies understand.

And the effect of this sentence was shocking.

A yuppie standing immediately to my left began bleeding from his ears. And then his nose. And then his mouth. And then his neck. And then something sprang from his chest. It might've been his heart. It might've been a rat.

A boy who couldn't have been more than seventeen flew straight up to the ceiling at what had to be twenty-five miles per hour. And then he fell back to the ground. And then back to the ceiling. And then back to the ground. And then his skull shattered into dozens and dozens of tiny white shards.

A young woman directly behind me yelled, "Oh, my God! My tit fell off! Jesus fucking Christ! My left tit fell off!" A young woman kneeled down to see what had happened to her friend's breast, and her head promptly exploded, covering all of us in the immediate vicinity with foul-smelling, boiling-hot gray and yellow goop.

And then the Beatles threw down their instruments and jumped off the stage into the fray.

As I watched Paul McCartney suck the bartender's brain from her ear, and George Harrison rip both the bouncer's arms from their sockets, and Ringo Starr pepper the defenseless audience with shuriken, John Lennon grabbed me by my collar, shoved me against the wall, ripped out my earplug, and whispered, "Welcome to the Poppermost, scribe. Enjoy the fookin' ride."

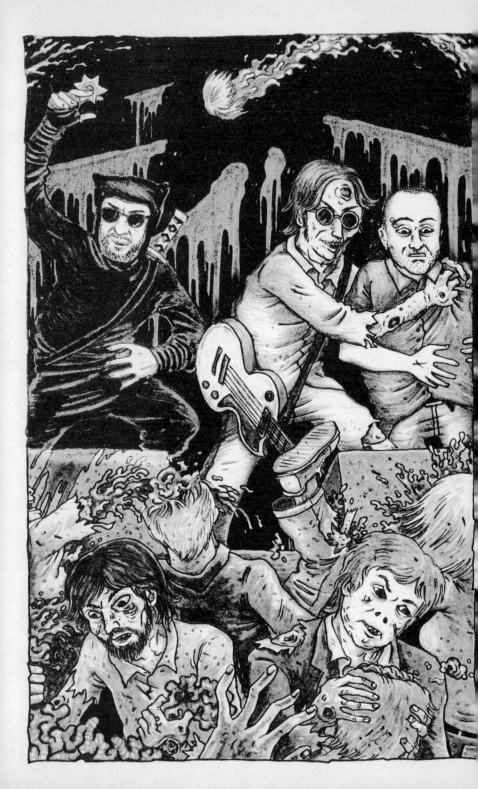

ACKNOWLEDGMENTS

The longer I do this whole book-writing thing, the more I realize that it's a group effort, and one couldn't ask for better teammates than my ubertalented editor, Jaime Costas, of Gallery Books; and my ultrakind agent, Jason Ashlock, of Movable Type Literary Group. From conception to execution to completion, their respective belief and creativity helped bring this project to life . . . and un-death. In any branch of the entertainment industry, you're lucky if one person totally has your back, and I've got two, and how fookin' awesome is that?

Isaac Adamson, C. J. Gelinas, and Jaime Woods pored through what Isaac called "the bat-shit crazy" first draft, and offered many musical, magical, and mystical notes, concepts, and jokes. They also corrected several boo-boos; any remaining mistakes are on me.

I'm a straight-up fan of illustrator/graphic novelist Jeffrey Brown, and couldn't be more thrilled to have him on board. He's the Billy Preston of *Paul Is Undead,* the dude who came in at the end of the

session and laid down a solo that took the jam to a higher, richer level.

Louise Burke, Jennifer Bergstrom, Anthony Ziccardi, Stephanie DeLuca, Richard Yoo, Felice Javit, and the entire Simon & Schuster crew has been nothing but exemplary. This is big-league publishing at its finest, folks. A special shout-out to Jaime Putorti for her sick, sick design work.

Cara Garbarino, your photo makes me look way cuter than I actually am. Folks, if you dig the picture, please visit www.TheAtelier-Chicago.com.

John Lennon, Paul McCartney, George Harrison, Ringo Starr, and George Martin provided the internal soundtrack for not only this project but the majority of my music-listening life. If they were to enjoy this book .0000000001 percent as much as I adore their songs, I'd be a happy boy.

And finally, infinite thanks to my beautiful, clever, intrepid co-pilot Natalie Rosenberg, without whose support and input this book wouldn't sing. I love you, yeah, yeah, yeah.